PASSENGER

Other books by
THOMAS KENEALLY

THOMAS KENEALLY

PASSENGER

Harcourt Brace Jovanovich
New York and London

Printed in the United States of America

Library of Congress Cataloging in Publication Data

Keneally, Thomas.
Passenger.

I. Title.
PZ4.K336Pas   1979   [PR9619.3.K46]   823   78–22258
       ISBN 0–15–171282–4

First American edition
B C D E

To Trish Sheppard
and
Iain Finlay,
Voyagers Themselves

PASSENGER

You remember the old myth about Eden. How Adam and Eve ate of "the tree of the knowledge of good and evil," and how the Ancient of Days, the Cosmic Link, the Substantial Boss, God Himself was pained at them for touching *that* tree of all those in the forest. He, It, or Whoever saw then that humans, who are built for innocence, cannot tolerate it. Listen, their blood vessels and the flow of their blood, their sinews, the wonderful tree of their veins, the magic reef of their nervous systems are built on a cellular structure appropriate to a decent and beastlike artlessness. But the bastards would rather be dead than innocent.

On the first day of my awareness, the strong fragrances of this tree of the knowledge of good and evil brought my mother to the Hologram Experimental Unit at Great Ormond Street Children's Hospital. Getting there, she had caught the underground to Russell Square. Going to Russell Square always gave her a girlish intellectual thrill, because it was near the British Museum, and reminded her of the reading room there, and of George Bernard Shaw and Karl Marx and other such people who used the reading room.

We crept up to street level from the tube platform in one of London Transport's sighing lifts. It had been a rainy morning in London, and the complexions of the people in the lift seemed, even more than usual, like complexions preserved in formaldehyde, bottled and left in some medical museum that has run out of funds. But my mother and the West Indian liftman looked at each other and understood straightaway that they were foreigners among all this dowdy flesh—my mother Irish, milk-white tending to russet at the points of the cheeks and forehead and when certain lights were on her hair; and the West Indian, of course, gleaming chocolate. My mother felt better for that smile. They maintained it between themselves while the lift emptied and until my mother had passed him. She needed kind smiles, poor sweet bitch. For neither of us then knew, though we soon would, what a studied barbarian my begetter, Brian Fitzgerald, happened to be. Sal's ignorance derived from her temperament and the culture she'd been raised in, in a pub in Clare and at the Sacred Heart Convent, Enniscorthy. My ignorance had better grounds. I neither saw, nor knew; nor in all my capsular magnificence did I have two opinions to rub together.

Under the onus of being a beautiful girl, and of making sure that she looked as happy as beautiful girls have a duty to look, Sal went dancing down Guilford Street. The sun was coming out but thinly, without any golden zeal. Mothers were starting to wheel their young into Coram's Fields. Old soldiers, at the gates to keep the city's pederasts away, nodded as the mothers and small fry passed. My mother took her raincoat off. She walked so fast her breasts jumped inside her blouse. Her skirt lay so nearly flat on her belly that no one would have guessed her pregnant, infused with me. I did not yet guess it myself.

There was no call for me to know anything of myself. I sat in the black duchy of the amnion. Through the blood vessels of the placenta I took bounties from my mother's

4

body—oxygens, minerals, carbohydrates. I controlled the extensive continent of my lovely mother, Sal, through the well-known expedient of the umbilicus. Only in places like Bangkok did they dare carve gods resembling me—blunt-nosed, intent, detached. In the manner of a pontiff praying or scheming, my hands were extended cunningly in front of my mouth. I had no idea that in the manner of twentieth-century monarchs I would ever have to abdicate and go out into the world as a private citizen. I had no idea at all.

I had no idea as she found the Hologram Research Unit in a basement behind the hospital and gave her name to the receptionist. No idea as a door opened down the corridor and a black-haired girl in a white coat called to her.

"Mrs. Fitzgerald, this way, please."

The girl in the white coat sat mother Sal at a desk and asked her questions. Listing the answers on a form.

"How many children did your parents have? Did any of your brothers or sisters suffer from mental retardation, brain damage, blindness, deafness? Were any of them spastics? What was your father's occupation?"

Sal, the good democrat, bridled at this last question.

"What difference does it make what my father's occupation was?"

"Dr. Ford . . . you've met Dr. Ford . . . he's interested in the way what people eat from childhood affects the brain configuration of the children they themselves eventually beget. We notice it in the holograms we take of the brains of fetuses in Liverpool. You have a whole generation of parents there who were raised on potato chip sandwiches. Unfortunately, Mrs. Fitzgerald, the protein people get depends on what their father does for a living. Hence the question."

Mother Sal laughed to show she wasn't going to be troublesome about my grandfather's profession.

"We got lots of protein, I'm afraid. My father owned a pub."

The black-haired girl began to question mother Sal about Brian's history. Occupation, journalist. Father's occupation, cattle farmer.

"Brian got plenty of protein, too. He grew up in the bush."

"South Africa?"

"Australia."

Old Brian. Old sunshine. The Marquis of Cunnamulla, this being the name of the town he grew his freckles in. And his balls that were too big for him. If you say *freckles* and *protein*, you have stated the concise history of Brian's childhood.

"Then there's this form," said the black-haired girl.

"What is it?"

"As Dr. Ford no doubt told you, the process is a perfectly safe means to determine a child's sex and cerebral configuration by means of laser beams. This paper simply says you won't sue us over the use of lasers. If however we burnt you with an ultraviolet lamp or dropped an X-ray machine on you, you'd have the normal recourse in law."

Mother Sal read the form and signed it.

"We had a mother whose child was stillborn. She tried to make a case on the grounds that our lasers had killed it."

In mother Sal's belly, not far from where I reigned, there ran one pulse of fear of which I was, as described before, unknowing.

"That isn't possible though?"

"No," said the girl with black hair.

Sal kept hoping that Dr. Ford, whom she knew, would come in. She was not much assured by the black-haired girl. But Ford was the director and wouldn't take any interest in this purely clerical stage. Sal was sent through into a changing room, where she undressed and put on a white smock. For a few seconds, she pressed her uterus with both hands and uttered a little noise, halfway whimper, halfway laugh. Then she went through into a room resembling an X-ray room and, as with X rays, had to stand by a plate, and hold her breath. It took longer, though. The technician ex-

6

plained it to her while she retained her breath for twenty seconds.

"The hologram's a photograph of interference fringes. If there's even a little bit of movement, the interference pattern on the plate gets jumbled. It's like one photographic plate that gets exposed over and over."

Sal did not answer, for fear of muddying the picture that would tell her if I were male, female, idiot, or highbrow.

"Thank you. Breathe out now."

It was while Sal stood there, and they peppered up my cortex with laser beams, that I flowered or declined into self-awareness. It didn't happen violently and I suffered no shock. But the rose or weed of knowledge opened in my hand, and I, as it were, fingered all its petals.

That's how much the bastards know about lasers, I decided. The history of Brian and Sal washed into me on the tides of Sal's blood, and straightaway my own instantly growing history began to roll out of me, unraveling down the vessels of Sal's body, unwinding itself like a moving fresco against the walls of her veins. Because that's the thing about self-awareness. It brings with it the yen to make memoirs.

So from the second of awareness, I was watching an unfolding cartouche. I was a child of the pharaohs, reading pictures of my ancestry on the walls of a temple. And the pictures moved and were full of irony. And so I witnessed and felt the hard core of Brian-love in Sal's belly, of which she was not herself fully self-informed. She might have flattered herself that one day she could clear Brian out if he became insufferable. Yet there it sat, in her gut. Terminal love. To erase and uproot it, I knew, he would have to work hard.

At the same time I knew about Brian. He sat at his desk at United Press, boiling down a release from the Home Secretary's department—some plans to get the British out of Northern Ireland. Brian hated this sort of work. He hated writing such portentous opening and connecting sentences as "The British Home Secretary today announced

7

plans for scaling down the presence of the British Army in Northern Ireland." He despised the task of rummaging through the littered sentences of the press release looking for something true or picturesque. There had been a time in his boyhood when he thought they didn't let journalists write this sort of thing until they, the journalists, had gone into the pit—in this case, Belfast and Derry—and marked the misery and tasted of the ashes. But Brian, whom millions would read tomorrow morning, had never been to Belfast.

I was aware he worked idly with the press statement, it lay side-on to his line of vision. After every sentence, he looked across the floor toward the desk where a lean girl with olive skin, a motion-picture reporter, was working, back arched, head held high, reading a press clipping she dangled from her fingers. For Brian liked skinny girls. He was frightened of women with substantial hips, women who looked natal, women of parturient lines. He would never have told anyone, but there was a sort of panic in him because lean, long-legged Sal was, within the next few months, bound to thicken and grow a mothering belly. And might never get back her borzoi lines.

All this I knew in seconds. Because, unlike a real child of a real pharaoh, my mind was not a building-block mind, my eye was not a one-picture-after-another eye. And as the naked histories of Brian and Sal coiled in through my umbilicus, I knew the ramified data of birth and death. Death did not rout me. I took account of it the way a child takes account of the extinction of dinosaurs. It was birth that seemed nonsense, it was birth that seemed obscene. All right, I resolved, it must be possible to avoid it. No walking round fearful, in the manner of Brian, for me. For after birth, your fear did not flow out of you on the ebb of blood. It got walled in, each walking man a zoo of vipering doubt. Which was ridiculous enough.

So the concept of birth was the only thing that came to me with the qualities of genuine surprise. The concept of sin worried me not at all. I took it as read and saw life therefore as a dazzling manufacture, a sort of dark, lush, biochemical tapestry—myself at its center—woven with consistent genius by someone or other until he got to the birth panel. The birth panel was the failure of talent and good taste. The birth panel was the descent into the lower state, the dumb limbo. And as I thought this, I knew that Brian felt the same way in disapproving of the death panel, seeing death as the blemish, the shit on the wall. But then, Brian was a man of immured fears, a specimen of what birth can do to a sensitive creature.

My perceptions now were arrantly awake. I never slumbered after the lasers went in. Or—to put it another way—knowledge kept running through me as I slept. I was, that is, the knowing sleeper. Sal could not prevent me knowing by signing forms acquitting Dr. Ford of legal blame. That's how much the bastards knew about lasers.

Mother Sal went back into her cubicle and got dressed. I sat in her unsurprised, but a different sort of fetus now. While the holograms were being looked at by experts somewhere beyond the partitions, Sal sat and worried about her book. If Sal were constructing this story, she might be tempted to make herself into a literate waitress and Brian into a shop steward. Something like that. She felt uncertain whether there was anything worth saying about B-grade middle-class people like herself and Brian. Two years past she had written a novel about a schoolteacher in the East End. It was called *Headstart*. It made no money, drew what they call genial notices, and condemned Sal to try writing another book. Two minutes self-aware, I knew what publishers were like with young and naive writers such as Sal. Not least Caledon Press, and its managing director, Sir Don Cale. Just by gasping a little as each new writer mentioned what his or her new book would be about, publishers kept whole schools of foolish young novelists researching, annotating, writing, revising, saying *fuck* at stuck typewriters, frowning at dictating machines. Sir Don Cale knew that a fragment of this coolie work would be able to be published, a further fragment would be profitable, and a further fragment again profitable beyond all telling, the subject of fabled paperback publishing deals in the United States. He risked nothing except an occasional letter about how much he admired Sal as a person and a writer.

Now Sal was no fool and she understood this. But you could not write for long months if you admitted that men like Sir Don Cale were speculating in the raw flesh of your aspirations. She submerged the knowledge down into her blood, where it became apparent only to me, her innermost apprehender and reliquary of all the secrets she kept from herself.

Down the corridor a door opened and Dr. Ford himself stood in the doorway calling, "Mrs. Fitzgerald? This way, please."

I already had my own sort of hologram of Dr. Ford, from the impact fringes that his features made on Sal's blood, on my blood in Sal's, on Sal's in me. In the same way I could tell that he was, more or less, the sort of thing Sal liked. A tall, Swedish-looking man. The blue of his eyes a little faded with close work, with scholarship. Some boyishness left in the way his legs moved and his hands dangled.

I felt, more or less beneath my feet, tickling my buttocks, the faint but piquant electricity of Sal's desire. I gave a small wriggle of protest, but I wasn't yet strong enough to distract Sal from lanky Dr. Ford.

"Good morning, Sal," he said to her in a friendly whisper. She brushed past him and went into the interviewing booth where earlier she had faced the crisp black-haired girl. The aura of the place was different now because Ford was there.

Now I mustn't pretend I feared Sal would seduce Dr. Ford in the booth, or he her. She was loyal to old Brian. And there were other reasons why she wasn't the sort who telephoned or eyed up some Viking like Dr. Ford and had him around to Hospital Road for an afternoon of juice and breathlessness. She had a sexual reserve which was part

10

Sal and part Ireland. She did not open the town gate just because someone asked her to. She yielded to a siege, yes, but there had to be some formality to it. That's the Irish nuns for you. They taught girls like Sal to begin with men by behaving like the Madonna, no matter how much the womb was throbbing. I was not complaining about that. I was very grateful to the nuns. I wished they'd spent some time on Brian.

As Sal seated herself, a little spurt of acid waste ran through me, something to do with animosity. Mine for Ford.

Moving to his chair, he asked, "How is Brian?" He and his wife—a pear-shaped girl, a wearer of ponchos—had met Brian and Sal at dinner at someone's place in Clapham. He'd got excited when he found out Sal was pregnant. It meant he could invite her to see his Hologram Unit.

"He's very well," said Sal. "And yourself?"

Himself was aware of Sal's suspense, but he gazed at her with the direct gaze not of a private man with a poncho-knitting spouse but as Director of the Hologram Unit, and kept her waiting, lips apart, for a while.

"Not to string out the agony, Sal," he said after some five seconds of said stringing. "As I told you our embryologist, Dr. Murch, can predict the probable sexual development of your child even at this early stage with a certainty in excess of ninety percent. Your child will almost certainly be a male. Does that please you?"

He wanted her to strike her forehead, groan, and behave like a lottery winner.

"I like the idea of a boy," she said at last. Smiling sparsely, sacredly, remotely as a cat.

I was again conscious of a certain electricity in Sal's belly, and did not know whether Sal was excited about me or Ford or both of us. I stirred once more. I put pressure with my foot against the amniotic wall. But I was small fry, and Sal was Leviathan. A fifth of a pound wasn't much weight to throw around.

What I detested was sharing Sal's excitement with Dr. Ford. I lay there swearing that I would not grow up to resemble Ford, who in turn resembles Brian a little. I would cure Sal of her weakness for lanky men by being squat and sturdy. She had been surprised to find that her tall men were sometimes rather meanly endowed. A tiny bole of manhood on a vasty oak. By being squat and sturdy with a good length and mass of manhood, I would win Sal away from tall miseries such as Ford.

"Also," Ford said, "the brain is well developed. The pictures of the left and right cerebral hemispheres show a normal development of lobes and lobules. Would you care to look?"

"I would."

"Some people are a little squeamish . . ."

"Not me. Isn't it my child?"

I was pleased to hear *that* question asked, my intimacy to her affirmed.

Staring at her with his lidded blue eyes, Ford produced the transparencies. If she had clapped he would not have been abashed.

"It's remarkable," she said.

"Yes."

"So clear."

"If you get a good hologram, it's usually a very fine picture."

"Isn't it . . . a darling thing?" said Sal.

I should say she was talking about the transparency of the brain, not the indecipherable area of my budding gender, which only Dr. Murch had power to read. "What are those creases here?" she asked.

"They're called sulci."

A chuckle came up quivering out of her belly. I felt its jolly resonance. "It's amazing to see them like that. The creases in your son's brain."

Ford chuckled too. "Yes."

Now she picked up the transparency of my lower trunk.

12

"These are magnified?"

"Oh yes, we magnify all our holograms. You must remember your son is only three and a half inches tall." And he laughed with her again.

"I can't tell anything from this photograph, Warren."

"How would you be *able* to tell anything?" he asked, indulgent as a wizard. "You'll be sent copies of these. And the embryologist's report. *Then* you can sit down with them, and try to understand how the results were obtained."

"You can't help me with them? Now?"

He raised his hand as a policeman might in traffic. "It's hardly my area, Sal. Interferometry's my strong suit. But be assured, your fetus is normal and male gender. You can trust our man."

You can trust our man! That's all the bastards knew about lasers. But at least, trusting the experts, she would get up and leave unctuous Ford. She would stroll back to Russell Square, being tempted to call to the mothers in Coram's Fields, "I have a son too."

"Do you want a sandwich?" he asked then in a half-choked, hopeful way. "Or some steak and kidney? You can get steak and kidney at the Lamb."

"Is it lunch time?" Sal asked.

"Yes, it is."

"That would be nice," Sal told him, smiling not remotely now but with a sensual broadness appropriate to the idea of steak and kidney. Yet secretly, very nearly with *my* brain, she was thinking, Another morning gone; and the question of Sal Fitzgerald's book and whether Sal Fitzgerald has talent no closer to an answer, and the question maybe not of much importance anyhow.

As they went out into Guilford Street, me with them, Sal saw the man she was always seeing. A few times a week she would step off a train or into a street and see him. A strange broad face, a little gnomish. A beard. He always wore a white roll-necked sweater and denims. In winter—she had been seeing him since the winter in which I began as a

13

simple yet ambitious cell—he wore a short black overcoat and an astrakhan hat. He was bald but wore the hair on the back of his head long and wispy, so that she was reminded of Benjamin Franklin. Because he looked like Benjamin Franklin and always wore the same clothes, he was easy to discover among any crowd.

There was always some fear but more excitement in Sal whenever the Gnome was sighted. And now in me too. Little bubbles of excitement. Aerating the sulci, Dr. Ford, tickling up the recently charted lobules.

The Gnome never seemed to be loitering. In fact, whether met in King's Road or in the melee of Oxford Street tube station, he was walking medium-paced or fast, going somewhere he had intended to go anyhow. Only a minor pause in his step showed that he felt the impact of Sal's recognition. Only the fluttering of his eyes showed he was either obsessed with her or, at least, very well paid for crossing her path.

Now here was a stocky man, stirring Sal one way or another. Not least because he had a tramp's look about him, the look of the lost, the look of the sort of man who has permanently a temporary ticket to the reading room at the Museum and goes there six days a week for lack of a home, a forum, a bosom, or a bed to go to. Yet his clothes were costly, better than Brian's. And his shoes polished and the face above the beard shaven. And he carried a new attaché case as if there was something worthwhile in it. Notes for a new life of Disraeli—something like that. And although he was a stocky man, as I intended to be, and although he'd forestalled me by walking across Sal's horizon before I could, I didn't resent him as I resented Ford. I felt somehow a sort of kinship.

Sal stood still on the steps. Brought to a stop by the flavor of the Gnome, the marked disturbance he made in her. Beside the Gnome, Ford was just homunculus candy.

Ford asked, "Is anything the matter?"

"I thought I recognized somebody." She turned her un-flecked green eyes on him. "But no," she said.

Ford coughed, for he wanted those eyes for cuff links. "This way."

Ninety minutes self-conscious, I already knew much about the hopes of seducers. And so I knew that Ford was thinking, She is ripe, she is ripe, and I the reaper! And his balls were suffering little tremors.

Turning the corner with Ford, Sal noticed the Gnome had passed the pub in Lamb's Conduit and was jaywalking across Great Ormond Street. This disappointed her. She was hoping that he might turn into the pub and buy his lunch there. And then she could have kept him under *her* surveillance. But the Gnome never did obvious things, like entering the same carriage or shop or pub as Sal did. That would somehow destroy his latencies. Sometimes Sal, seeing him, thought that if they ever faced each other, it would need to be at her initiative.

Now you might say she shouldn't have been disappointed to see the Gnome move on. The Gnome might be a killer. But Sal was a strange girl with a strange imagination. It was hard to predict what would stimulate her.

And the pub in Lamb's Conduit would have been an interesting place for keeping an eye on the Gnome. It had those head-high beaded glass panels you could open to give your order to the barmen, then close to maintain your privacy. This would have suited a peekaboo style of keeping an eye on someone, of taking an angled view of the Gnome across the bar.

She absorbed her regret. Ford got drinks and a plate of steak and kidney for them both.

"Feeding the inner man," he said, gesturing toward her belly in an embarrassed way. "Now that you know it *is* a man."

Sal smiled (but at least did not laugh) at these crippled witticisms. The sight of warm and piquantly low-grade pub food had made her forget the Gnome a little and swung her attention back to the Director, Hologram Research Unit.

Ford said, "Tell me. How is your book?"

"Some days I don't manage two hundred words."

I could have told him that. All the information was innate in me. She wrote a sentence, for example, then found herself on her feet, reading a letter, say, or the dust jacket of a book, or sharpening a pencil. Or just scratching her hip or feeling her breasts. When alone she felt her breasts a lot in a mysterious way. As if testing whether she was still there. Sometimes she just stood still and farted for a while. You must remember there are fewer opportunities for beautiful women to fart than there are for men. So—not to waste her privacy or her idleness—she voided herself of wind.

"May I ask what it's about?"

Sal flinched a second. "It's a parable really," she said.

"Oh?" He said it as if she had uttered a statement of astounding talent. He thought she was ripe, you see. So he was willing to pretend she was Herman Melville.

"I mean, the story's about a crowd of people on board a ship. The ship's moored in Cork Harbour in the summer of 1799."

"1799. That's a long way back."

"The whole thing is a parable, you see. Of the present."

"Ah. Where's the ship going?"

"Well, it's full of political prisoners, you see. You know how Australia started off as a penal colony. And eventually the ship will go to Australia."

"Australia?"

"Brian's from there."

"So he is."

"Yes. His great-great-et-cetera-grandfather was one of the prisoners on the ship."

"Oh? It's a real ship?"

"Yes. Its name was *Minerva*. And Brian's great-great-et-cetera-grandfather was in the hold."

"I see." The news depressed Ford. As if the tough ghost of Great-Grandfather Fitzgerald was going to stand between Sal and him. "Do you know much about this great-grandfather?"

"Yes. But I must stress. I don't intend to write a historical novel."

"Of course not." It was the last thing he'd accuse any pretty woman of.

"Till the Irish rebellion of 1798, this Fitzgerald was a servant to a rich naturalist in Wicklow. From the naturalist he learned some revolutionary opinions imported from France, and the elements of classifying species, and other tricks of trade. The naturalist was also a revolutionary and a drinking friend of Danton's."

"Remarkable. That's Danton who . . . ?" Ford laid the edge of a greasy knife against his own neck. It left a trace of gravy.

"Yes. When the rebellion began, the naturalist and Fitzgerald joined the rebels. The naturalist died of pneumonia in the field. Fitzgerald was captured, shipped to Cork, and put in the hold of the *Minerva*. Now the *Minerva* stood at anchor in Cork Harbour from February to August. There were Fitzgerald and one hundred and fifty others locked aboard it."

"Ill-treated, I suppose," Ford asked, idly interested yet willing to be riveted by a good story of flogging or rape.

"Not particularly. The ship was suspect though. It had run aground the previous winter. But more than that, everyone in the hold, everyone on board, knew he was sailing to an unknown society. The way we are sailing toward an unknown society. The Irish convicts were full of a vague demoralizing dread. The way we are. That's what the book will be. An essay on dread. Our dread of the coming society."

"And what will you do for erotic interest?" Ford asked, forcing a chuckle. "In the book, I mean."

Even Sal, willing to be lenient, still thought, Christ!

"There were thirty women in the hold. Prisoners. Some of them whores. Locked away forrard."

Ford sensed his question jarred her. "I'm sorry. I didn't mean to belittle . . ."

"Please. Don't worry." Sal found she had done her duty by the steak and kidney and pushed her plate away. She would not waste on him the truth of the *Minerva*, that its imprisoned people occupied benches used a year or so before for slaves, that each prisoner had a space of six feet by eighteen inches to lie down in, in that limbo of a place, come dysentery or high seas. And at the end of it an unknown continent. A continent from which no reports came. About which there were no books. Of which there were scarcely maps.

"As it turns out," she said, thinking aloud in the end, "there's a sort of parallel between *that* Fitzgerald in *that* hold and the Fitzgerald I'm carrying in my womb. *Minerva* was by and large a trusty ship. As I hope I am."

There was a quiver in her voice. Genuine. It was for me. Sal worried some nights that there'd be famine and rolling catastrophe in the eighties. Me? I was not going to starve. Even if there was famine. In me stood an unbeatable will to get sustenance. I had only to keep *that* pristine pure and bright. And not let Brian and aunts and teachers dilute it with the stale waters of their weakness. I would have food, yes, it would come to me in view of my superior knowledge of myself. I pumped my confidence out of my belly, over the border, into the sovereign state of Sal. She smiled. At Ford, yes. But the smile was really for me. For her blood came to me trembling and I sent it back to her reassured.

Meanwhile, because for the moment she was all naked feeling, Ford felt he had a right to lay a hand on top of hers. And what he said, he said quite well for a clumsy bashful man.

"I think," he said, "that your womb, Sal, would be a delightful habitation for man, born or unborn."

Of course, Sal reddened. After suffering education on the chaste, some would say dry, laps of Irish nuns, it was hard ever to become so worldly that you can hear strange men talk about your womb and not flush a little.

Now, facing the desire of Dr. Ford, she fell back on the

dictum uttered by handsome Mother Angelica of St. Brigid's College, Enniscorthy, in 1962, when Sal was a senior girl.

Sal remembered the twilight that year, the season and herself ripening, and Mother Angelica inviting her for a walk in the garden.

"Sarah," said Mother Angelica, "I tell you this because you are pretty, and pretty girls have greater trials than plain ones. Some of the nuns themselves don't understand these things, because when they were girls, they were plain, and of course have continued plain. That is their good fortune, it helped bring them safely into marriage with Christ. When I was a girl, and men wanted to feel or take my body, I'd always put on as sincere a face as I could muster and say, 'I'm very flattered.' I found it always made them more human. It made them think of you as a fellow being and not just as an object of lust. Best of all, it implied that you were tempted, that they had had their impact on you. That they had got at you in spirit. And once they thought that, they felt flattered themselves and were willing to let you be. I would like you to remember that for when men *try it on* with you, so to speak. Because they will, I'm afraid, poor child. Even a pretty nun cannot altogether avoid male suggestions, sometimes from the most unlikely directions. A pretty worldling is *doomed* to meet seducers."

Sal *had* spent a part of her young life giving Mother Angelica's answer to boys. Partly as homage to Angelica, with whom she'd half been in love since she was twelve.

She was now no longer half in love with Mother Angelica; she no longer kept the faith she was raised in. But she had never got over this—that when she was asked for her body, for a few seconds her consciousness went. And in the vacuum, Sister Angelica spoke for her. "I'm very flattered . . ."

But it was not only because of Angelica that she gave Ford a rebuttal. In the cooler areas of her mind she feared taking lovers and complicating the nexus with Brian, at a stage when Brian was doing enough complicating for half a dozen people. Also, she kept a little of the afterimage of the Gnome. Though it did not seem to be an erotic image, yet it somehow lessened the allure of Dr. Ford.

"Warren," she said further, "it's not possible at the moment."

"Come," he urged. "Lovemaking won't affect the child."

"It isn't *this* child I'm worried about."

"I'm an expert observer of married couples," Ford said, his speech flowing along better now that he was half piqued. "You'll have to face it in the end, Brian doesn't give a damn about you."

There was a tickle of anger in Sal. I myself shivered with the delight of it. "If you want to have an affair, set about it, Warren, but don't bad-mouth my marriage as well, please."

The chieftain of the lasers bit his lip, contorted the line of his mouth. "I'm sorry."

"I think you'd better raise this whole question at a happier time."

"You're attracted to me, though?"

Mother of God! The expletive ran through Sal's blood and mine in unison. "Of course. A man of your intelligence doesn't need to be told."

I kicked my toe in the direction of the chorion, trying to punch the message through. Clear him off, Sal. But it's always been Sal's method to adjourn seduction scenes, to leave possibilities open. "Is your wife all right?" she asked, as part of the dialog of adjournment.

"We have a good arrangement," said Ford. Two hours self-aware, I know that everyone said that these days. And I was learning, of course, the truth of those lines of William Butler Yeats available to me through the anthology of Sal's nervous system, through the memorabilia of her blood, about how lovely women often eat a crazy salad with their meat.

On their way out of the pub, the crazy salad asked Sal, "What happened to Brian's great-grandfather in the end?"

"In Australia he was sentenced to a thousand lashes. To

be given in series. He took four hundred, and then was nursed back to health and took the rest in two lots."

Ford released his breath through his teeth. "Why did they do that to him?"

"He was supposed to have said revolutionary things to the other convicts. Also, he claimed that kangaroos were homosexuals."

"You're not serious?"

"Yes. They thought it was a revolutionary thing to say. They knew God wouldn't permit animal sodomy to occur under the British flag."

Ford laughed. "You're a strange girl," he said, as if she had been a contributor to the eccentricities of that ancient convict Fitzgerald. "Delightful though," he assured her.

"It isn't me that's strange. I tell a strange story, that's all."

I suppose the same applied to me.

At the time of my first awareness, Brian and Sal lived on the third floor of a house on Royal Hospital Road, SW3. Clytie Heatherton-Meadows owned the house. From most of its front windows you could see the Thames, very close, but the river rarely managed in this age to look the way it does in Turner paintings, and sometimes contrived to flow grayly even when the sun was on it.

An Irish bogtrotter like Sal, a lad from the end of the earth like Brian, both liked to have a Britannic hyphenated name for landlady. They also expected Clytie to be an eccentric; it's what they paid their rent for. Clytie in fact had no trouble being an oddball. As visible tribute to the fact that she was a bottled-in-bond British eccentric she kept a great wardrobe of mid-1940s robes. She wore very little of more recent manufacture. Whenever Brian complimented her on her clothing, she said, "Yes, it's twenty-five years old." '44 to '48 must have been her heyday, and highhey her day must have been.

Two and a half hours self-aware, I knew of her other

oddness. She was a monkey fancier. She had a Brazilian brute, large as a five-year-old, called Ran Singh. He sat in a wired-off stateroom opening straight onto Clytie's living room. Shaking the bars of his stateroom, he hissed at guests, fell in love with lady visitors, tried to bite Clytie's grandchildren. Being bored, he excreted a great deal, and Clytie —who had never shoveled shit for anyone else in her life— entered Ran Singh's coop with a little Georgian fire shovel, burnished copper, and cleaned up for her monkey.

When we got back to Clytie's place, early that afternoon, I was sitting happily, my ear up against the uterine wall. Not to hear anything. I didn't need to overhear anything when my blood was chanting like a monk, making its own Matins and Lauds. "Sal, sweet Sal. I ride in the estuary, in the warm Nile of your blood." That's the sort of thing I was emitting. "I bud in your dark cave, sweet Sal."

All the time I had kept half a lobe on Brian, on his dull morning. Now he was onto his first pint in a pub at Ludgate Circus. There were half a dozen other giants of the press with him. Talking scandal and sex and the Middle East. The girl who wrote about the movies refused to have lunch with him and for that reason there was an edge of bitterness in the way he told his dirty jokes today. I did not note the jokes. They were some sort of audible smear on someone else's horizon.

When she entered her flat that afternoon, carrying the unsuspected freight of my awareness, Sal caught the fatty tang of her kitchenette and saw the dusty sunlight falling onto the floor of the front room, and suffered sudden melancholia. And me with her. My first touch of *weltschmerz*, it yet felt as familiar as the umbilicus that entered my gut. It seemed to me then that I was sweating. For some seconds her blood carried no oxygen to me. In panic, I hit at her. Why so? I asked myself. Why so, when the blues were mine as well and, by bunching the muscles of my abdomen, I refused whatever oxygenous froth Sal sent my way.

Then I knew, the knowledge came chugging to me through the placenta. She was not just frightened for me, that with strong bonds I should be bound down into hunger and misuse. She was—for but an instant, mind you, and not as markedly as Brian—frightened of me. Would I mouth her breasts to the extent that they no longer fitted the breast-canons of the age? What also of my small fatiguing hands? Of my throat and its sharp demanding music?

Meanwhile, such little oxygen, oh Dr. Ford, was coming in through the villi and my lobules were yawning. I slipped into a miserable daze. I dozed.

I woke an hour later and considered a canny, chemical revenge. Should I take from Sal a ruinous share of phosphorus, of nitrogen, of carbohydrates, and wait the twenty years, the thirty, the forty? My phosphorus, my nitrogens, my carbohydrates would still bloom while Sal sank to haghood. Overthrow! Biousurpation! Should it interest me?

It didn't. I knew that we sat now in Clytie's living room. Sal and Clytie each had a sherry. Ran Singh was watching us all from his cage. Clytie had the color television up close to his bars so that he could watch "Jack-a-Nory." But he only liked Westerns and war movies and the chorus girls in the "Black and White Minstrels." He stood on his squeaker toy, holding his parts and watching Sal, to whom he like Ford had always been attracted. Clytie always said she would have gotten him a mate if the expense hadn't been so prohibitive. But the little man who brought Ran Singh out of the Amazon basin was now in jail in the lower city of Salvador, because Ran Singh's species was a prohibited export. The Brazilian government had a bad press when it had a press at all, but I strenuously agreed with its efforts to keep bastards like Ran Singh in their verdant and native squalor, well up the Amazon.

Though Clytie blamed the lack of a mate for Ran Singh on her supplier being locked up in a hot jail, Sal suspected, and so did I, that she just wanted to guard her boy, Ran Singh, from the sharp teeth of some savage lady of the appropriate species. So—no ravening, jungle-tough, mustard-hot mate for Ran Singh.

At the moment I woke, Clytie was talking not about her

champion simian excretor, but about her daughter, Rowena. I knew, because Sal knew, that Rowena was now an elegant woman, Sal's age, and a fair clue to how mama Clytie must have looked in the year Rowena was dropped, and Singapore fell, and with Singapore the Honorable Eugene Heatherton-Meadows, Clytie's first husband.

"One tends to be soft on them," Clytie was saying. "You remember how they were, lying on the delivery table. Covered with membrane and muck. But day one isn't too early to let them know you won't be exploited. I mean, they understand better than they let on."

"Understand?" Sal asked. "Are you sure, Clytie?"

"If there's one thing about babies, it's that they keep on forgetting to look limp and at a loss. You're always catching them out at times when they rather resemble visitors from another planet. A more developed planet than ours. And have you ever noticed twins? They look—I mean—like two Renaissance cardinals plotting. Conspirators."

Sal said, still blue, "Yes, they do. But that doesn't mean they are conspiring."

"You think not? Well, I let Rowena know very early. As my mother let me know."

"How do you do it?" Asking this, Sal knew that she could never use clever tactics against a child. She would love me too wildly. Her understanding of this and my understanding of her understanding buoyed me beneath my buttocks, and helped me adopt the posture of a satrap at his ease.

Reclining in her angular gown, Clytie ground on. It's a wonder she didn't write a book on the training of the young. National Socialist Press could have run it in their spring list. "How do you get the message across? Why, you tell them. Their lack of understanding, as I say, is just a pretense."

"Oh?"

"As soon as Rowena could walk, I got a cat for her and a cat for myself, and I was very affectionate to my cat, and she was to hers. So she learned that our lives were to be parallel, not merged."

Sal gave a grunt of approval, more because she liked the contours of the words "parallel, not merged" than because she agreed with Clytie.

"I know you think I'm barbarous," said Clytie. "It was the only way I could give her anything. If I'd been forced to give more, I'd have hated her. The way so many *good* mothers . . ." I clenched my stomach a second, and yet again. I was trying to emit a thin mist of rancor and to infect Sal. I seemed to succeed.

"Then you sent her to boarding school," Sal stated, so flatly that it was a sort of judgment.

"Of course. What else? Keeping them at home out of sentimentality? Are you grateful to your parents for keeping you at home?"

"Mine weren't quite average. I mean my father spent a fortune buying cheap yearlings at the horse sales. He dreamed of being the man who bought an unexpected champion. All he's ever managed to buy so far are the expected flops. Now my mother's a very practical woman. So they fight a lot and always have."

"How novel."

"Brian always reminded me of my father."

Clytie laughed. "The dreaminess you mean? Or the same interesting rough grain?"

"You were talking about Rowena."

"Yes. I was about to say they try to punish . . . and what's more, outflank you. Rowena, for example. The school cat had a litter. Six kittens. Rowena took one at a time into the woodshed at Cheltenham Girls' Prep and beheaded them. Then presented herself to matron. Gore-encrusted tunic and plaits. Imagine. The headmistress wanted to expel her. Thank God, I had friends on the Board. I said, if she's expelled, she'll think for the rest of her life she can reap substantial results. Just by beheading things. I know you think I'm a monster."

In his cage, Ran Singh began making demanding noises with his squeaker. Clytie's long hand, cupping its sherry glass, began trembling. Was it Parkinson's disease? Or the memory of Rowena as prep school executioner?

"Don't think it doesn't take effort, integrity," Clytie stated. "Just because I'm not sentimental about them. The Egyptians weren't." And, on the strength of her parity with the pharaohs, she half-emptied her sherry glass at one large yet stately gulp.

"The monkey . . . ?" suggested Sal.

Clytie looked over her shoulder at Ran Singh. He stood with his squeaker bear in one hand, squeezing, squeezing. Sal felt sorry for him. His eyes were as blank as the eyes of toy monkeys sitting among the children's clothing in shop windows.

"You're sentimental with the bloody monkey," said Sal. She managed to tease out the intonation of the words, so that they finished just short of being an accusation.

"One can be with the monkey. Without doing harm."

"The thing sits in its cage and masturbates."

"My God! If you're going to complain about that . . . What about the corgis on the streets?" The trembling hadn't lessened. Clytie got up and began pacing the length of a wall-high portrait of her great-grandfather's family, tall, well-structured Georgians, the children a tight-bodiced girl and a boy in satin knee pants playing with a Pekingese, the father leaning on a hunting gun, the mother passive on a bench with fruit in her lap, and all of them placed in a landscape of classic gardens and bounteous country where hares were peeping and dashing from the hedges. "You really do think I'm a monster."

Sal uttered a tight little laugh that gave her away.

I thought I could see the discharge of Clytie's anger. It was like a disturbance, I suppose, in a magnetic field. Three hours self-aware, I was about to hear the worst statement I'd heard yet.

"You prim bitch," Clytie began. "I can foresee the mean- ness of it. The dishonesty. Brian hung over. Walking it to the tobacconist's of a Sunday for its ice cream. Taking it over the river to Battersea Park. Putting it on the merry-go-round. Smiling at it as round . . ." She made a sweeping movement to indicate the action of a merry-go-round. ". . . round it comes. *Be happy, you little bastard.* Dismembering it with your unhappiness. As you shall. Because I can tell what you really want."

"What? What do I really want? Tell me!"

"In the cautionary tales of your girlhood it was performed by cynical doctors and brutal nurses in back rooms. Now you can get it on the national health."

Again there seemed to be a cut in the oxygen. When the blood flowed into me again, it felt like blood from a bruise, bad blood. Clytie's lethal suggestion had got into Sal's arteries.

Sal stood upright, just as tall as Clytie, screaming as well as I could wish. "How dare you, Clytie! How dare you make projections for my child!"

I desired my old blankness back again. The blankness I had had till mid-morning. The blankness of Ran Singh which Ford had stolen from me. I went through the tumbled fragments of Christian mythology that lay about in the forum of Sal's brain, looking for a god, not the vast and ultimate, but a tough, active, intervening deity. With such a being I could brew up a curse against the Director, Hologram Research Unit. For, because he wanted Sal, he had invited her in to be disarmed by his lasers, and in the authoritative shadow of his satanic machine, had found in himself the fiber to put the word on her. Perhaps he worked in this way with many a pretty and not-too-heavily pregnant girl. In that case the Hologram Research Unit was merely a state-subsidized branch of his libido, which *per accidens* gave me the chance to hear Clytie whistling up my death.

My account of the quarrel with Clytie was being paid out like a kite string along Sal's vessels, and almost as soon as it occurred. There it met not listeners, not readers, but heedless corpuscles. If, however, I had listeners, I would have to say, dear listener, dear reader, you no doubt have labeled me in moral, political, and other terms—you have called me antiabortionist, an enemy of Zero Population Growth, and—in a world where thirty million Indians will die before I am born (if I consent to be born)—a sentimental pleader for the rights of fetuses. None of that am I. Let others make their own pleas. I am a pleader for myself. I want no sharp knives for me. For me, the deep possession of Sal that I enjoy.

Anyhow, Sal had rushed out of Clytie's living room and was on the stairs, making for her own flat. Clytie, already penitent, followed her and throttled a section of the carved balustrade by way of contrition.

"Sal, I'm trying to be helpful. With all my advice about children. I mean, Rowena's quite happy with her whiskey importer. Telephone her."

"Go to hell, Clytie."

Clytie made pleading noises. "Ran Singh is my sore point. You know that."

But Sal had slammed her door, locking Clytie out. I felt better now for being away from that monkey and all those tall paintings. Sal sat by the window hugging her belly; I could feel the deep impulses of her fingers. She began to croon.

"Oh my tiny love. Oh my deep one. Oh my boy, my little dancer."

Such sentiments were enough for me.

And the sun sat with us like a kindly neighbor, sitting low and lazy over Battersea Fun Fair, soothing us with its little curlicues of ultraviolet. Sal thought, Beneath *that* sun all western London looks like a healed wound. And the river, this once, looks like mercury. The Thames thermometer. Deep into London's anus or armpit, and registering for once a golden quietude.

We thought, Battersea Fun Fair. Where bloody Clytie says I'll (he'll) have unhappy merry-go-round rides. Bugger Clytie. Yet we neither of us trusted Brian. It was our knowledge of Brian that had given point to Clytie's scenario.

It wasn't any use Sal getting dinner ready; she was sure that today he would call and say something like, "Sal love, I'll be late. A party. To meet that Rumanian doctor. The one who can cure old age with hormones. I might take the treatment myself." That sort of afternoon call, it seemed to her, had become more common since I was discovered to be *in situ*. Her little dormant dancer.

He did all his quick womanizing at these parties. Not often with benefit of a bed. The beds at most parties—not embassy parties where the beds are always locked away, but at ordinary parties in ordinary habitations—were usually covered with overcoats or belonged to children. Overcoats crushed, and as for children, Brian was so frightened of them and their aura that he could rarely pleasure a woman in the presence of nursery prints and under the manic grins of teddy bears. In sum, nursery furniture made him feel sacrilegious if not under threat.

The parties had been three times a week these last few weeks. Though Sal was aggrieved, she thought the party-going had more to do with Brian's drinking than with the rutting instinct.

I who knew had been forced by knowledge already, in my first day of awareness, to feel paternal about Brian's pitiful success with girls. Since Sal first came home from the clinic after her positive pregnancy test, Brian had gone back to the boyish idea of *Methods*. One of these was, for example, to arouse a sort of friendly hostility in the chosen woman. For this he needed the presence of another man. The sort of man who was the best catalyst was one who fancied himself as a good somber listener. The appropriate man stood, pretending to the girl that her work on some social column, fashion section, Sunday supplement, financial page, captivated him. The girl would be surprised to find Brian, my true begetter and hefty antipodean, already looking drunker than he was, already looking racy, tie already loosened, grinning like a pirate at her side, listening in in a way that put some stress on the sober respect the man and she had been building for each other. Out of the angles of their eyes, they would both watch Brian, their talk would lose its rhythm.

"Sounds bloody boring," Brian would be likely, at last, to say. The girl and the somber listener would flinch. "Sounds a wall-to-wall yawn to me, love. Like my job and his job. Like anyone's."

The girl might then tense her nostrils. "I wouldn't be surprised if your job was a bore. Boredom to the bores, so to speak."

And Brian would laugh. He had an affable, meaty laugh. There was a lot of his raunchy cattle-breeding ancestors from sunny Queensland in his laugh. And no malice to it. And it was more than sound, more than an ack-ack of the larynx. You could say it had a smell tò it: brown acreages, woodsmoke, cow dung, sweat. People were deceived by it into thinking about frontiers and the wild and free life. (I supposed I too would grow into such a laughter, although as yet I but smiled, smiled. I had, nonetheless, better cause to find these things funny than Brian did.)

Poor girls—natives of Finsbury Park, or, at the worst, wild Devon—took from his laugh a vision of the awful Channel country in southwest Queensland where he grew up. They did not understand that he laughed and breathed in fear of three-inch, thirty-five-gram me.

"I admire you for sticking at it, love," he might then tell the girl. "For being enthusiastic and all that. But Jesus, you don't have to pretend. Something has to be done to fill the wait between womb and tomb. Just because the only alternative is motherhood, you don't have to tell me that you find your bloody newspaper some sort of golden kibbutz."

The good somber listener could often be depended on to say something professional now. "A lot of journalists get fulfillment from their jobs. Male and female."

"Most get pay," Brian might lazily opine.

"If you don't get anything from yours, you ought to drive a bloody taxi."

Brian by now had no doubt. He engaged the girl with his eyes. His mouth might be wet, his tongue licking in and out. "My love, you are a beautiful and intelligent creature. You know how news is made up of great events and non-events. You know what your job is: to mash the event or nonevent down to a cretinous pap. Your proprietor sees news this way. And you're brighter than he is."

The girl might answer, "I agree with him. You ought to be driving a taxi."

She might utter a bitter laugh as she said it, yet it would sound indulgent as well.

"You don't," Brian would tell her, "get so much free booze driving taxis."

"That's disgusting." But as she said it she would be already amiable.

Brian was now free to turn to the straight man. "Why don't you get the lady another drink? Seeing you admire her work so much."

"Why don't you get stuffed?" the straight man would say.

"No," the girl could be expected to announce, "I would like another." Her glass would go to the straight man, who rightly suspected that it signified his marching orders. "Do you mind?"

When he went, the girl might begin surveying Brian and her eyes possibly coruscated a little. They would talk more, but just when Brian saw the straight man turning from a waiter and holding high more liquor for the girl, he would grab her elbow.

"Come!" he'd say.

If my account were not streaming out like a moving hiero-glyphic in the loggias of Sal's blood . . . if this were in fact an account to be read by outsiders, I would not intend that Brian's Method should appear as advice to the seducer. It wouldn't necessarily be any use to anyone else to grab girls by the ulna and radius, and say, "Come!" To say, "Come!" the way Brian says it is a gift of sorts. He says it as if historical imperatives are gnashing like Dobermans at his backside. He utters, "Come!" as Caesar uttered it to Antony on the morning of the Ides, as Lincoln uttered it to Mrs. Lincoln the night of their frightful visit to the theater.

To the grasped girl, Brian became for a second a des-tined being. They slipped out of the room like emigrés of fate, not like two people stealing off for a fast grope on the conservatory floor.

Six hours self-aware, I already knew of the mysterious silliness of women. I knew it through tasting the marrow of Brian's apprehensions and of Sal's. Silly women, pretty and plain, let Brian have them. Feeling enriched, feeling *at last a real man!* He had them on tables hastily cleared in someone's studio. Among the telephones and copy, appointment diaries and newspapers on someone's desk. On the steps to the cellar. In washbasins! Among pots of semigloss on shelves in garages! In revolving chairs, where the climax of the man of destiny and his grasped girl might cause mad spinning.

Yet though I did not admire all Brian's avid grinding, I yet loved the bastard in a strict and helpless way. His long-tailed spermatozoon, sailing up Sal's tube toward a meeting with her naive egg, carried with it a cargo of Brian-love. When the meeting occurred and the cells began to split and grow, I was then too simple a creature to withstand that merchandise. Therefore I feared, now that I had the power of fearing, that he might go off with one of those cellar-stairs girls. And since he was doing what he did I wished he would do it for its simple raunchiness, but understood he had taken to it as an escape from Sal as mother and from three-inch me!

And when he buttoned himself up they sometimes complimented him and hoped to enjoy him in less extreme conditions.

"Ah," he might say, not too arrogantly but parting his legs, "the old Queensland sugar banana!"

It was strange that if a safe bed were found, if the girl asked him home to her spinster flat, he felt at risk. It was as if he functioned on the likelihood of people breaking in to distract him from the girl to whom he had said, "Come!" His love at leisure, his love with the comforts, he kept for Sal. His fly-by-night love was for the washbasin women. That was his concept of marital fidelity.

Sometimes, though, he risked a nine-day affair. At the end of it the girl said, "And to think I thought you were a man!" Then he trotted back to Sal as happy as a boy let out of boarding school.

Now Sal did not choose to know all this in exact terms. She would not choose to know it tonight if he telephoned her and said he'd be late. We would sit together, she the mother, I the successor of the poor frantic boy. And together we would think, He's going through a stage.

Now, in the sun from west London, Sal chose to do some writing while she waited.

With the minor dyspeptic fear that might be common to all writers, she went to her desk, opened the folder, and squinted at the foolscap pages in front of her for portents of talent. Her handwriting covered every page. She could see by the way some of the words formed, the way *n*'s and *m*'s, *y*'s, *r*'s, *k*'s became wispy at the end of words, how uneasy she felt with the material and how, in the teeth of all the feminist manifestos, her literary passions had been curbed by motherhood.

Yesterday she finished a chapter. Maurice Fitzgerald, fabled and many times great-grandfather to that random copulant, Brian, arrived aboard his convict ship. Sal wrote him as a sort of Gaelic Che Guevara. He ate the revolution with his rations, his sleep was for the revolution, and for the revolution he beat up another convict called Boyle.

There were whores and pickpockets chained forward in the women's portion of the hold, and like a good rebel Fitzgerald looked on whores as symptoms of an uneven world. In the world after the rebellion there would be no harlots. Meanwhile there was one called Dymphna in that convict hold. There was also a sweet vacant girl called Molly whom Maurice Fitzgerald wanted, but not immediately, not with the impatience that is typical of his many-times-great-grandson, Brian.

In what she wrote now Sal wanted to point up all manner of crafty ideas, such as that the guards are as surely imprisoned as are the convicts. It was of interest—to me anyhow who probably overprized her talent—to read a new chapter.

"In the Cobh of Cork [Sal wrote] it is a dazzling morning. The daylight is soft, furzy, full of drifting offshore pollens.

"There is no wind, so the scuttles are open, the better to air the prison. Fitzgerald and the other men, even the women forrard, must wear their ankle chains, for a prisoner might readily get out through the scuttles, to swim Cobh Harbour or drown trying. The light steams in the prison mess deck. In the women's section forrard there's a lot of chatter. But back here the men are quiet. And the ones who were brought aboard yesterday are silent with a silence of disease proportions. Three of them catatonic. They have been in solitary cells in Cork prison for the last three weeks. This morning they couldn't be roused, so they still lie on their bed tray, tethered by chains and anklets to the bulkhead. The duck-egg morning falls on their bodies like an extra blanket. They snore, but with their eyes open. This is normal in prison ships when people are first put aboard. By evening they will wake and look about for food. In the name of reason, Fitzgerald will have it waiting for them, there on their mess tables—the morning's cold oatmeal, the biscuit, the lobscouse . . ."

You see—and it is I talking, the cunning fetus—Sal has documentary evidence that this chained Fitzgerald had some grandeur to him. In Australia this grandeur suffered genetic erosion to the point where Brian now stood, bearer of all that was left of it. But I, I promise myself—I am the inheritor of all Fitzgerald's Jacobin probity. If you're tough enough, you can enforce and imprint a certain destiny on your chromosomes.

"Fitzgerald [Sal further wrote] sees his friend Dennis and another prisoner hefting the caldron of hot oatmeal down from the well deck. They talk to the sentries in the Irish language. In a way the soldiers are the saddest Irishmen. As likely to be flogged as anyone, they have to keep a red and foreign uniform tidy and pretend all day to be interested in the sovereignty of a fat and insane German. They feel guilty, too, that *they* are not prisoners. The prisoners know that, Dennis knows it, and is jaunty and self-important with the big oatmeal caldron. Because he belongs to the best corps (you would think), the ultimate regiment, the captured rebels.

"But Dennis has been in Cork prison since the spring of three years ago on the grounds not of belonging to the Council of Dublin or possessing forbidden pamphlets written by dangerous Frenchmen, but because he lifted a bag of flour from an estate near Newmarket. Petty lifters and whores however have honor in the prison hold, because Fitzgerald has said that criminals are welcome rebels, rebels not yet informed of their cause. To help enforce the dictum he has already knocked flat the prisoner Boyle, who looked on the harlots as mere harlots.

"Sometimes the Irish conscripts look in through the bars like orphans, hissing jealous insults the way orphans do. It all makes you reflect on the nature of freedom. Now, with his key, a conscript soldier lets Dennis and the other orderly into the prison hold.

" 'Coming in?' a prisoner calls at the Redcoat boy. But the boy locks up again.

"Dennis laughs as he and the second orderly edge the oatmeal onto the mess bench. They do this easily because they have no chains on. There is nothing like a sudden absence of iron anklets to make your movements fluent.

" 'That old harlot Dymphna,' says Dennis, still in Irish, the south Irish that bards, kept warblers, and lapdogs on the estates of sensitive Irish lords found barbarous. 'She wants us to say—in a whisper, she said—that if anyone cares to give her their oatmeal, they can nail her against the walls of the ship. What she said is, don't tell Fitzgerald.'

" 'Then why are you telling him?' Boyle asks.

"From forrard, on the other side of the well the soldiers stand in, Dymphna yells, 'No giving away secrets back there.'

" 'By Jesus,' says Boyle, 'it's her trade that she was raised in. Either pay her the oatmeal, Dennis, or pass the god-blasted message on to another man.'

"To quieten Dymphna, the soldiers started knocking on the wooden wall forward of the well. The women are behind that wall, twenty raucous presences and a further ten who don't speak at all.

"Fitzgerald calls, 'Let us have you for free, Dymphna darling. A free gift for free men. Every man back here needs his oatmeal.'

" 'Not me,' says Boyle. 'I'm not free. And I'd rather go down that pink cave than eat the damned oatmeal.'

"With one ironed foot, Fitzgerald stands on Boyle's ironed foot.

" 'Those gentry from the aft cabins, they'll be down soon.'

"He meant the respectable rebels who traveled above decks and in the poop cabins. The rebel general Holt, the parson Fulton, the surgeon O'Connor, the renegade British Army officer Allcock. They had been sentenced to death but their sentences commuted to nothing as decent or nasty as life in the prison hold. They had instead been exiled. One day their exile would be revoked and they could sail home. As they would gratefully. Because there was not one clear-headed rebel among them. Rebellion was a fit of which they had been cured now. Sure, they had done one or two brave things in Wicklow or County Dublin and now they thought they were exempt from further duties of subversion. They visited the hold each morning to meet the men who had rebelled in lowlier ways, had broken curfews or been found drinking with United Irishmen, or been herded up to make a round number of arrests after some little riot in some little town. If the rebel gentry found their fellow countrymen in the hold to be in good order, food fragments stored, no shit on the deck, no cursing, no suggestive offers from Dymphna or the others, they praised you. If they found the dormitory trays fouled, puke on the mess tables, and some bare-arsed rebel halfway up Dymphna, they looked pained, as if you have proved to them once and for all that they had been foolish to take to the hills for you in the mad summer of '98.

" 'So,' said Fitzgerald to Boyle, 'no pink cave for you.' "

That then was the way Sal wrote the first afternoon of my consciousness, the room darkening as she sat making a myth out of an ancient Fitzgerald and musing on the tatty reality of another one called Brian. At last stretching herself and sitting back dissatisfied. Poor man's Camus! she thought to herself. Yet she smiled, forgave and caressed herself, remembering my boyhood and my perfect brain.

Through which I already understood that for the born, there were no simple joys. For the unborn, nothing but. Even the couplings and partings of nucleotides and enzymes in the DNA sanctums in my spawning cells clouded my face with pleasure. Enzymes had sweeter and more skillful sexuality than was dreamed of by Brian. I was diverted too by the ribosomes. Springing like champignons from the golden floor of my proteins, taking off like hot-air balloons, trailing carnival ribbons of amino acid. If I concentrated I could taste the fragile instant when the chromatidia aligned themselves in the core of a cell like two sides of a house of assembly. Their mad decision to migrate, one party to the farthest south rim of the cell, the other to the farthest north, engrossed me. My mouth was tight in the tremulous second when, by their pushing, they split their world in two. So now there were two cells, a dizzy and reckless multiplication of me. Yet, each time it happened, I found that in their haste and frenzy, in all their bioideological rush to sunder, they had each brought with them in clear symbols their prize heritage. In their hands, so to speak, the sage chromosomes held the formula for me, which no crisis could alter or distort. No wonder I enjoyed life.

To boot, I rode the warm estuaries of Sal's blood and heard it sing in me. I adverted to the charming deftness of my inexorable kidneys and the crafty manufacture of my gut.

From all these bedazzlements the born were distracted. By crowds and timetables, by buses and giraffes, by each other and by death. Pleasure grew clumsy in the born, self-conscious being. Pleasure grew self-questioning, tormented. And the mute blood, till the day it clotted the heart, ran unadmired.

Sal turned on the television. At Wimbledon they were in the fifth set of a men's singles. A stumpy Central European player reminded us both of the Gnome, the little man who—in his way—stalked us. What nationality was the Gnome? Sal wondered, posing again the questions she had already posed. Did he have a wife or woman to wash his polo neck? What was his dwelling, what his trade? Did he follow us on behalf of an institution, an agency, an arm of government? Or was Sal an obsession he had got together out of his own brain?

At the expected hour, just before five, Brian called. He announced, in a way that almost invited Sal to be joyful with him for the opening, that there was a party to christen United Press's new computer. He would be late an hour, two at the outside.

"It's getting less funny. These parties I don't go to," said Sal. But she was a gentle girl and her tone, even now, was teasing. Oh too tolerant Sal.

Eight hours thirty minutes self-aware, I felt more than she the risk of losing Brian to some harsh infertile girl.

"You wouldn't want to dignify a rort like this, love," Brian told her. "Only staying a moment myself."

"These moments you stay add up. You're doing twelve hours work a week for the cr'ater."

"Now!" He didn't like her talking of whiskey this way, as if it were a mythic Irish beast. Perhaps because the beast very nearly had him in a corner.

"Come home soon," she said. You knew the man was twisted to shrug off such invitations. "Come home not smelling. All right? Because . . ."

"Because . . . ?"

"I've something wonderful to tell you."

"*Wonderful?*" Even the word frightened him. Since she became infused with me, he no longer trusted her *wonderfuls.*

"It's the child."

By his telephone, the wild colonial bull flinched and squeezed up his eyes.

"I visited that hologram unit today," Sal persisted.

The bastard was actually short of breath as he asked, "Oh yes. What did you think of it?"

"*What did I think of it?* I wasn't the Duchess of Kent, you know, visiting worthy institutions. It's a question surely of what it thought of me."

"I suppose you're right," Brian told her. He did not understand himself why he waited for her words as for a blow.

"I'll only tell you if you're really interested."

"Of course I'm bloody interested."

"What if I told you the child is male? What if I said its—*his*—brain shows a perfect configuration?"

"Come on, no Irish rhetoricals. Is it the truth?"

"It's the truth."

"Well . . . you must be very happy."

42

"You must be too." She uttered it as a command.

Through the telephone at Sal's ear I felt the reverberation of his frown. "It's a . . . a relief to know. Not that I expected . . ."

The yellow miasma of his disappointment got beneath my sealed eyes. Did he want a monster? Didn't he know how genetic errors burden people? Did he hope I'd be imperfect? Well, no. If there were ever a man to eschew expense and anguish it was the old Queensland sugar banana. But to hear I was whole and perfect made me too real, too close.

I wanted to warn Sal, to say don't tell him any more. For her tidings would make him look for girls. I nudged her uterus uselessly with my toe. I tautened my mind like a catapult.

"A boy," said Sal. "Maybe you'll want to raise him in the sun. In Australia." Sal was a sentimentalist.

"We'll see, love."

Now he needed to get away to his party.

"Enjoy yourself, darling," Sal told him, as if he had earned enjoyment.

While Sal got the veal from the refrigerator, I felt again the bile in my mouth and waved my crumpled fists. In a garage of a town house in Hampstead, Brian was humping a cadet from the *Express* on the bonnet of a white Renault 10. Registration number BN4.7563.

The good news had of course forced him to it.

One day—September 25, 1963, it was—Brian took part in an ambush and understood, for the first time, that he was not the darling of nature. Since that day he had always suffered a sort of asthma when people like Sal told him that the unbribeable processes of nature were taking him over. The process, for example, by which sons become fathers and at last see that there is no other and buffer generation between themselves and the pit.

What I learned about Brian from the ambush was that

he had at a time possessed the qualities of a knight. And since now, so long after the ambush, he was enjoying a girl between the headlights of someone's little French car, I needed to remember that he was once a chevalier.

Brian came of a family whose origins were convict but who, by the 1870s, were grazing cattle on a station large as Cornwall, carrying six head of beef per square mile. They were people whose thrust Brian had largely lost, though perhaps the girl on the Renault's superstructure might not have believed so.

In 1942, when Singapore fell to the Japanese, my grandfather, Wallace Fitzgerald, as tall as Brian but fuller in the bones, had been away soldiering in Egypt. A world distant from Alexandria, his own homestead paddock lay naked before the intentions of the Japanese High Command. He would never recover from his feelings of helplessness in the desert. From that year on his reading of Asian affairs was that all Asia lusts for Australia. Soon this axiom developed and became more refined. All Asia was turning monolithic and Marxist and was lusting with ideological ardor for Australia.

This view was taught in the grammar school Brian attended for five years. The convict ancestor's Jacobin sentiments had been traded in by his progeny for a wan attachment to the Anglican faith, and Brian as a schoolboy felt little fervor for any doctrine except the doctrine of lusting Asia. In the first years of his puberty it took on a religious heat for him, it was his brain's burning bush. He belonged to a secret group who would meet in a toolshed and masturbate together and plan the thwarting of Asian communism. Only selection as center for his school's under-fifteen rugby team saved him from this sticky and fanatic group.

At the university he had joined the Young Liberals. (In that country the conservatives called themselves the Liberal Party, so a suspicion old Maurice Fitzgerald, the convict, once uttered, that in this southern land titles and meanings might be turned upside down, was in part justified.)

Following his graduation and for one year of mixed joys, Brian worked as a cadet journalist on a Brisbane daily. He was a pious student of foreign affairs. For him as for his editor, foreign affairs meant what China and Russia were doing in Asia to imperil Australia, that great Asian capsule of European values.

In that year, Brian wasn't what is called *good* with girls. (He is now, I suppose!) On the North Brisbane rugby team he had been dropped to the reserves. Indonesia was in receipt of arms and aid from Russia. Diem, strange darling of America's Asian vision, was suffering from the Viet Cong.

Brian began reading T. E. Lawrence. (If he'd read more D. H. he might have been saved the ambush.) *Seven Pillars of Wisdom* reacted almost chemically on his obsession. He even wondered if he might be meant to be an Asian Lawrence. He wondered too whether, even should he become first-grade halfback for Norths and, after beating South Brisbane 50 to 3, be awarded some milk-white club concubine, it would be enough.

One passage of Lawrence's he underlined and learned by rote. "Arabs could be swung on an idea as on a cord; for the unpledged allegiance of their minds made them obedient servants . . . they were incorrigibly children of the idea, feckless and colour-blind, to whom body and spirit were forever and inevitably opposed. Their minds were strange and dark . . ."

At the end of the 1962 football season (September in the Antipodes) Brian fancied himself as a possible crusader in Asia. He would traverse its ideological deserts and sow them with meanings. When in the end he got to Asia—the part called North Borneo—he would find no ideological desert but rather something his geography books should have prepared him for. A jungle.

That spring, he joined the army. In the last summer of his innocence, he took the three-month officers' course at a place called Portsea. Here, in a college above the sea, was the back door to the professional army. It offered no promise of unlimited promotion; there was another military college for that. A college with a course years long. But Brian felt he had a right to be impatient in the Lawrence manner. Lawrence hadn't, after all, been a Sandhurst man.

At Portsea, Brian studied jungle warfare and went on toughening hikes. Letters from his father, as well as instructing him in certain Asian facets, decried his enlistment. "And watch out for Asian whores," Fitzgerald, his father, wrote to him. "In the Balikpapan campaign my company suffered two wounded and sixty-three V.D. cases. The women of southern Borneo chew betelnut and are as ugly as sin. But it doesn't put some people off."

His father's letters undermined him. Wasn't the Asian peril large enough for a twenty-one-year-old boy to make a career of it? Was the one risk a risk of infection?

There was also a worldly schoolteacher, a trim girl with brown hair, who played tennis with him and was a hoary fornicator. "There's no monolithic communism," she used to tell him. "The way there's no monolithic Rotarian movement. Why don't you sit back and take in the sun? I know what you think. You think, what is there to Australia if there is no threat from Asia? There's nothing if not that, you think. There's blandness and boredom, that's all. So you have to create a threat to save yourself. It doesn't mean the threat exists."

He should have learned sense from her curving mouth, her spotless and suntanned quarters that had a quality to them that was senior and droll. She was a sensible girl. Her name was Beatrice Porter, and in the end she dropped him because she couldn't bed down with his opinions.

Brian felt happiest, and least challenged, in the library at Portsea studying the tactics of Filipino guerrillas or jogging beside an NCO and grilling him about the former emergency in Malaya.

Once he heard a lecture about Indonesia from a young interpreter called Lieutenant Ball. He rose and asked Lieutenant Ball where Sukarno stood in relation to Russia's plans for Asia. Ball said politely that such a question had no meaning. Asian statesmen didn't think in the same terms as our statesmen, said Ball. The glossary of the cold war meant little to them. Later, in the officers' mess, the conversation went on. "Then what is Sukarno really after?"

"Succulent Indonesian snatch," Ball said.

Ball, the girl, his father. He was happy to lose himself in the jungle warfare course. He did very well in the rain forests. He arranged crafty ambushes in coastal jungles in Queensland. He suppressed claustrophobia and sat alone in an underground burrow the way the Viet Minh used to do and the Viet Cong had done since. But his faith was pockmarked now. Answers such as "succulent Indonesian snatch" had pitted it.

The infantry battalion he joined was to undertake Malaysian duty in the middle of the last *annus mirabilis* for fine-grade anti-Communist conviction, 1963, the year consecrated to Kennedy's outbidding of the Russians in the matter of Cuba.

As if someone sensible were plotting Brian's education, Brian found Lieutenant Ball in the officers' mess of his new battalion. At first their talk was cool, for Brian mistrusted Ball's whimsy, and Ball believed Brian to be a little mad.

Brian said, "You're coming to Malaya with us?"

"North Borneo, Sabah," said Ball. "I think it will be Sabah. That's the only place where Malaysia and Indonesia share a border."

Though Brian was hurt that Ball didn't know he knew that, they became friends.

Brian was engaged by Ball's gentleness, even his cynicism. "I've got simple aims," Ball announced. "All I want to do is take up a lectureship in Indonesian in the new year. Until then it will be my job to tell any Indonesian infiltrator found on the borders of Sabah to put down his Russian carbine. In doing so, I intend to exercise all the pith of a Bahasa Indonesian Ogden Nash."

"A time server, are you?"

"Too bloody right."

There were more assaults on Brian's faith: when Captain Murdoch spoke to the company in which Brian was a platoon commander, he uttered Brian's tenets. And when Brian heard them as delineated by the captain, they had to them an unhinged sound.

"Indonesian terrorists!" said Captain Murdoch, briefing his troops. (For I had now access to that strand of nervous gristle in Brian's brain where Murdoch's speech was recorded as on magnetic tape.) "Indonesian terrorists. Armed by atheistical Communist Russia. Armed with the best of weapons. M41's. Thirty-round magazines. Indonesian terrorists better bloody armed than you. Pawns of Russian strategy. When the Malay States federate, these Russian bloody puppets will cross into Sarawak and Sabah. Every rubber plantation and police station that they raid, every patrol they attack, will mean a victory for a corrupt bloody Slav sitting in the snow thousands of miles away. The bastard's name, my friends, is Khrushchev. Sukarno has told us what he intends to do if the federal state of Malaysia is formed. He and Khrushchev think the fucking Malays will be a pushover, and he's right. He thinks the fucking British with their bad teeth and poofter officers will be a pushover, and he could be right there too. What does it mean to those pale bastards if Malaysia is threatened? Nothing. What does it mean to us? Everything. A victory for Khrushchev close to Australia's front door! Will we let it happen? Sukarno fears we bloody won't. Let's prove the bastard's fears correct."

At the end of briefings, the company would often applaud Captain Murdoch. At the end of the applause one day, Lieutenant Ball, stretching and yawning behind a hand, asked a question. "Sir," he said, "about our rifles. Will the fire-select levers be unsoldered when we go to Sabah?"

The fire-select levers on the company's rifles had been soldered at "Single Shot" to prevent soldiers from firing automatic bursts on maneuvers and wasting the ammunition of the Commonwealth.

At Ball's question, the captain paused and squinted. "This battalion, this company, can defeat any scratch bunch of Indonesians even with single-shot fire."

"Is it the Defence Department's intention to prove that principle?"

Murdoch looked at the roof. "No. The bloody levers will be unsoldered when you get to Jesselton."

But the levers never were. It was to prove some thesis in Murdoch's meaty head that they remained welded on *S* for "Single Shot."

In a hotel room in Jesselton, a balmy town on the northwest coast of Sabah, a Malay girl called Betsy asked Brian why he had come to Borneo. Brian, bending over the hooks of his jungle boots, commenced to tell her about far Khrushchev and the world plot. Yet after a few seconds he stopped. He saw not only that the girl could not understand him but that the formulas he was using hung in the air like some improbable item of European finery on which mold would grow by morning. What he was saying, he understood then, was no longer organic to him.

An hour later he sat staring down at the froth of a beer on a hotel veranda. He said to his friend, "It's a local argument, isn't it? This argument between these people?"

"In many ways."

"And we're just bloody policemen."

"The idea disappoints you?"

The idea left him bereft.

Ball took Brian's elbow and pumped it as if disappointed young men could be easily reinflated. "Don't be a funny bastard," Ball told him.

But I think Ball understood Brian's pain. That all his fervor was gone, that now he had nothing but to settle down to the normal avocations of those who lapse from some high and arrogant faith. Booze and whoring.

Ball at last grew embarrassed at the deep purchase the nails of his own forefinger and thumb had taken in the flesh of Brian's arm. He let go, a millimeter at a time to begin with.

"This has been an education, hasn't it? Listen, mate. What will you do?"

"I've got some sort of rash on my feet. Maybe I can get out on medical grounds."

"Of course," Ball admitted, "it's true that in the diplomatic sense—in terms of the international game—Khrushchev *would* be fairly pleased if Sukarno puts a scare into Malaysia."

Brian raised his hands and very nearly blocked his ears. He had lost the fundamental creed that bound him together, that had for a year or more drawn his brain so taut that it had the unity and shine of a spearhead. Now Ball offered him a trite little commentary on Asian affairs! "Bugger the game!" Brian managed to utter.

On September 25 that year there was a patrol in the rotting forests along the river called Sabatik. A Dusun guide led them down an ancient hunting trail among wet monkey puzzles, beneath lawyer vines hoared over with a fibrous green mold, and over the silt of the mangrove swamps. The way made no sense to someone not born to it and sometimes they went thigh-deep into black waters. If they cared to look they could see aquatic leeches, olive but brightly banded, jerking toward them over a surface of jet swamp drainage.

In his jungle boots Brian was nurturing foot rot. He knew it was progressing in its climate of sweat and foul water and tried even to foster the growth of the appropriate molds by sending telepathic impulses down to his extremities.

Before mid-morning these telepathic patterns were interrupted by a radio call from a British helicopter. A fishing boat of suspicious contours, said the helicopter pilot, was moving up the Sabatik estuary in the direction of a timber mill. The pilot had swooped on this boat without causing it to turn back. Now he would keep a distant eye on it and guide Murdoch's men to intercept it should it put in.

Brian thought, Two weeks ago that sort of message would have meant something to me, would have come down on the bumpy tropical radio waves like a divine election.

I remember better than Brian how Murdoch's detachment stumbled on another hour under guidance from the helicopter. Better than Brian I remember the screens of mangroves and the ripe stench of mud. And how without warning they saw, through a gap in the greenery, a fishing boat overloaded with young Indonesians. Better than Brian I remember Brian's few seconds of prurient excitement at seeing tarpaulins draped over weapons in the bows. He was such an innocent, had grown up in such a bland country, that even in his loss of belief he thought still: No person of true talent gets killed at random in police actions up rivers in Borneo. In a great battle of ideologies, perhaps. But not in a local brawl. So he felt safe on account of his talent and felt that Ball was safe.

I remember better than any of those voyagers the exact contours of that sound when the boat kissed a sandbar near the mouth of a side stream. I remember better than anyone the pale tight smile of Captain Murdoch. With movements of the head, he marshaled his soldiers behind the mangroves while the boat lolled on the sandbar and the young Indonesians were busy on its decks, like bona fide fishermen. Better than Brian I remember how Brian watched the mudskippers drowsing on the rich silt in front of him. He had leisure to inspect these ancient fish, for he believed he knew what would happen. Ball would take the loud-hailer from his back and advise the Indonesians to stand still. No doubt, the Indonesians would obey.

Brian's position lay in a mesh of mangrove roots, in his hands (his hands being small) a small biddable Owen gun. Watching the Indonesians with little more interest than a cop watches shoplifting schoolchildren, certain of a quick and undisputed arrest, he heard Murdoch whisper to Ball.

"I'll tell you what I want," said Murdoch. "Tell 'em in English that we're here. Lay down their arms and all that. Then tell 'em in Indonesian."

"In English first?"

"That's right. They're the bloody trespassers."

"They'll panic."

"They're the trespassers," Murdoch said. "Do what I bloody say."

Had they argued they might have been heard, even over the rant of swamp birds, by the interlopers. So both Ball and Brian kept silent, thinking, Well, a fast burst of English. Then the real stuff . . . the sedating words Ball had been schooled to utter.

Better than any born man I remember the ways the Indonesians wasted their time, talking, laughing, as would authentic fishermen. But how at last the deck tarpaulins were dragged back and revealed a mounted gun which no one, however, bothered to man. How automatic weapons were brought up from the hold, and some twenty young invaders stood about on the deck or on the silt, inspecting or lazily fingering them. Better than Brian I mark the instant in which Murdoch nodded Now.

Ball meant only to tell them to stand still, but the first sound of the language of Shakespeare and Milton stampeded the visitors. Though some of them had trouble, being unfamiliar with the Russian mechanisms in their hands, others had already cocked the weapons and now began firing. On me? Brian asked himself. On me?

In Queensland the sky is so large and the earth so vacant that a man stands out, and a man of talent stands out like a grand city of the plains. And you don't shoot at such irreplaceable objects as Queensland men of talent.

Without knowing it Brian himself fired his Owen gun. The Indonesians, caught firing too high into the vegetation, fell and slapped and flapped on the mud. Why is Ball kneeling by me? Brian wondered. At the end of his magazine, he looked at his friend. Ball had suffered a frightful wound in the throat, although not quite so—his throat had rather been altered and the gullet torn away. His life's blood ran over his bottom lip. Brian could not believe the force of its escape. That after resting docile in the veins through childhood and high school and the trials of young manhood it would escape so furiously.

Driven by this new insight into the properties of blood, Brian locked a new magazine into its cavity. He was crazed, he was frightened. Ball, clever Ball, had put his brow against the silt and died. God help not-so-clever me, thought Brian.

Better than Brian dares remember, I remember the Indonesians whom Brian slaughtered with his second magazine and with half a third. Better than he dares I remember the mud which drank the gore yet no more accepted the cerebral matter poured out by the victims than silk accepts mercury.

Behind his sights, Brian already knew he could never feel safe in spirit or body again. No ideology and no measure of talent could save you from certain besetting truths—the pace of escaping blood for a start; but also the blunt fact that events were indiscriminate as runaway cement trucks. Just because everyone has to know *that* in the end doesn't mean everyone has the talent to break the fact into digestible bits and flush it through his bloodstream. Brian has never had any such talent.

When the firing stilled, the dead terrorists dared lie on the silt displaying ears so pink and translucently perfect that you were reminded of shells on a better beach than this one. That's it, Brian drunkenly told himself. Cling to imagery as to the only refuge from the crude fact of death.

Having lost his innocence all those years before he knew of me, he these days felt in a guilty way that a father ought to have an ideology to display, enameled and seamless, to his children. Hadn't his own father had one?

This was yet another reason for his being scared of me. He didn't want me to see him empty-handed.

5

In that first evening of my consciousness, not counting the events of my cells and my blood, the next event was Brian's arrival. He came in at a quarter to nine hungry to be held by Sal. With the girl on the bonnet of the Renault, his seed had seized up. Therefore he felt foolish and worn down by the world. He carried in his hand some poppies which had come in fresh from the countryside last night and now rose from his fist a little withered after a full day in a railway station florist's.

Sal welcomed him as he wanted to be welcomed. Her blood, as she held him, made certain affirmations: Yes, this is the man, the love of my nerve endings, of the pit of my belly. I could feel the special voltage of her Brian-desire tickling my spine.

They sat together then, eating the veal and drinking a bottle of cheap Portuguese wine, a special from Wineways. They watched a particular comedy show on the grounds that Sal thought Brian liked it. Yet he had grown somnolent

54

before the first vocalist appeared. His harsh day of making, breaking, being broken was at last absorbed down into his dazed cells.

Sal's hand lay on her belly imposing a soft quietus, and I could feel her fingertips—not as a pressure but as five golden presences. The first astounding day is over, I told myself.

But suspicion surfaced, sharp-nosed, otterlike, in Brian, and without warning he lunged at the lower right-hand corner of Sal's bookcase where her small reference library in matters of conception, gestation, birth was stacked. He picked some of these books up and peered at the index of this one and that. A half-minute madness had touched him, the idea that I might be self-aware had taken him over, and I trembled at knowing how potently I resounded even in his after-dinner sleep.

"Don't you want to watch them?" Sal asked, indicating the television. "Your favorite goons?"

Brian's answer was to read aloud an index entry. "The Psychological Conditioning of the Embryo."

"I'll switch it on to 'Man Alive,' " Sal offered, mistrusting this fit of his.

"I was wondering about this joker and his benign laser beams."

"Dr. Ford?"

"What if those lasers have gingered the little bugger up? What if he knows me better than you do? And you too . . . you better than you know yourself?"

One might ask where that idea came from so pat, so punctual. I could answer only that as Sal carried me in her womb, I must also have inhabited some sac in Brian's brain.

"It's like light passing through your hand." Sal was used to him taking up questions in this half-fanciful, half-crazed way. She never knew how to ease him out of it, except to point him to the Scotch. He'd already been pointed to too much Scotch for one day. "A laser can find its way among the molecules. Breaking nothing, taking nothing. Leaving nothing either. Ford guarantees that. And Ford is—after all—a scientist."

So, mocking him, she was pleased to see the mockery settled him down. He was merely half serious when he said, "Oh yes, one has to admit that journalists don't have the stature, the hand in history that scientists have. For—to name a case—devising blasts to sizzle a maximum of human flesh, brewing up bombs full of anthrax bacteria, tinkering with people's cells and finding emulsifiers for napalm and . . . and all the rest of their sweet bloody arts . . ."

They laughed together, though he did of course light some mental candle for those vanished Indonesians. The laughter jollified the little pellet of my heart. Yet he still retained it as a serious question: Did I sit in Sal privy to the manner in which his manhood had stalled an hour or more ago in a garage in Hampstead?

His suspicion, I could tell, derived from a diabetic aunt of his who had died in the drought summer of 1953. Aunt Cecilia. Mrs. Fitzgerald, driving into Cunnamulla to shop on a Friday, would often leave young Brian to sit and chat by his aunt's bed. Aunt Cecilia had always been indulgent to Brian—even then he worked his charms, in fact they were charms more appropriate in eight-year-old boys than they are in a man of thirty-two seasons.

But Aunt Cecilia, stricken by diabetes and beached on her gleaming brass bed, had ceased to be the kind of husky mischievous aunt a boy needs. There was an intrusive smell about her now, not a nasty one, but one that signaled to him that she had become a transient. She was now—not through any great change in her face—difficult to look at, and he could not joke, boast, tussle with her.

The room was kept dark, for in darkness there was a chance of cool, but Brian could hear red dust thudding against the draped window, the red dust for which the Japanese Empire had lusted and which now copiously flew on a scalding wind.

"Brian," Aunt Cecilia told him one such torpid Friday, "I am going to die. Did you know that?"

"Yeah," he said. Squirming.

"So that you might think we'll be lost to each other. But I am at peace with God. And I tell you that I'll look over you, every second of every day. Would you like that?"

"Yeah," he said, horrified. But his father and mother had raised him to be polite. "Thank you, Auntie Cecilia."

"Of course," she said, qualifying her promise, for she had returned to the old faith, "I may be some time in Purgatory . . . I was a wild girl when I was young . . . but from the moment I enter God's presence, I will look after you."

Aunt Cecilia died of blood poisoning before the wet spell began, and throughout the winter he refrained from picking his nose, conscious of Aunt Cecilia's supervision. He tried to avoid excreting but that only led to laxative dosages from his mother, and so he besat the lavatory seat red faced not only from his tortured bowels but also for shame at being surveyed by ranks of dead and heavenly Fitzgeralds.

Now, twenty-four years later, he cringed at the possibility of observation by unborn and kingly me.

Sal sniffed, rose, found a page in a particular book. "The scientific study of embryonic defects," she read, "has disproved the ancient belief that physical injury, repulsive sights, or horror affecting the mother may cause the deformity of the child. There is no connection between the mother's nervous system and that of the infant by which ideas or impressions in the mother's mind can reach the child . . ."

"It doesn't mention though . . . ideas in the father's mind. Impressions of his. Experiences . . ."

"The father's?" she asked, frowning. It seemed almost that he had intruded on something private to her.

"For Christ's sake, Sal, I provided some of the matter for building the little bugger." He said it as if he were proud of the achievement, as if he might go down into Hospital Road and boast about his fatherhood.

"Well, yes," she conceded.

And half joking still, to cover up for still being half afraid, "Consider the lonely sperm," he said. "The prodigious journey he makes. Across the Pons Uterinum. His colleagues dying all round him. Going under like shipwrecked sailors. And there he is at the mouth of the ovarian canal. Lean now. A crazy little barb. Obsessed. Fated for the flanks of Moby Ovum."

Sal shivered, though with delight. It was this kind of whimsy that had first made her take notice of him at a party in Holland Park three years before.

"Who says the little hero carries no knowledge, communicates nothing? Who says he . . . the . . . the boy . . . doesn't tune into me on gene radio?"

Aroused by this fantasy, Sal began to caress him in her long-armed, strenuous way.

"Oh Sal, I missed you today," he whispered, but remembered that his body was still flavored with the sap of little Miss Renault.

"It's been a sweaty day," he said then. "Let me shower, eh?"

Merriment rose in me, not entering from the placenta but radiating from my core, my founding cell. And merrily and without malice I thought of how willingly Brian would take my place after his day of blunted labors, how more-than-he-knew pleased to usurp me once he'd finished his shower, rubbed Brut on his genitals—as was his habit—and taken Sal to bed.

I laughed at him as silently and temperately as, one golden morning, Tiberius might have laughed at some shaggy barbarian from beyond the Danube.

After they had fallen asleep, on one of those cooler summer nights, I observed them, laid out on their backs, as one might observe a knight and his lady laid out on their backs in some old church in Norfolk. There was moonlight on the left side of Brian's cheek, on a bulge which the doctors call a mandibular condyle. That was the place where the provosts in Jesselton broke his jaw in 1963.

For when Brian stood with Murdoch among the perfect ears of slaughtered Indonesians and Murdoch instructed Brian to search the corpses, and Brian refused and hurled his automatic weapon at Murdoch, the hair trigger of the mechanism had done its work and discharged one accidental bullet into the air.

Murdoch therefore arrested Brian for attempted murder of his company commander and, after the wounded had been bounced away across the cyclonic sky in a helicopter, and before Ball's body and his shattered loud-hailer had made any such journey, Brian was lifted out, dazed, under a dazed guard.

The court-martial acquitted him, suspecting that his broken jaw had not come from a fall downstairs as the medical records pronounced. The court-martial reprimanded Murdoch for his strange procedures, but by the time the reprimand was spoken, Brian's foot rot, nurtured throughout the trial, had put him in hospital.

Now, a dozen years later, he still suffered from it in a mild way. I suspected that he must have infected whole changing rooms of footballers, tennis and squash players in those years since the ambush.

Because of the rot, because the provosts had been premature in handing out mandibular condyles, he was given an honorable discharge. After that he could not risk staying in Australia, for he feared the tone of Australian journals, that they might push that naive world view he had lost and remind him too grievously of the Sabatik, of arguments he should have waged with Murdoch, of Ball, and the Indonesians whom he remembered as translucently beautiful young men in those pieces of their bodies which remained whole and waxlike after the shooting. He felt he had nothing to say in his own land, that he would be too easily pained there and silenced. And editorials he thought he might read there frightened him in advance.

He sailed for England. Two years later his agency asked him to return to Australia, but he refused.

One night after he had married Sal—all Fleet Street telling him in chorus what a lucky bastard he was—he saw a television documentary about Murdoch. Known to the Viet Cong as "Black Beret," Murdoch commanded a battalion of Montagnards. He had become a legend in Phuoc Tuy, et cetera, et cetera. There was vivid footage of Murdoch speaking with an urbane British correspondent.

"Are there many like him at home?" Sal had asked. But Brian did not answer. His palms itched. He was galvanized.

At the end of the documentary, the correspondent re-created for the viewers the death of fabled Major Murdoch, shot in the face while displaying himself to the Viet Cong.

From that evening, Brian had begun first to think more neutrally about the country he'd been born in and then to let certain congenital images of it work on his brain. There was an image of skies of such taut and metaphysical blue that you wondered if they might not at any instant split and deposit some god or son of God on the ocher cattle pastures beyond Cunnamulla. There was an image of rain forests more pleasing than those of Borneo, and of tropic waters in Whitsunday Passage, a blue that differed from the sky blue and spoke of woman and sense and the shadows of fishes and that held the warmth of the sun. If ever he dreams, these are likely to be the landscapes of the good dreams.

Perhaps sentimental Sal was right. Perhaps, as the ancestor called Fitzgerald traveled south in the *Minerva*, I shall one day travel for the same landfall in the saner hold of Sal.

Saturday afternoon Clytie, Sal, and I went shopping. I
moved in King's Road like someone who had been ac-
quainted with its crowds and geography a long time. But
seventy-five hours self-aware, I knew as well as Sal where
the Boots was, the post office, Elliot's Shoes, the newsagent
who, if Sal were nostalgic, could supply her with *The
Hibernian* and *The Irish Press*. I knew that Lyons was
across the road from Peter Jones's department store but
that Clytie would not crowd in there for a cup of tea and
would rather crowd into the tearoom of Peter Jones's. Like
a veteran shopper, I knew which floor that tearoom was on.

So, a little after three, we found ourselves at a yellow
table screened by palms, "beating the menopause rush" as
Clytie called it, ordering tea before other women, struck by
shoppers' fatigue, came staggering up to the tearoom. The
quarrel Sal and Clytie had had two afternoons back, all that
reckless talk about having me expunged, had been forgotten,
even—very nearly—by me.

"Tell me," said old Clytie, squeezing a lemon over her

Earl Grey, "are they sending Brian on many foreign assignments lately? I was just thinking—you wouldn't want one to coincide with the happy event."

I abhorred Clytie when she uttered words like *happy event*. It was another of those things I seem to have been living with far longer than seventy-five hours. The hand of poor George, Clytie's beloved surgeon, must have itched for a scalpel when he heard Clytie utter such words in her style of withered drollery. Unless he found that sort of thing erotic.

"Brian can usually avoid them," Sal told her. "He doesn't like flying, you see. He would go to any trouble to avoid flying . . . once he went to Narvik by train. It took him four days as against four hours . . ."

"My God! Afraid of flying." Clytie laughed as if she had at last found something endearing about Brian.

"My second husband was a bomber pilot," she went on. Any wan pretext did her when she wanted to go over to autobiography. "Now that was something to wonder about. One never knew from day to day how one stood. We'd already decided to divorce, but it didn't seem very sensible instituting proceedings when he might be killed any day."

"Why did you want to divorce him?"

"He was one of those people who wanted a child a year. Imagine me, a broodmare. Anyhow, I can remember him saying to me: 'Clytie, I'm likely to shuffle off any day. Why waste money on a solicitor?' He surprised himself by surviving. Continually. We stayed married longer than we ever would have in peacetime. And then VE-Day came. So I said, 'Adrian, it's time.' And I went and had the papers drawn up. Then, a month after the war, he was killed delivering a plane to Germany. Not before impregnating poor Clytie."

"I'm sure you were soon snapped up," said Sal. For she knew how dazzling Clytie must have been then.

"Not in my *enceinte* state." Clytie played with her lemon rind. "Of course the child was premature and lasted . . . maybe ten days."

Sal was thinking, Clytie's certainty, the way she's at peace with her past. Will I ever be like that?

Two tables away, a tall woman maybe three years older than Clytie saw us amid our thin defense of palms and recognized us. Leaving her table, she hobbled up to us smiling in a manic way.

Clytie said, "Oh Christ. My mad cousin."

The mad cousin sat down avidly, and without being requested, in the third chair.

"Clytie," she said, settling her blue linen coat about her, "I was at Mass this morning in Farm Street and said a prayer for you. And here you are."

"That's right," said Clytie. "I had a visit from the Virgin Mary. She said, 'Go up and take some tea at Peter Jones's. There you'll meet your dotty cousin who's worried about you.'"

"Clytie, Clytie," soothed the cousin.

Clytie explained it all to Sal. "Her husband left her after twenty years of martyrdom. *His,* to be exact."

"No, he found a girl more beautiful. It happens a lot."

"Does it?" Clytie asked, making a face of wonderment. "How are those young Jesuit gigolos you invite to dinner?"

"Let's not argue, Clytie."

"I should tell you, I'm still the whore of Babylon," Clytie told her. "It might be dangerous to talk to me at all."

"Please, Clytie," Sal implored.

"You're Irish?" the cousin said to Sal.

"Yes."

"Did you see the article on the Virgin Birth in the latest edition of *The Month?*"

"No. No, I didn't."

"Toss it in, Elspeth," said Clytie. "She's not that kind of Irishwoman."

"You aren't a Catholic?"

"I was."

"You must miss it," Elspeth decided.

"No."

"Oh yes, you do. You know you do."

"No, I don't."

"I know you know you do. No one who has had it and lost it ever gets used to the loss. You come back to it when you're dying, or when your husband leaves you. And there are reasons to come back to it now you're pregnant."

"Reasons?" Sal asked her. Sal felt tremulous and might soon be angry.

"Who else will protect your baby at this stage in history?"

"I'll protect it."

"You are not enough. You'll see."

"For Christ's sake, Elspeth," Clytie said. Showing some sensitivity. Thinking, Let's not have any more upsets about this bloody fetus. "Do you really believe it's a world where pregnant girls walking down King's Road get inveigled down some cellar steps by an abortionist?"

"The situations are much more complex than that. Say, for example, our young friend here was certified."

"I don't think that's going to happen."

"Say it did. Say some psychiatrist decides she's psychotic. It happens to the sane, oh yes. Mortimer tried to have me certified once. He even got a tame psychiatrist to say that I was a clinical case. Oh yes, it happens. And so the psychiatrist says to our friend's husband, your wife is a hopeless case, your child should be aborted. And the husband, confused and wifeless, agrees, and the whole force of our institutions seems aimed against her unborn child . . ."

Clytie said, "What a melodrama!"

But Sal sat still, as pregnant women always will when someone, even Clytie's crazy cousin, undertakes to brief them on the potentialities of their state.

"Have you ever been in a psychiatric hospital?" the mad cousin asked.

"No," Sal lied. But when Sister Angelica left Enniscorthy for America, Sal had begun to tremble and be inconsolable, and they had put her in a sanatorium for two days' rest.

"Once you have been . . . well, it's like having a criminal record. Certain rights are suspended."

Clytie stood up. "What a shame we have to go," she said. "Come on, Sal."

The cousin was hurt. Clytie, the subject of her Farm Street prayers, was snubbing her. "Some landladies hate children," she told Sal. "Rather than one child, they'd sooner have a house full of monkey droppings."

"Sod you," said Clytie. "You dotty old Papist! Coming, Sal?"

Sal wanted to. "Well, Elspeth, it's been nice . . ."

Clytie led us across the tearoom floor, weaving among tired shoppers who were chewing their lips over where to sit. Beyond the antique department, we reached the lift. Sal looked back and saw the cousin in the blue coat wiping her eyes at the table. Under her armpits and breasts, Sal began to sweat with grief. It was a question whom the grief was for. I didn't know, though it struck me pungently.

"How does she know I'm pregnant?" Sal asked Clytie, for Sal fancied herself as being a willowy childbearer. "Does it show?"

"No," Clytie reassured her. "She has a mad way of knowing things."

The lift reached that floor, sighing. When the doors sprang open, Sal turned to them as if she wanted nothing better than the warm huddle of shoppers. She propped, however, for the Gnome stood just inside the door.

"Going down?" she asked him in a small voice.

"Sorry. Up." His voice too was small in its manner, and aghast because he could not have planned to face her that way. The vowels of the two words he uttered came out with an alien softness, neither Irish nor British.

Another failure of breath occurred in Sal and so in me, and we suffered the impulse to hurl ourselves in with him and travel against all reason, upward—escaping Clytie and her cousin. There was a hushing noise, as if to tame our urge, and the doors closed.

"An interesting-looking man," said Clytie. "He liked you too, Sal."

"Did he?"

"You ought to have a friend. Especially in pregnancy. Most women need the added reassurance. You know. As they lose their girlishness."

"I'll give some thought to it, Clytie," Sal promised her, looking away to the table they had left. Elspeth still sat there, her eyes locked in a close focus, almost crossed. Anyone who had ever been a praying Christian could tell she was praying.

Lest she be tempted with that despair which to some people can be more attractive than the call of the flesh.

The name of Clytie's beloved was George. He liked Brian better than Clytie did and, often on Saturday afternoons, had him down to watch the sport on the color television. This is my afternoon, Ran Singh, he would say to the monkey and turn the rump of the set toward Ran Singh's cage. No "Jack-a-Nory" this afternoon, he'd say. He was just a little pleased to be able to deprive Ran Singh of colored pictures for once. But, being a broad-faced kindly man, he was not vengeful enough with that simian oaf. "For Clytie's sake," he was always saying to guests, "I love a bloody monkey."

Just the same, on Saturday afternoons he drank malt whiskey and watched the sport. And whenever Brian sat with him, they enjoyed being knowledgeable together about horses, tennis players, leg spinners, or halfbacks.

Brian spoke easily to George. George never looked you in the eye, unless you were a frightened candidate for orthopedic surgery, which was George's specialty. At the start of nearly every sentence his throat rumbled in a way part growl, part cat's purr. It was a reassuring sound that prepared you for the meat of his sentences, especially so if you'd come to consult him about bone doctory.

There was nothing wrong with Brian's bones, but Brian had come to consult him anyhow.

That afternoon George and Brian had been watching

cricket. Dutifully in charge of the monkey while Clytie shopped, George squinted now and then through a portico at Ran Singh's caged stateroom and rumbled.

"Ran Singh! *Ran Singh!* Don't do that."

Brian, although his legs were spread and a third glass of whiskey stood in his hand, although there was a knowing glint in his eye and he watched the West Indian batsman the way Zeus must have watched the fumblings of mortal men, was no way at his ease. The frightful thing was, I understood, that Ran Singh reminded him of me. Because Brian had no pabulum of dogma to feed to me, he foresaw our future as a matter of crap and cages and turning the back of the television toward me.

I strained my face forward in my private sea, in Sal's womb, as we awaited the down lift at Peter Jones's. Some weeping mechanism came into play, for the first time, behind my sealed lids. If Brian could have seen my face he would not have used a Brazilian monkey as metaphor for me.

"And so it's a boy?" George rumbled at the end of an over of pace bowling.

Brian grunted, pretending to be interested in the field placings. He had another peck at his malt whiskey.

"Benign laser beams you say?" George went on. Field placements bored George. If he were captain of England he would tell his bowlers to bowl only on the leg side of the wicket and stack mid-off, square-leg, the gully and deep fine leg. Why didn't anyone ever do that? It could change the whole axis of cricket. If surgeons had to work within such fixed limits, surely bloody cricketers could.

"What should I do?" Brian asked him.

"Ran Singh! What do you mean what should you do?"

"About this . . . terror. It isn't an average terror, George. It isn't a fear of just being inconvenienced. It's more primal than that. It's like the fear of dying."

"Oh, you mean your fear of the toddler?"

"My fear of the unborn," said Brian.

"Yes."

"Well, should I see a psychiatrist?"

"I don't know. Wait for it to be born. Maybe that's the cure."

"Is it?"

"Oh yes. You'll be forced to behave in a fatherly way. Society will force you. And then you'll find yourself enjoying it. Without admitting it, everyone still thinks a lot of men who produce sons."

"For Christ's sake, what do I do? Leave the maternity ward, go out to a party, plow some girl? Swagger home from Sloane Square station? It won't happen that way. I'll be gibbering. Like that bloody monkey. I know I will."

"No you won't. He yorked him! Did you see that?" At the Oval a West Indian batsman had nearly lost his wicket. "In my whole career I've never seen one father-to-be sit down gibbering, to use your quaint verb. Well, there was once. But it was different circumstances."

"A father? Gibbering, begging?"

"It was in Yugoslavia. In 1944. My orderly got a partisan girl pregnant. Now there was this rabid commissar who had partisan ladies who fell pregnant shot by firing squad, you see. They also shot the impregnator if they could find him. So my orderly was gibbering. With justifiable cause. It wasn't a pathological fear, like yours. It had a base in reality, you see. The reality being the kangaroo courts the partisans used to run."

"You helped him of course."

"I take it you aren't asking me for that kind of help . . . ?"

"No. Of course not."

"Well, then, I got the girl into my hospital and talked to her. I told her how to feign an appendicitis attack. Which she did. The commissars were very snoopy, so I had to take out her appendix although it was in perfectly good health. Then I squeezed her uterus, you see. It was the first abortion I'd ever done. The first abortion of that kind anyhow."

"What kind of abortion do you mean by *that kind?*"

"An abortion of convenience."

Brian began palpating his whiskey glass. "You call that an abortion of convenience? When two people were going to be shot?"

"Oh yes. It would have been better to smuggle her away to Italy. By trawler, say. She could have had the baby there."

"You sound as if you've got high principles."

George looked about him, as if his principles lay around on some shelf and he was checking their safety. He looked at Ran Singh, at Battersea Park and its sun, at the river, at the books and whiskey bottle on his left, at the ancient glassware he collected, but kept behind locked armor plate in case Ran Singh got loose. "Oh yes," he said. "High."

"Those two will be there till stumps," said Brian. Kindly —he was trying to divert George from too acute a memory.

"Only it wasn't my orderly," said George. "It was me. It was my child. I've got so used to telling the story in polite company when I'm pissed that I have to say *my orderly*. I say *my orderly* without thinking. I aborted my own child, you see. Quite a kettle of fish, emotionally speaking. I mean we tried to get the girl out, smuggle her away to Italy. But the partisans had their eye on her. They were always too sharp for us."

"It had to be done," said Brian. He was thinking, I came to be comforted and here I am comforting. "I would have done it without thinking twice."

"Oh yes," George chuckled. "But according to you that would have been merely putting the knife into your enemy while he slept."

Brian shrugged but made a motion of his hands as if, given the right training, he would squeeze an impregnated uterus with dispassion and even a little regret.

"Do you love it?" George asked.

"What?"

"The fetus. Your son."

Scratching his razor rash, Brian answered, "In an abstract way."

"Pallidly?"

"If you like. I mean, it's not here, is it? It's like God or something. An absent deity."

"And you're fornicating more and enjoying it less?"

"It's pitiable."

"I don't need to tell you what you're at. Perhaps you despised your father. Now you are about to become a father and, ultimately, despised. You think the cycle can be halted by fucking bouts. You don't need that explained." George screamed across the room at the monkey. Brian did not bother to observe why. "*Did* you despise your father?"

"I don't know. I never thought I did."

"Tell me this. Was he what is called faithful to your mother?"

"Yes." Swift as a sword, Brian answered.

"How do you know that?"

"I . . . I can't imagine him being unfaithful."

"You ought to be able to. He's just another man, you know."

"There was an incident like unfaithfulness," Brian said. "I mean, when I was a kid I thought it was a kind of unfaithfulness."

"Yes?"

As Brian told him there occurred to me in King's Road as well as to my true begetter some blocks away the beguiling smell of hot sand in Queensland. And the smell you had when starfish and seaweed, jellyfish and plankton came in high onto the beaches on the tides of dawn and were fried all morning and noon by the sun. Every summer the Fitzgerald family would go down to the coast to a place called Bowen. They would pitch a large tent and Brian and the others lived like Peterkin and his friends on the Coral Island, with the added convenience that in the evenings my grandmother had the day's fish ready cooked for them. Brian remembers as do I how every morning his father stepped into the vast coral lagoon and began to swim. Mrs. Fitzgerald and my aunts and uncles and Brian himself, all variously interested, saw him off. The children could swim like seals but anything they did was paddling beside my grandfather's great stroking. Three miles out he would swim and three miles back. The water was dense and warm with the animal warmth of plankton. Sunlight revealed the sandy bottom. Some locals worried that at that time of year the sea wasps came in over the reef but Brian's father swam at large anyhow.

The sea wasp is some sort of jellyfish, a tangle of purple tendrils. Many animals, in fact, living in a colony. Sometimes the colony got broken up on the coral and strands of it would float on the surface. If so, my grandfather, in making his three-mile traverse back and forth across the lagoon, was more or less trolling for tendrils. He was a mile out one morning when a strand of sea wasp wrapped itself around his arm. His organs seized—his breathing, his vision. A fisherman found him, comatose yet afloat in the rich waters, and brought him in. They gave him some serum. In a week he was better. "You'd think he'd been to Peking," Brian told George. "He was full of talk about his encounter."

"Encounter?"

"He thought of it that way. In the next sea wasp season he went out courting the beasts again. He wasn't disappointed."

"What did your mother think?"

"I don't know. I think she was angry. But we used to boast about him at school."

"And the second time satisfied him?"

"No, it didn't. There had to be a third time. He had to meet the intact colony. One day when he was swimming way out in the Passage, he found the queen, the complete animal. She wrapped herself around his arm and chest. They had to fly him out in a helicopter this time, to a hospital in Brisbane. They had to put him in an iron lung."

"He got better of course?"

"Yes. And he never went for those long swims again. Not at that season of the year, anyhow. He got to know some officers from the military camp there and started to use their pool instead."

"You know you *do* talk about it as if it was a fling," George accused him. "An attachment he got over . . .'"

"Well, she's a deadly mistress," Brian said. "Medusa."

They were thinking it out when Clytie came in, calling no greetings. George rumbled in a way that said, There's an end of our Saturday and the serenities of watching cricket. Clytie went straight through to Ran Singh's cage and put her hand through the wire, inviting Ran Singh's incisors. "You should be with her, Brian," she called out.

"Why? Has anything gone wrong?"

"We met a cousin of mine. You know, George. Dotty Elspeth. Sal didn't say much. But it disturbed her."

Just quickly enough, Clytie withdrew her hand from the cage. "Don't try it, you little beast."

Rubbing her hand, she turned around and walked toward them, squinting at the level of whiskey in the bottle that had been full before she and Sal went shopping. "Well, you *should* be with her. Away half the time, pissed half the rest. What are you bloody men for, anyway?"

"I can tell, Clytie, that you're just trying to mask the profound attraction you feel toward me," said Brian. But he realized he had not settled a certain question. "Well," he whispered to George. "Do you think I need a psychiatrist?"

"Will you go?" Clytie squawked at him.

A month of self-awareness passed, like all mortal time, even for me who had no other duty than self-awareness. Already I was educated in the transience of things. Yet the magic chemistry of my building went on without pause. I was indeed Tiberius in his royal box. My stadium grew about me. Slave elements coupled on the sawdust for my delight and there were biogladiatorial contests. The tax of Sal's blood was processed in the honest placenta to become my bread and my breath.

Brian frowned as much and stayed as fearful as I had come to expect. And often, on his way home from the Hologram Research Unit, Ford called in on Sal. He was of course infatuated with her. Sal let him keep visiting for reasons I did not like to read—now that her state was faintly contoured below her waistline, she wanted a lean blond man for whom she felt a tepid interest to come panting in one afternoon a week.

Whenever she answered the door and found him morbidly smiling on the steps, she would say, "Come in for a drink and don't expect anything else." She was as merciless a girl as Sister Angelica could have hoped for.

Graciously he would reply, "You're still merely flattered?"

On the stairs their talk was forced, loud, jovial. For Sal never wanted Clytie to think something pallid and predictable as Ford came as a lover. Clytie and Sal had this in common—they prided themselves on liking rascals, wild men, men of husky content.

Ford himself climbed the stairs in this loudly innocent way because he was sure he'd have to climb them one day soon with stealth, as a secret soother, with a bellyful of nectar and what passed for a stiffened manhood.

Upstairs he always sat in too-studied an ease on the floor by the Thames-seeing window. Look what a simple boyish man I am, he seemed to be saying. Director of the Hologram Research Unit but here I am laying my arse and long legs on your humble floor.

"Would you like me not to come again?" he always asked at the end of a silence.

Sal wanted to say yes but found herself saying something different. "I don't say so," she would say.

"No. You're lonely, aren't you?" She wouldn't answer, yet it was the truth. What a world it was out there when a fine girl like Sal had to let a technocratic dimwit like Ford into her house.

"I'll drop in again on Thursday."

"Good. Brian will be home."

"Friday then."

"No. Make it Thursday."

"You aren't serious, Sal . . ."

I squirmed so much in these elliptic dialogs that Sal would begin to sicken. There was a point beneath my left foot which, when heartily punched, nauseated Sal. It presented itself to me by accident during one of Ford's visits and now I could not stop punishing it whileever Ford was with us. I wondered why she did not notice his suspicious sexual humility, the vulpine way he lowered his head beneath the slanting light, the strange blue cores of his eyes.

The silly season in Fleet Street was over now and the world had come back from its holidays, churning, moiling. The autumn looked benign, yet on a given morning I myself became sick with a Brian-sickness, fearful with his fear. He came home at noon and Sal, answering the door with a pen in her hand, found him pallid on the doorstep, and without the wit to use his own key.

"Well," she said. Her viscera, me included, leaped in small ways at the sight of him. Because of his fear and his terror of and (to be fair) pity for warring mankind, he kissed her thoroughly.

"Haven't you heard?" he asked.

"Heard?"

"The Syrians and Israelis began to fight three hours ago. The Egyptians are moving." He touched both hands to his knees and frowned. "Are my beige trousers back from the cleaners yet?"

"My God, they're sending you?"

"Rawden insisted. They would have sent Cummings but his kid's having an eye operation."

She comforted him. There was his fear of the battlefield to be absorbed, not so much of bursting shells but of what might be seen there. Then there was his fear of flying. "It's easier to believe in a flat earth," he said once, "than to accept that those great bloody lumps of metal can stay way up there." To a vulnerable boy like him birth was probably the terminal shock. He had never got used to the chancy uterus of earth and ether. But the furious ascent of jet planes threatened to remove him even from that.

"My darling," Sal told him. "I'll pack. You have some whiskey."

Brian was quick to obey. While she packed he sucked up enough Jameson's to see himself sentimentally, a man savoring good whiskey on the rim of a war that is not his business but will claim him just the same.

"You know," he said, "whenever I'm in any sort of danger you're the only person I think of, Sal. The only person I want to come back to."

So gratified was Sal that she handled his colored jockey briefs tenderly. Poor and too easily exalted woman.

He went to the toilet and returned to Sal red faced and in his shirt. Little of the antipodean tan of his childhood was left and, with the aid of the whiskey, he reminded her a little of the pitifully lecherous men you met at dances in Ireland.

"Is there time?" he asked.

His department chief at United Press had told him earlier this morning: "The Syrian Air Force won't guarantee the safety of passenger jets. But that's just to scare journalists away from Tel Aviv." Brian's too-active blood assured him that the plane would fall from the sky. He therefore wanted Sal's lean sweet limbs once more before the fire and the impact, before his flesh was tettered by jet blaze and scattered on the earth.

"If you don't take all day, my love."

"I won't take all day," he promised.

As Sal knew and the girl on the Renault could have told us, he sometimes took too long laying his seed down. But today he was wild and fast. I waited through the vibrations while Brian thudded his love home in the manner of a man under sentence. Yet, thoughtfully, they coupled on their sides so as not to put too much weight on me.

"My lovely long mick lady," said Brian. "Will you pray for my safe landing?" Sal thought his fear had been settled by the honest means of whiskey and carnality. So she gave a light answer. "To which God?" she asked. "Seamus O'God? One word from me and he'd do whatever he wanted. Of course I could try Sir Alistair God K.B.E. but I think he's got too much good taste to meddle with airlines."

Brian's jaws went bravely through the business of laughing but he thought, We might as well have made love through a hedge, faceless to each other. Because she doesn't really know how scared I am.

And in that moment he suffered a desire for me, to see me before he went, before a Syrian fighter shot the blades off an El Al engine and they went knifing through the fuselage and fatally across his lap. *He wanted to see my face!*

Though for the past two hours his emotions had done credit to Mrs. Miniver, it was only now—on wanting to see my face—that the bastard tried to shake off the sentiment.

We drove him to Heathrow. Sometimes he would shiver, and fear and indigestion rattled in his belly. I felt uneasy myself because Sal drove so wildly in her shabby little car, the steering column aimed fair for her sternum and lungs and the richest poolings of her blood.

As he passed through the plywood security barrier in front of the immigration desk, he looked back at her. He wondered how he ever needed another woman, he wondered how he ever feared me. Angry at being cast off as a destiny somewhat better than death, I stabbed just once the spot that communicated nausea to Sal.

Back at Clytie's place, Sal began to clean up the mess she had made in packing. In her hurry she had left briefs with withered elastic, handkerchiefs with shredded edges, shirts with worn collars rejected on the bed and the floor. She saw that the old briefcase he took uselessly to work had fallen on its side. Lifting it, she found it unusually heavy. She squinted inside to see what was making the weight.

There was a large bottle of Drambuie fatly nesting in the middle compartment. She frowned because Brian was not a liqueur man, we were not a liqueur family. Hooch suited to quantity consumption was what Brian spent his money on. Sal however shrugged and extracted the stubby bottle from the case. Written large across the label with a felt pen was a message in Brian's handwriting. *To Christina, Scotland's second secret recipe.*

Sal staggered about all afternoon, bullying herself toward tranquility, failing at it. Brian is a rhetorical fellow, she said. He is likely to write such things without meaning them. He is a charmer of middle-aged and old women. Perhaps this Christina was but a butt for his blarney. But what Sal knew was that Christina was young, the sort of pitiless metallic girl Brian went for. And that sometime that morning, in a liquor store, he had bought the bottle lovingly for her which only a war and the terror of flying made him forget.

I tried uselessly to transmit the facts to Sal. That in a Paddington flat Scotland's second glory had argued with her new love, Brian Fitzgerald, two nights before and, for want of a better weapon, directed at his head the gift bottle of whiskified syrup. Managing to snatch it out of the air as it traveled toward his forehead, he had put it away in his case and come home to Sal.

It became a miserable afternoon, for in her state of animal hurt she began to drink the stuff. To toast the ceiling, saying such things as, "Here's to secret recipes." "Here's to the others." She feared there had been or would be others because Brian's temperament assured it. Once disloyal at all, he would go on to diverse betrayals, on a wide front.

At Heathrow, Brian's delayed flight was taxiing now. Strapped shoulder to shoulder with other journalists in the plane they had already occupied for an hour, he drank Scotch from a flask that was handed to him, and passed it on. Welcoming them aboard, the captain told them, "for the benefit of the nervous," that there was no danger, that they would come in to Tel Aviv from the west and be well clear of all aerial conflict.

The man strapped in at Brian's side began to annotate the captain's statement. "That's so much bullshit," he said without intonation. "Have you heard about the new Egyptian missiles?"

"No," said Brian. He disliked the man, who seemed a journalistic type. Fifty years old, been to all wars and on all junkets. Old brown suit with a flaky detritus adhering to it—cigarette ash, dandruff, or both. His collar yellowed just to show it took more than the slim pretext of world crisis to make him change his shirt. Me at fifty? Brian wondered, forgetting that he'd already decided he would die today.

The man told him all about Egypt's most recent gifts and purchases of missiles, ground-to-air and air-to-air. There had also been recent Syrian purchases of jet fighters. Poor Brian was blinking, retracting his stomach, making less of a target of himself. It was as if he believed the Arabs' new armaments could affect the takeoff of his jet even here, at Heathrow.

But the plane rose straight and unwavering and was soon a small shadow on the face of the suburb of Staines.

By then Sal had got halfway through the sickly bottle. She felt overheated, the air pressed around her with a fibrous density. "Won't hurt the infant," she muttered. "Won't hurt the unknown fetal prisoner." She knew *that*: the Romans erred when they said that Vulcan was born lame because Jupiter was drunk while begetting his blacksmith child. That the Carthaginians were wrong in constraining the newly married to stay off wine in case their firstborn proved defective. The alcohol Christina hurled at Brian two nights ago was now used up quickly by the fairgrown body of Sal. I did not even feel a sting nor any minor brain ache.

Though I could not quite hope that the Syrians might get Brian's plane, it would have been nice if, as his jet approached the Middle East, a fighter plane came sniffing at them, just sniffing at them, no more. I would have wanted the journalists, the stewards, the hostesses to see him whimper. That was justice.

At half past five her doorbell rang. It was sure to be Ford. An ambiguous groan usually came from her when Ford called by. Today I found we were bouncing downstairs. Through the open door on the first landing Sal could hear Clytie chatting with Ran Singh, Ran Singh uttering his squeaky cantatas.

Immediately Sal opened the front door, Ford could tell she was a different woman today. She put an arm loosely around his neck.

"Did you bring me anything?" she asked.

"No. Sorry."

"So! You're not as generous to strange women as Brian is?"

Ford, at least, had the sense not to answer. I winced for her pain. The sentences came up her round throat like sharp little cubes. They made a strange impact on the foyer walls. Ford didn't worry much about that. He could tell he was in with a chance.

Sal made such a noise going upstairs that Clytie appeared in her doorway. You had to say this for Clytie: she was not a gossip and she found a sisterly, not a perverse, enjoyment in discovering that wives were going upstairs with strange men.

Sal called out too gaily, "My friend Dr. Ford. My landlady Mrs. Heatherton-Meadows."

Clytie and Ford nodded at each other. Inside Clytie's rooms Ran Singh emitted a series of shrill grunts, as if he could smell the sexual expectation in Ford.

"You know," said Sal, "what it is to have a husband away at the wars."

"Oh yes, I know," Clytie admitted without too much warmth. Ford could not prevent flushing, notably on his tall forehead. He did not breathe properly again until Clytie wished them well and closed her door.

Upstairs, Sal asked him if he wanted some of the liqueur.

"Before dinner?" he asked.

"This isn't the bar of the King's Head, you know. You've got to take what's going here."

"I'll have some," he said.

"Just lay yourself down by the window as is your wont," she ordered him. "I'll bring you some of the juice."

But when she brought him the liqueur he looked at it without appetite. "Has Brian left you?"

Sal nodded. "By going to the Arab war. And in more notable ways."

"Is there anything I can do?"

"Don't be coy," she said. "You know what you can do."

I ground my fist against my sealed left eye. For there was no joy in her. Even Ford could tell it. He sat there feeling like an uncle.

They spent the afternoon in talk about the war. After dusk, Sal turned on the lights and the television. Cairo had been bombed, the air battles and the tank battles that had been fought many times in the Negev and on the Golan Heights were being replayed again. But Brian was still intact, sweating his way down over the darkening sea. For otherwise it would have been mentioned—a planeload of journalists, men of influence.

As the news finished and became the Morecambe and Wise show, Prince Charlie's tipple began to work on Ford. He touched Sal. "Don't worry," he said. He began fondling her hair, which was, of course, like the hair the young autumn wears. His hand felt cool to Sal, who was steaming like Bombay with the liqueur. She pulled him to her as if he were no more than cool linen on a tropic night. She desired not him but his even temperature.

One month self-aware, I squirmed at the banalities Dr. Ford now uttered. "I've been thinking of this so long." "It's been worth the wait . . ." Yet because he was about to hold that corner of the earth's beauty whose name was Sal, his statements induced in *him* the same creative excitement that the Eclogues might have in Virgil.

And then all the ordained things happened. He found her breasts, he was their unworthy and ham-fisted priest. I felt the sluggish current of his hand across her belly. Of course, he hoped she would do his unzipping for him and extricate his genitals. But in the end he was left to do it himself. The second he touched her pubis I began kicking that little groove of nausea beneath my left foot. Yet because she was aroused, the bilious message did not get through to her. Her head, though, felt as vast and risky to her as a hot-air balloon.

"Will we go into the bedroom?" he asked.

"Oh yes, please."

Her urgency came from a need of somewhere stable to put her head. But he thought she was all stumbling and tottering desire. He became jaunty.

"Easy as she goes," he advised epigrammatically, steering her.

Hands over eyes I jammed, kicked, jolted, lunged, smacked, spurned, kneaded, trampled, heeled, and pounded the spot which now that it was in truth needed had lost its efficacy.

Undressing, Sal did not even feel the fury of my leg. Her intent to slum with Ford preoccupied her.

Nor did she look at Ford as he undressed. She suspected rightly that his skin might be pale, despite his yearly holiday in Corfu, his shoulders bony, his chest faintly cratered with some earlier acne. She didn't want to be put off by aesthetic considerations. So it was, against all the protest of my limbs, that lovely Sal and witless Ford lay down together for intimate purposes. So it was that his angular hip impressed the belly I inhabited.

Once he penetrated, the closeness became insufferable. It wasn't that he lay due atop her, bearing down like an adversary. I wish he had. Like Brian, he lay side on, as thoughtful an adulterer as you could hope for. If I gasped, it was simply in distaste.

My spurring and stamping had got fainter but now Ford's vegetable love possessed him and, straddling her, he lost all reason. His stiff man-root became an ally as it and my foot hammered from two sides at the sinews from which a queasiness might arise. And at last Sal groaned, but not in passion. I kicked and kicked now. Bile shot into her throat. She began to choke, with Ford still heaving on her. By reckless swallowing she got back her breath and at last could say it. "Stop. Stop. I'm going to be sick."

He wouldn't stop, and the bile burned the fine layers of her throat and seared the passages at the back of her nose. Him? she thought. The Director of Holograms? He should be able to switch himself off. Her chokings could well have sounded to Ford like some form of acclamation, some sexual applause. His prick, after the example of his lasers, would split Sal and take no account of the inconsequentials.

Sal could say, "Please, please." But he heard these words too, put together with fragments of breath, as an erotic plea. A speckled yellow panic entered Sal's vision and I saw it too behind my eyes.

As Brian waited for his luggage at Tel Aviv, a voiceless scream of weird frequency escaped me. It ran in constant circles over the Chelsea Embankment into Wandsworth. Back over the Thames again it made the drinkers in the Phoenix blink but had instantly crossed again to Battersea Park Road and so on a widening circuit through the Royal Borough of Kensington and Chelsea, through Clapham, through the City of Westminster, tickling the ears of guardsmen in Birdcage Walk and policemen in Kennington. Then it was piercing Soho and the walls of buses in Putney and so it ran, and nowhere seemed to make a solid impact.

What happened then is almost too painful to whisper, even to Sal's discreet plasma. The barely rendered-down liqueur burst from her stomach, flooded her throat where she lay, face up and choking. The sour reek of the liquor appalled her sense of modesty. But Ford, his head on the offside of the pillow and—for all purposes—in another hemisphere, was not appalled. The floor of his brain gave way in a manner that frightened and exalted him. He found himself in a gothic and heretofore unvisited chamber of his libido. Here the sicked-up oddments of Sal's unhappy stomach seemed to be a concession from a victim. He went at it all the harder. My scream whistled through Kingston, Beckenham, Walthamstowe, and Wembley and no one came. Not—if I can forgive myself the pun—even Ford.

Sal fought him but was of course weak now. At the center of her mind she considered in an academic way how the fetid rationale of their coupling had yielded up rape. As well as in the spasm in her throat, she could feel the threat of murder in the way he was pounding at her yet could not release his seed.

Soon I was aware of a fourth person in the flat. I wondered how he had got there, for our bell had not rung. I felt the radiance of this intruder, his brotherhood, penetrating me from the living room. He entered the bedroom more deliberately and therefore more slowly than I would have wanted, but once there, slipped his arms under Ford's armpits and locked his hands behind Ford's neck. Holding him thus he lifted him and threw him against Sal's dressing table. Ford got up to fight but my brother the intruder kicked him on the hip. Bunched and livid and groaning, Ford howled on the carpet.

Sal kneeled and gagged. For shame, she held a soiled sheet up to her throat, but the intruding Gnome now found her a towel and, after a second's pause, began to wipe her face briskly, dispassionate as an orderly. "I didn't mean to drop in like this," he told her. His eyes were on the corners of the room as if the embarrassment were all his. Sal had no voice to reply. The Gnome's voice was soft and of American intonation.

He picked up Ford's clothes, helped him upright, pushed him out of the bedrom. "Put these on," he could be heard telling Ford in the living room. "Quick as you can."

"I'll have you for assault," Ford promised in a constricted voice.

Two minutes later the door of the flat closed and then, distantly, the heavy front door of Clytie's house. Ford and the Gnome had gone off like associates. But Ford was of course limping.

For half an hour Sal lay still with her eyes closed, bunched on the unfouled side of her bed. Though I sent out soothing emanations, she did not seem to feel them, at least, not for that first hour of her distress.

At last, still naked, she went out into the living room. On her desk was a note written in letters one inch high. It said, *Don't be frightened. I'll send someone to clean up.* She wasn't frightened, even though he had a way with locks and could break in at will. He should have said, *Don't be ashamed.* For in shame she stood hunched, her arms crossed and her hands folded each beneath its opposing armpit. Yet she remembered the way he'd wiped her face with the towel so readily, without prejudice, like brother cleaning sister.

Meanwhile, in the bar of the Tel Aviv Hilton, Brian felt jaunty through having survived. There were at least a dozen other journalists around the cluttered table where he drank. One of them a beautiful woman from Swedish television.

Sal was still sitting naked and half off her chair when her bell rang. She thought she mightn't answer it, but then remembered the note. She went looking for her bathrobe and, finding it, hurried downstairs. Her legs felt large and too brittle beneath her.

At the door stood a little West Indian woman. Five feet high. Thirteen stone. When she saw Sal, the hair still wild, the face looking bruised, she frowned and smiled at the same time. As if she were saying, These fellers—they really put us through it, don't they?

"The boss sent me around to clean up."

"The boss?" said Sal in a bemused way.

"He didn't upset you, did he, love?"

"The little man?"

"Nobody's little to me, love. But he didn't do nothing of this, did he?"

"No. Of course not. Come in."

As they limped upstairs, they could hear George and Clytie loudly discussing their day against a background of Ran Singh's crooning and the rant of television. It seemed to me that the voices of the Arab and Israeli experts on the BBC had taken on some of the stridency of Brian and his brothers and sisters in their boozy den in the Tel Aviv Hilton, where Brian was making his usual inverse approach to the lady from Swedish television. "What's wrong with you, love, that you've got to be there with your camera? It really has to be a massacre for you, doesn't it? Or tribes of swollen-bellied kids. I bet you've never filmed a flower or a girl on a bike. Oh yes, love," he said, all lazy eloquence, "you go on as if your fine lines, your—your *beauty*, if the bloody word must be used, are fed by a world of woe. The mulch that makes you bloom is the world's chaos."

"Oh yes," she said without anger. Because she wasn't listening to Brian. He wanted to tumble her in a punishing way. But he had no hope. She was the sweetheart of the mediacrats and could choose whomever she liked in this rowdy pen, any of those high-paid Americans she'd known in Vietnam.

Entering the door of our flat with Sal, the small Barbadian woman crooned more sweetly than Ran Singh. "I got some broth. The boss said I should bring broth."

Being fed the broth, Sal said, "The boss. You must know his name. Where does he live?"

"Oh, I'm not allowed to tell you, baby. When I went to work for him he said to me, 'You can drink my Scotch while you're dusting, you can use my loo, there's only one thing I won't forgive. And that's handing around my name and address to people.' He hates having an address. The man won't answer most mail he gets."

The little woman moved to the bedroom door.

"Don't go in there," Sal called, remembering the mess. But little five-foot was already in there, discovering in her own right.

"Oh you poor thing," she called, finding the mess. "Oh honey."

There was a froth of anger in Sal now. "You don't mean that. The way whites treat you. And I'm a white slut."

But the little woman moaned at such a harsh word. "Missus, we're all sisters. Doing dreadful things to keep men happy." She appeared again, making for the bathroom with bundled sheets. "I'll rinse these."

In Tel Aviv, a man from the London office of the *Sydney Morning Herald* turned to Brian. "Mate, you really ballsed that one up." For the Swedish lady had left him not only in mid-sentence but in mid-clause. A tranquil rising it was, no heat to it. Across the littered tables she had sighted an old colleague.

"The lady will be back," Brian said. "I could see her eyes."

"You didn't even make a dent."

Brian watched the woman smile her remote smile as she reached the chosen table. She was the butterfly of the Apocalypse. In the southern deserts tank commanders were taking positions tonight, sighting on each other by radar, making subjects for her. While she idled, hardly drinking, rationing her smiles, her responses, in a bar of the Tel Aviv Hilton. Tomorrow she would photograph tonight's howling deaths, reducing this one or that to the dimensions of a prize-winning press photograph. From New York to Stockholm she won press trophies from each of her wars.

Disgust at her and at himself sent Brian's belly into spasm. He ran for the lavatory and, staring into a mirror, wiped his sweating face with a paper towel.

In Hospital Road, the Gnome's daily help was back from the bathroom. "The sheets are soaking," she said.

"Will you stay with me?" Sal asked on impulse.

"Sure I will."

For half an hour my limbs had been working to soothe Sal through the amniotic wall. But now I knew the company of the unborn was no salve to her. That I could not restore her as much as those exquisite bastards, Brian and Ford, had deranged her.

Our visitor settled Sal on the sofa and kissed her forehead. "I'll make some tea, I think."

Yet before she could get to the stove there was a telephone call from over the river in Clapham. The Gnome's daily answered it. "Is Mrs. Fitzgerald there?" the caller asked. "Mrs. Ford speaking."

Sal shook her head and sheltered behind her long hands. Yet the telephone was close and she could hear.

"Mrs. Fitzgerald's out at the moment, missus."

"Did you have anything to do with it?"

"I . . . I don't . . ."

"The assault on my husband I mean."

"This is my first day here, missus. I don't know a thing about assaults."

"You might tell Mr. and Mrs. Fitzgerald and whoever else was involved that my husband has hernia damage. You might tell them I consider they should pay the bloody medical bills."

"Medical bills," said the little West Indian, as if memorizing a neutral message. "That all, missus?"

Mrs. Ford hung up before we could begin to wonder what narrative of the afternoon Ford might have given her.

Long before she woke in the morning I was moving in her with some urgency. I saw, strung out along the channels of Sal's lucid blood, the profile of all the doubts I carried concerning our survival. Yesterday Sal all but drowned under Ford's weight and my sharp scream, lacking in decibels, had nonetheless hooked in the Gnome. I was now like someone who has seen his savior's face.

Sal, however, woke this morning without expecting anything. A bubble of despair was released from her stomach, coming up foul, last air from a sunken submarine whose dead crew sit about rotting.

I would not let her get away with slumping there. Squirming, I began exuding a message in her direction. Don't lie all day on *this* bed, Ford-foul, Brian-betrayed. Today, I know, the Gnome will be about, looking for you in public places yet trying to escape you as well. Today is the day we trace the Gnome.

Sweating in the belly of a helicopter, sucking on his furry tongue, Brian lurched south toward Khan Yunis. Beyond which the Israelis (so they said) had won a great tank battle overnight against the Egyptians' left flank. The stunning noise and heat in the body of Brian's helicopter distressed him. He bloated with gas and diarrhea, terror, lust, blunted talents. Whose savior is he? Awash in Sal's waters, I sweated beneath my secret skin, remembering how the best authorities Sal had so far read all told me that after I left her womb, that zone of wisdom, Brian would prefigure for me god and pontiff, huntsman and general, sage and magician, fakir and maker. That once born, I would not see through him again until my balls dropped.

Sal called out, "Are you there? Are you there?" half hoping the Gnome's housekeeper would bring in a cup of coffee. But there was no one there. When a knock came at the door, Sal believed it was the little lady back from the shops. I felt more blithe when she rose to answer it. On her feet was the first thing, then into a skirt and her long leather boots. Then out of doors. To wander would be enough. We could rely on the Gnome, as ever, to present himself.

Clytie and George stood at the door. Seeing George, Sal wondered if it were a medical visit. "Could we use your balcony?" Clytie asked.

George said, "It's that bloody Ran Singh."

Sal could see that there were tears in his eyes. Clytie went on, discomfited, shrill.

"He's got away. He's up on the roof."

"It's humiliating," said George. A strange, helpless shame held him. It was as if he'd been let down by a son.

"Last time," Clytie said, "he got into a house two doors down and fondled the housekeeper's leg."

Again I cringed from the fatuous born ones, from besotted Clytie and George who should have known better. Wasn't he supposed to be a fine surgeon? Wasn't he the British wizard on infantile hip-socket injuries? Hadn't they flown him out to Jordan last year to fix up some gammy infant prince? Yet here he was pinked to tears by some useless item of Brazilian fauna.

"Please come in," said Sal. "Will you excuse me while

I get dressed?" For she understood now that being out today would be a little more tolerable than being in.

Dressing, she could hear Clytie shrilling, George rumbling at the monkey on the roof. After a time she found she had put on the right clothes and had makeup in her hands. An instinct told her she would run today, whether to someone or away she did not know. But to honor the instinct, she chose low-heeled flexible shoes.

Just as she had them on, there was an impact and clatter on the balcony. Sal hurried out and could see Clytie and George, standing pale among a tangle of aluminum and wires that had been dropped on them from the roof. One of the wires had cut George's cheek open.

Before we knew what the tangle meant, I experienced one of those him-or-me feelings about Ran Singh. I hoped the police would bring a rifle and snipe him down from the tiles.

"Now you won't be able to see how Brian's getting on," Clytie called to Sal. For the mess of metal was the television antenna.

"You should call for the fire brigade," Sal suggested, lightly, as if she had not agonies of her own. She looked full into George's eyes, moist and dismal.

Clytie closed her eyes, the sort of eye-closing that meant *not on your life.* "It would only flatter the little sod. It's just like Rowena and her kittens."

"If I had a net and an extension ladder," said poor lachrymose George, "I could get him down."

Clytie opened her eyes on his brave offer but did not make a fuss of him. She had always lived with valiant men and took guts for granted. "Would a tablecloth do?" she asked George.

George shivered. "He bites a lot though."

Clytie whimpered.

"I know," said George, "how much he means to you. I think the Osmonds have an extension ladder."

He came back through the flat and went downstairs and down Hospital Road to borrow the thing. A tile clomped at Clytie's feet. "Oh, don't be such a stupid little prick, Ran Singh. I'm the only one who really loves you in the whole of SW3."

"I'll go now," Sal told Clytie.

"Certainly." Clytie was a little cool. She had sniffed out the low-grade vein in Ford yesterday and wondered why Sal had taken it to bed with her.

As we stepped out into Hospital Road, we saw George and fat Mr. Osmond hauling a fourteen-foot extension ladder across the pavement. George so blinded by exertion and disquiet that he did not see Sal tramping west and then around the corner of Flood Street, like someone meaning to catch a number 19 to Piccadilly.

Sal decided, however, she could not face the arterial pulsing of King's or Fulham roads. At the corner where, according to a blue plaque, Tobias Smollett wrote *Roderick Random*, she turned back and so we were headed toward the gardens behind the Royal Hospital. It was half past ten of a cloudless morning. Those pensioners who were allowed out to buy or cadge a morning pint in the pubs around about were now strolling out the hospital gate in their uniforms of navy blue and red. There were all sorts of fatherly crinklings around their eyes when they saw a beautiful girl like Sal, depressed and all the more erotic for it, striding close to their loveless dormitories. If they looked for a smile from her on account of the Royal Hospital's being so womanless, today they did not get one. So on they went.

On the corner of Smith Street, she stood still, sapped of all propulsion. Abandoning this fine late summer day and all its potencies, she turned down the lane between the hospital and the Military Museum. Not only had she decided she would not meet the Gnome down in these isolated gardens. She had decided she didn't deserve to.

It was tranquil in those gardens where Sal walked with her anguish. A few wealthy Chelsea paraplegics were shunted about by paid companions. All parties seemed appeased under the thin sun. The crippled at ease with being so, the shunters at ease with their servitude. An old man clutched a crossword as if it were a letter from a habitual and cozy lover. There were mothers and children. Petulant and knowing children of three months, petulant and unknowing ones of three years, plump and vacant, already half worn down to fit their mean world. To sense toddlers through the long periscope of Sal's optic nerve was always a depressing event for me, akin I suppose to a visit to a graveyard for Brian. You got that feeling of unbelief. Was it possible that what they now were I should one day be?

On the far side of the gardens stood a line of tennis courts, only one of them in use. Two sparkling white men played singles there. Even at that distance Sal was briefly distracted by the clear competence, the sharpness of their strokes.

In a house in Khan Yunis on the edge of the Negev, a young Israeli press officer described the ghastly tank conflicts of last night. He was a boy of obvious American origins and spoke in a calm, seemingly nonpartisan manner.

"After lunch," he said, "we'll be traveling southeast of here. You'll see a lot of disabled tanks. A short excursion will tell you that the Arabs have added to their losses by abandoning a number of their tanks . . ."

Brian and I both thought how sensible those 3 A.M. Arab conscripts had been. Brian, and therefore I, remembered a saying of Napoleon's on the manner in which euphoria and bravery washed in and out of the bodies of men: "Few men are brave at three o'clock in the morning." Well, thought Brian, it's 3 A.M. for me most of the time these days.

Sal circled the obelisk in the park. For a few minutes it seemed she was tethered to it and would stroll, locked concentrically to it, all day; while in the white house in Khan Yunis, Brian decided he would not visit any battlefields, even yesterday's. He wondered if he could pretend to be sick.

The shadow of the obelisk shot Sal off at a tangent, aiming her for the tennis courts. As she made for the two competent tennis players, she noticed for the first time that her brain had already begun rendering down the business of Brian-Christina-bottle-of-Drambuie the way the patient earth rendered down its worst events so that the only place they still lived was bloodlessly, on library shelves, between scholarly covers.

I know that if this tale were meant for people's diversion, if it were more than an echo in Sal's corpuscles, I could not get away with saying that one of the two tennis players was the Gnome. Long before Sal herself was aware of it, when she was still a hundred and fifty yards from him, I had taken the impressions his stumpy and bouncing body made on her eye. I knew before she did that they were the correct calligraphy for the Gnome.

She stood with her fingers hooked in the wire of the courts. It gave her the look of a political prisoner. For some time the Gnome did not see her, his partner being the first to notice her. Immediately he dropped four points and the Gnome took the game to love. The Gnome did not smile at this minor triumph. You could tell he knew how to play games. Nothing existed for him but the net and the white lines and the ball.

But when they were changing ends the partner pointed Sal out. By the way he muttered to the Gnome you could tell he was explaining how that strange woman at the wire had distracted him.

Sal stared at the Gnome and the Gnome watched her sideways. He muttered something to his partner, canceling the game. From the back of the court he picked up a sweater, a wallet, a racket cover and, still apologizing, moved to the gate. Sal waited for him like Magdalen waiting for Christ. Thinking, more or less, If he speaks to me, I'll be whole again.

But the Gnome did not turn toward her once he was through the gate. He began running. He pretended to be doing it for fitness rather than escape. He even turned his head to look into the open square of the Chelsea Hospital yard, taking long note of Christopher Wren's magic geometry.

Sal's belly clenched. Me in it.

"Wait!" she called out. But so low that only the Gnome's confused tennis partner heard her. She began to run herself. As I've already noted, a long-legged girl, and in flat shoes. Of course she gained on him. She didn't care if Chelsea pensioners or young mothers wondered what she was doing. Therefore she gained on the Gnome.

In the laneway toward Royal Hospital Road, anyone could have seen it was a case of flight and pursuit.

I loved her to run, though there were experts to say it was bad for our condition, the same way they insisted that lasers had no effect. I was the one who savored the rhythms of her long legs, of her easy elastic sinews. The Gnome ran earnestly, with his head down, like a badger. Sal like an antelope.

On the corner where Oscar Wilde used to live stood a Safeways. The locality had degenerated from epigrams to placards saying DANISH BACON 45P HALF POUND. Here the Gnome pulled himself into a small blue car. As if he were used to fast escapes, the blue car was unlocked. Before Sal reached Safeways he had driven away.

A man about Sal's age but with lush mustaches was climbing into his car as Sal galloped up.

"Oi," he called. "He run out on you?"

Sal said nothing. She stood in the middle of the intersection panting.

"Come on," the man said. "We can catch him."

She climbed in beside the man, still not speaking. She was in the mood where you take it for granted the human race will lay on transport to meet your need.

Pulling out, he said, "See, it's my lunch hour. So I don't mind helping my fellow man out."

"Very kind," Sal told him.

"He ran out on you, love?"

"Yes."

"Where'll I drop you then?"

"Just follow him. Look, he's turning toward Fulham."

The Gnome was still well in sight. Sal could see him hunched studiously at the wheel.

"Look, I don't want to be heavy with you," said the man with the mustaches. "But here's my card. If he gives you any trouble, which he's mad if he does, I want you to feel you can call me like."

"Very kind," Sal said for the second time.

"Does he let you out? Like, we could have dinner tonight, say?"

"Not tonight. I'll ring. He's going right down Old Church Road."

I too was studiously hunched. I knew we would catch him. As we turned left into Old Brompton Road, Sal believed the Gnome didn't know she was following. He was sitting upright now, looking about, pausing at zebra crossings long enough to encourage housewives into making the crossing. It was a slow journey through Earl's Court and on into the borders of Kensington. At the corner of a dead-end street called Pembroke Gardens Close, Sal ordered her driver—provided as he was through forces of cosmic mercy —to pull up. For fifty yards away the Gnome was parking, extracting his racket from the back seat, entering a tall old house.

"You've been very kind," she said, getting out.

"But you'll ring, won't you?" the man with the mustaches asked. Already he was thinking that he'd invested too much petrol in this vague lady.

"I give you my solemn word."

"What's your name then?"

"Betty."

"Had a sister called Betty."

"Good-bye."

She ran across the pavement, appearing to the man with the mustaches to be a woman freely running, who might stop running at any second and stand akimbo, catching her breath. In fact she ran on rails, like the 7:50 from Leeds to King's Cross, like—in other words—predestined machinery.

The front door of the Gnome's house was shut now. There were but two buttons to press. One said *H. Finn*, the other *W. Jones*. Convinced, as romantics tend to be too easily, that the fates confer picturesque names on deserving folk, Sal pressed the *H. Finn* bell. A woman's voice spoke out from the little amplifier grill above the bell. "Clarice?"

"No," Sal said.

"Oh. Who did they send this time?"

"I . . . Is Mr. Finn there?"

"There isn't a Mr. Finn. Mr. Finn and our son both perished in the Battersea Ferris-wheel collapse in 1958. Who are you?"

Sal thought she had unleashed a portent on herself. Her head full of the carnival wreckage, she backed away from the buttons.

"Are you still there?" squawked Mrs. Finn. "I say, are you still there?"

But Sal would not answer.

"Mm," said Mrs. Finn. She was used to finding that people were frightened off by news of Mr. Finn's fun-fair death. Without making any more appeals, she switched off her intercom. Sal pressed the *Jones* button. Immediately, as if it had been waiting by the buzzer through all the chat with Mrs. H. Finn, the Gnome's heedful voice answered.

"Hello. That isn't you, is it? Mrs. Fitzgerald?"

"Sal," said Sal.

"Sal."

"Thank you for sending the . . . the woman yesterday."

"Oh . . . it's nothing."

"Thanks too for earlier on, when you . . ."

She had squatted and talked directly at the fine wire grating of that metal mouth. It reminded her of the confessional gratings of her childhood and though blood had gone to the rims of her ears as she mentioned yesterday, she also felt lightened.

He said, "I don't know why I went to your flat. I don't know where the impulse came from. Let me say you ought to tell your landlady that the lock on the front door is too

97

simple for a house like that. It's a 1902 Beasley . . . another and better age . . ."

The grating spoke no more for a full ten seconds. Sal couldn't think what to say to encourage it toward utterance, but her lips moved, making trial passes at speech.

At last the Gnome said, "It ought to be clear to you. I want to see you but I'm afraid. You should be too. There's a plate in my brain. The normal electric impulses get confused by it. The circuits are artificial."

"It doesn't matter," she said. "I feel we're old friends."

"If you knew the half of it," the Gnome told her with a little laugh. "No, you ought to clear out."

The door before us sighed open. The Gnome, at odds with his advice to her, had pressed the button.

"I'll go away then," Sal offered.

"Go away, little mother," the Gnome told her.

"Yes," Sal whispered, pushing the door wide, entering a white hallway and rising on the staircase.

Gnome Jones was waiting, standing at his open door one flight up, still wearing his tennis rig. A panther, symbolic of some sporting-goods company, was sewn melodramatically on the left pap of his sweater. He did not—in spite of whatever interrupted circuits governed his brain—look like a probable carnivore.

"You climb stairs too fast," he called, and as she arrived took her elbow for a second as if he needed to believe in her fragility. Together they passed inside. The living room was white-walled. There were a few unremarkable plush chairs. He steered Sal to one of them and placed her in it, and—in Sal—me. Already she could see there were no pictures on his walls, no ornaments or books on the shelves. It seemed he was a man who sought no evocations except perhaps for those that rose from Sal.

I felt in my own gut the fast quaking of her heart as she inhabited that deep chair.

In a hall at the west end of the town of Khan Yunis, in the direction of grieving Egypt, the correspondents lunched with their Israeli press officer. The food—cold cuts of meat, kale, rice—had no savor for Brian. There was a girl, however. Down the table from him sat a neat, brown-haired little woman of—very likely—his own age. Her correspondent's greens hung baggily on her but in a manner that promised trimness beneath the fabric. She had a subtle and underfed face of the type Brian usually ignored. Is she beautiful? he wondered. He felt sure she was but could not say why. She evaded all his categories.

The press officer, it had been ascertained, grew up in Santa Monica. As he ate he made certain admissions. "You get the feeling," he said, "that we can deal with recurring Arab attacks and even with the leverage of the Arab oil producers. But the deep-down danger is the breaking down of the quality of Israel by migrations of Sephardic Jews from North Africa and Turkey. Ignorant? . . . oh, my, you've got no idea! It takes three months of instruction to teach those guys to flush a toilet."

No fools, the correspondents understood at once, that no matter what they might hear in the desert that afternoon, they already had a nice story. *"Racial conflict in the kibbutz. An Israeli Army officer admitted here today, within sound of the guns which have once more though narrowly repulsed the Arabs, that deep prejudices separate the Sephardic and Ashkenazim Jews in townships, kibbutzes, and settlements. Last month in a kibbutz close to the Syrian border, three young Sephardim were savagely beaten by Ashkenazim youths, etc. etc. . . ."*

If the young officer's heedless words were a gift, they were a gift Brian did not choose to accept. He watched instead the woman farther down the table, how she closed her eyes and winced. She must herself be—one way or another—Jewish.

When the meal was finished and they left the mess, Brian jostled to get on her flank. He made sure he boarded the same army truck, not helping her over the tailboard, since women journalists often objected to belittling gallantries of that nature. He was so close behind her that he was able to pretend to look about the truck selecting a seat before choosing with a counterfeit yawn to sit beside her. At her side, he believed, he could tolerate the afternoon.

Seated, he put his head up against one of the uprights, which in chilly or rainy weather would support a canvas canopy. He closed his eyes. War- and world-weary, I take my sleep in interstices of time. As the truck pulled out he banged his head so loudly that the girl must have noticed. To stop himself blushing, he talked at her directly.

"Who're you filing for?"

"*L.A. Times*," said the girl. But she did not sound Californian.

"Your accent . . ."

"I'm Australian. The same as you . . ."

"How can you tell what I am?"

"The walk. The voice."

"The walk. Jesus!"

"I'm a Jew from Western Australia," she told him. "A poor one. My father works in an asbestos factory. Nonetheless, I'm familiar with the mechanisms of the water closet."

As Brian laughed he noticed how her deep eyes sparkled in an age and profession in which eyes were brick walls.

"My name is Brian Fitzgerald."

"Mine is Annie Newman."

"Annie Newman," he said, too heavily, putting too much of his tongue into the syllables.

"Try not to say it like that. Let's be friends, just that. I live with a man in London."

"You're a still pool," said Brian. "You're a gift on the battlefield, Annie Newman. If they let me sit here forever with my hand on your knee, I'd be happy."

It came to me in the Gnome's apartment that there was a new kind of fever to Brian's words. He *had*, driven to it by his divers terrors, found a woman whose knee sufficed. Just the same, from reverence as well as because of the jerkings of the truck, he did not touch the small firm knee beneath the camouflage trousering.

"And you're a type," said Annie Newman in a low familiar voice, as if they had known each other five years. "The terrible journalistic stud bull. Please be yourself and not just a stud."

Even this banal advice resounded in him. At once he denounced typical behavior forever and chose—God help us!—to be the essential Brian Fitzgerald. With this woman, he had decided, he could face the omens of the war and the small warm challenge of me, the biochemical formula of all his fear. On the jolting seat he decided to fall as thoroughly in love with Annie as he could manage.

"Do you realize," she asked him, trying to slow the pace of their infatuation, "we're going to a battlefield? There'll be the corpses of young men . . ."

"Yes. Yes, there will be." Will there be? As on the banks of the Sabatik?

The desert ran flat and stony, the stones sharp and crystalline and hurtful to the eye. Fallen fruit of the sun tree, Brian thought, taking to imagery as to wine, inspecting the stones beside the road. Harsh manna that snaps the teeth.

Brian and Annie kept their shoulders together; they were coiled to see awesome things yet so pleased to have each other. Looking idly past Annie's back he noted that one of the stones was a blackened head, tongue out, lying on its side. His stomach, a province not yet penetrated or soothed by love of the girl, sent a spurt of sour matter into his throat, and only a quick locking of his mouth saved him from spilling it on Annie Newman's shoulder.

"We're here," she told him. She nodded at the scorched ruin of a large tank by the side of the road, Islamic characters and a scimitar and crescent showing fire-stained on its superstructure. Brian could feel the girl trembling beside him, as full of complex shudderings as a small silver aspen or an animal.

"I say, is this road mined?" a journalist asked.

"No, there's no risk," the press officer declared, though the truck had slowed to an amble.

"Perhaps it isn't mined," said a know-it-all voice which Brian and Annie both hated on hearing. "Perhaps it isn't mined because your forces did not anticipate this depth of penetration by the enemy."

The boy from Santa Monica said, "I can't be sure why this area isn't mined, sir. But if it's important to your story I can certainly ascertain the reasons."

Brian and Annie turned inward to each other to look over the railing at the battlefield. "It's all right," whispered Brian. There were a few corpses strewn on the desert but most of the tanks seemed intact, their tracks in place, as if the Egyptians drove them so far just to depot them here.

"Excuse me," said Annie, turning inboard, raising her chin, showing her long alabaster throat. "Excuse me, did all these tanks just surrender?"

"No, ma'am. I think you'll find most of their crew inside them."

"I see," said Annie in a fluting voice.

The truck braked. Brian was thrown most heavily against her flank, which quickly yielded, the way familiar flesh might yield, schooled flesh, flesh accustomed to his pressures. He smiled a second and the bile drained back to his acidic gut.

"Dead inside them?" someone asked. "Their crews *dead* inside them?"

At the question, an Israeli guard armed with a carbine dropped the tailgate and they were all invited to dismount. Brian jumped recklessly, turning his ankle but swallowing his curse and reaching up for Miss Newman.

She shook her head, half sat, and vaulted. The press officer led them off to an apparently whole tank some fifty yards off the tar. Under its skin of dust its paintwork seemed new and unscarred. Brian had by now taken Annie's hand though his eyes were nearly closed. The heat from the desert floor scalded the undersurfaces of his body, the underknuckles, eyebrows, and gullet.

"A fifty-ton T57," the press officer announced. "A gift from the Soviet taxpayer to the people of Egypt."

The journalists stood back a little, even the photographers who danced around the tank clicking. For there were still martial emanations from the massive and—it seemed—operable machine. The press officer was first to approach and circle it, squinting at its superstructure. He stopped on its far side, raised his hand, and burned it on the hot armor.

"Look at this," he called, and the whole party crunched around to join him in looking.

"It's like home," Brian muttered, kicking a stone. "It's like the stone deserts."

"Yes," she said.

The press officer pointed to an exactly made hole in the tank's front apron. "That's our ten-millimeter armor-piercing shell. It often takes a perfectly formed disk of metal with it when it enters. In the seconds before the shell explodes inside the tank, the disk goes scything around the interior. No one would deny it's a savage weapon. But you don't have to be reminded of the conditions of our struggle."

A small man, lumpy and bald, straggled a step or two closer to the tank, leaving the huddle of journalists. "I asked you. You mean there are men in there?"

"I said so," said the officer.

The small man made a sound of disapproval with his palate and, hobbling to the tracks of the machine, began to climb the wheels to its superstructure.

"Sir, what are you doing?"

The small man did not turn back to answer. "Verify," he said. "You want I shouldn't verify your lovely ten-millimeter armor-piercing shell?"

Brian and Annie Newman heard behind them a voice say, "It's Krazniak. A New York Jew but an Arab-lover. What do you think of the man?"

Little Krazniak opened the hatch, making small darting movements with his fingers, like a cook handling hot dishes. "I don't think that's advisable," said the press officer, but Krazniak's work compelled a number of his colleagues forward and even Annie Newman and Brian crowded in. "They should stop him," Annie murmured. Her mouth stood open, there was a snarl on her upper lip.

Protecting his hands with an infantryman's floppy fatigue hat, Krazniak eased the lid up, while the press officer argued against it and already had his khaki handkerchief in his hand.

Such a fetor rose from the junked remains of those Egyptian troopers who had brought the tank here that Krazniak was taken by it beneath the jowls and hurled bodily from the superstructure. Strangling, some people managed to get out imprecations—"That fucking hophead!" they said, or "Jesus, he's a lunatic!" The press officer made a fistful of his own nose and mouth and signaled journalists to back away from the reeking machine.

For some reason Brian's eyes took the shock for him and he began to weep. Annie Newman though was gagging and doubled up and Brian walked her away by the shoulders, saying, "There, there. Get it up. There, there." For a second he saw her as widow and himself as first comforter, a role full of opportunities. Onto the stones at her feet she spat a piteous green slime.

"What's it about?" Sal asked intemperately after they'd sat, taking each other in at length. "Why do you follow me around?"

"Do you mind?" asked the Gnome in his oblique way.

"I've never felt at risk. Do you love me in some way?"

"In some way," he agreed. His hands held his knees, each taking an exactly symmetrical grip, but his still green eyes stared crookedly at her.

"Come, Mr. Jones," said Sal, blushing. "We live in a worldly city. Desire in all its forms is uttered millions of times a day."

"Desire," he agreed, tickling his knee. "Desire, yes."

But they both knew there was no average desire here, nothing that could be satisfied on a mattress. He got up, took her hand, putting a strange pressure on it. And through the pressure I understood at once. He suspected he was me. He had fantasies of enjoying my kingship and thought that once he was delivered he might then put pictures on his white walls and place books on the shelves. Until then he would invest little but money and his tennis arm in the outer world.

I was flattered, disarmed. And—since humans have it on good authority that a man cannot again enter the womb—secure.

"I am an orphan," he began, as I knew he would. "They tell me my mother gave birth to me at a table in a diner called Caruso's in Pittsfield, Massachusetts. That was in the spring of 1935. It seems she was very young and didn't know she was pregnant. She was traveling with her father at the time. They were taking a load of maple syrup down from Vermont, from Montpelier, where he had a little farm, to the distributor in New Haven. I have even discovered from my research into the subject that boiling syrup down was an activity that suited his temperament, sitting by a great caldron, waiting for three hundred gallons of sap to boil away to some eight gallons of syrup, and I suppose that kind of patience is inherited. My mother ordered sausage the afternoon of my birth in the Caruso Diner and her father told her, 'Watch out, Chrissie, it'll give you gas.' She was only sixteen and gave birth very quickly, within two minutes of the first pain and in the first panic.

"I suppose that's a circumstantial amount for an orphan to know about his mother. Yet when I was young in the orphanage I suffered from the conviction that I'd given birth to myself, that I'd been a larger and more complicated me and had split in two and the lesser of the two was me and the greater had gone to an appropriate destiny. I began to see my other on the screen from about 1941 onward. He was a drummer boy in *Gunga Din* and *The Charge of the Light Brigade*; he was a jockey in the turf classics. I was happy for him. I thought he deserved to be deified in movies. That was my obsession then—before I even had the plate in. It ruled me. It even enriched me. I think."

The narrative had Sal engrossed. It appealed, I suppose, to her Celtic imagination. At the same time she breathed wildly; she knew how mad the Gnome was and thought she'd be redefined by his madness. She did not yet know how, but she wasn't leaving without finding out.

"I'm not telling you this," he said, "to elicit pity. Because when I was twelve I went to a foster home, a childless couple in Connecticut. They took me in to help pay for the husband's flying and he used to let me go with him most Sundays, taking off from the airport at Danbury, always climbing north toward the Berkshires, always circling some of the fine old houses in places like Great Barrington and Stockbridge. He'd drone around at a respectful distance and summer parties on the vast—*really* vast—lawns would raise their eyes to us. 'There,' he used to say, 'they're looking at us, Warwick. We have claimed the attention of the people of Mammon.' In the autumn when there weren't any parties on the lawns, he sometimes used to give the controls to me and we'd bounce above the hills—red and gold at that time of year. About this time my ameba obsession—if I can call it that—began to peter out. I could see movies without spotting my other side. My brother. His career in movies was finished."

"You became a normal child," Sal supplied.

"I thought I'd found a family in the McQueens. But one Sunday when I was on a Scout outing, Mr. McQueen took his wife up for a plane ride—it was her birthday. According to the newspapers he dove on and buzzed three garden parties in western Massachusetts that afternoon, causing the people of Mammon to run indoors, no matter how many cool airline tycoons stood on the croquet lawns yelling, 'Don't go inside, don't go inside!' In the end Mr. McQueen caught his undercarriage in a high beech and tipped forward into a stone fence. He and his wife both perished in the crash. The police discovered from the family doctor that Mrs. McQueen had cancer of the stomach. It was funny that such a quiet man as McQueen should be buried as a dread flier.

"There were other foster parents and I did well enough with them and eventually went to MIT on an orphan scholarship. It was about that stage that the new obsession set in. I *had* a mother. But she was no past mother who dropped me without knowing in the corner of a diner. That was an unworthy scene, something from a melodrama, and it wasn't my scenario. No. The truth was I was not yet even delivered. I had a future mother. I would stumble on her. I started to inspect all pregnant women. I was like God looking for a woman to act as crucible for his son. Except my needs were simpler and they were desperate needs too. In the streets of Boston, Irishmen and Italians would come up and ask why I was staring at their wives. I knew I'd recognize the woman in a crowd. I knew there'd be an aureole of rightness about her."

"Me?" Sal asked, squinting at him. "You're telling me there's that . . . aureole of rightness . . . about me?" For a second she felt she was seated on one of those high desert points on which bushes burn and a dazzling onus descends. She wanted him to say she was elected and with the same mind wanted to beg off.

As for me, I clenched my mighty and minute fists. I had an ally outside the amnion, beyond the walls, behind the lines of my enemies. I had a counterbalance to Brian. The pumpings of my fists were self-congratulation.

"Wait!" the Gnome ordered. He closed his eyes for some ten seconds, during which he trembled a little, reminding me of me and my quiet weeping behind closed lids.

"I became," he went on at last, "my company's representative in Saigon and did wonderful business for them there. When the CIA were employing everyone, they employed me and put me on a retainer. I took the retainer seriously. I was still looking though. I'd look at peasant women and at refugees. But the contours were never right. They never fitted the . . . *refinements* of my obsession.

"In the meantime I spent one evening watching an arms depot at Tri Huan Duot and filmed Americans and Vietnamese casually stealing arms from it and paying the guards off before driving the plunder away. After I gave my report and the film to my superior, the first attempt on my life was made. A grenade was dropped from a balcony into an open truck I drove. I saw it even before it hit the seat beside me. I flew from the cabin like a robin, I swear I took wing. I had flown into a wall like a swallow into a barn, I had fallen dazed, all before the thing exploded. It's known for children to die prior to birth, but the self-aware child doesn't permit it . . ."

How I liked him and hoped my liking would infect Sal if that were needed. He took wing when threatened because he had ambitions that rang like bells—to re-achieve my stature, to rinse his brain in the falls of Sal's blood. His drift was wise, which was more than you could say for Brian's.

"The plate?" Sal suggested, tapping her head and then wondering if it was bad taste to allude to his affliction.

"It came," the Gnome went on, "from the second attempt on my life. My main search, you must understand, was for the woman. But in the meantime I kept superficially busy—earning my retainer. I discovered that there were establishments where you could change every U.S. dollar you earned into a dollar and fifty cents in occupation money. There was a tailor's shop to the north of Saigon that seemed to be a laundry for all the city's dirty money. A U.S. Air Force major introduced me to the Indian tailor, who was always working on a bona fide suit, whenever we entered. We would give him our U.S. dollars at two P.M. on a Thursday, be paid one and a half times the amount in occupation money, go to a bank and change this amount at par back to American dollars, return to the Indian, sell him those, being again paid too generously in occupation dollars. So we'd spend all afternoon traveling from the Indian to a bank and back again, pumping up the value of our dollars. We'd stop for beer at four P.M. Because you need to pause in an exercise like that. He was like me, the major, a man of what you'd call humble origins. Money had been an iron reality for his parents and for him himself as a young man. The Indian was showing us that money doesn't exist as a structure, that it's gaseous, that its impermanence matches that of a thin-walled helium balloon. We could inflate a five-hundred-dollar wage to twenty thousand dollars in an afternoon without rushing. We never quickened our pace; it seemed indecent to do so. We sat after four drinking beer and my eyes would wander to the faces of passing women.

"I wrote a report omitting my friend the major's name. I mentioned acquisitive officers from whose hands a sea of dollars washed away through the tailor's shop and touched shore God knew where. I was thanked and told to go on patronizing the Indian and observing him. I observed he had a cataract of the left eye and a total lack of nasal hair. While learning this, I became wealthier and wealthier. I asked the authorities if they wanted me to keep these illegal moneys in visible note form. They told me, 'No.' 'Observe,' they instructed me again. One thing I observed was that the tailor's bank was never broken. You—as I once did—could start at two P.M. with twenty thousand dollars, and on your last visit toward four, his daughter could go into a back room and return with a suitcase of dollar bills. Of course, once we got to that level we didn't frequent corner banks, the major and I. We made use of the short-term money market, borrowing a suitcase of notes by arrangement at one-thirty, returning it with interest at a quarter of five. The limitations on our wealth-making were purely in terms of portability—how many notes a man could carry from A to B and back without risking pulled muscles, holdups, police intrusions . . .

"After a year of this kind of work I was worth somewhere in excess of two million dollars and had to resort to Swiss banks as an efficient way of filing my items of evidence. And need I say that on the busiest afternoon, rushing from the money market to the Indian whose bank could not be broken, and certain banks as strange as his but working symbiotically with it in the mulch of the world's dirty money, I was searching, the search was everything, it drove my legs, it made me watch the clock, a clock in my viscera.

It told me how old I was getting and yet hadn't been delivered to the world.

"Once I made the mistake of appealing to an army psychiatrist about my problem. He told me, swore to me in fact by the dry vermouth in his glass, that marriage would adjust the balance. In that spirit—I admit it with some shame—I married Angie, a clerk from the embassy in Saigon. She was a gentle, square-faced, blue-eyed girl. Her parents had been Polish. In the first month of our marriage two men came to visit us in our flat near the cathedral. They said, 'You have to expect a little currency disequilibrium in a situation like this one we have here right now.' They had rings on their fingers. They raised their hands like priests. You know the kind of men. 'You see, if we took action we'd have no way of proving your good faith. How much did you say you have, Mr. Jones? In bank accounts?' 'I'll turn it all over,' I said, but they went on making these movements with their hands, they were conferring on me the high priesthood of wealth. 'No, you keep it.' 'What's to stop me,' I asked them, 'turning this two million into fifty right there, in the back room of the tailor's shop?' They said, 'Nothing. Nothing will stop you if you are discreet, Mr. Jones. Nothing will stop you except the limits of the people you deal with. And it is not our mandate to interfere with free enterprise banking.'"

Sal wanted to speak but could not break into his even, formal account.

"I think those were the most miserable days of my life," he said. "I could feel the weight of that money. But even more, I was aware of Angie's pain. Her eyes went over me trying to define what was missing in me. She didn't understand that my lack was a basic one—I had never been adequately introduced to the world. That there was a quiet womb somewhere out of which I might be born sometime but not yet . . .

"I knew I was in some danger when I read in the press that my friend the air force major had been shot dead while holding up the tailor's shop in Gia Dinh. I knew the major was no thief. He was building a modest million, he wanted to buy an electronics company in Phoenix and when he had he would have joined a service club. Quaint criteria of honesty if you like . . . but there we are! I arranged for Angie and myself to stay with friends in a villa in Vung Tau and on the way there with poor Angie at four P.M. one afternoon, the same hour I used to drink beer on Thursdays with the air force major, I was confronted by three trucks traveling astride the highway toward me, occupying all the space between the highway fence and the hillside. I avoided them by driving through the fence. I was in flight again, high above terraced fields. Angie did not survive. I did. At some metallic cost . . ."

He touched his brow.

Sal, still short of breath, wanted to force the narrative pace. She was like a person in love begging the beloved to get to the point at which she enters and transforms history. "And then you came to England," she murmured, with fractional thought for the mangled Angie.

"In my long coma I encountered you in a botanical garden, among luscious tropic growths. Great—if I may say so—" And here he bowed his head and coughed and made a little canceling movement across his lips with his forefinger. "—great phalluses of the Monstera deliciosa flanked you. I woke content and had to be reminded of the accident and poor Angie. The meeting would occur. I didn't have to plot it and work on it any more than a migrating bird has to work on the pattern of his navigation. I came to London. I was certain—without having to tell myself I was certain—that London was the appropriate city. And our orbits touched, didn't they? Again and again without any of my planning . . ."

His hands still lay over his knees, formally, not familiar. And his story was told, formally yet subtly familiar. He must have been an earnest little orphan; I could imagine how scrubbed he would have arrived at the doorsteps of new foster homes, blinking and bowing. I could imagine him eating, private and neat as a cat, in the orphanage dining hall.

"When you are delivered," he murmured, a man uncomfortable about the size of the claim he now made, "I'll be delivered. I'll be after forty years a child of this earth, I'll be able to make demands and marks . . . you know. It isn't too great a desire, is it? It isn't too much of an . . ." He did not raise his shoulders in shrugging, instead retracting his head. ". . . an obsession?"

Sal smiled at her own lap. His craziness worried us not at all, exalting us instead. Though he placed a weight of motherhood on Sal, of brotherhood on me, we felt flattered. It came to us how unsafe we'd been before he stated his kinship. They hadn't killed him with all the artifices of grenades, of walls of oncoming trucks. So we felt allied to his toughness. The deal had been stated. For the small symbolic price of letting him be born through Sal, he would be my external knight, my champion, my guarantor.

To show my willingness for this contract I spread a hand against the walls of Sal. And while my fingers were so placed, the Gnome rose, walked to Sal, and, like a husband in one of those Dutch family portraits—say by Van Dyck—placed his hand on Sal's belly. It was a barely touching, merely ritual placement, not at all like the meaty probing of an obstetrician. Yet it passed radiantly into my fist.

"Are you in any danger?" he asked her.

In Tel Aviv, Brian, sharpened by love, had filed copy an hour early. Two days back it would have been a matter of pride with him to keep to the bar until a half hour before either deadline or his allocated time with the radiotelephone. Now, using the time slot of an unpunctual French journalist, he enunciated his dispatch into that device. "Young lives canceled in a microsecond by a disk of steel . . ." It was a dispatch written in a high heat, it had a new gusto to it.

He never regretted that he was no prose master. For he could tell that people were attracted by the boyishness which stood at the center of his sad circle of talents. If the talents had been higher, Annie might not have been beckoned by the central Brian. As, a little later in the day, she was, mewling toward an upshot astride his thighs in the Tel Aviv Hilton.

Brian, it seemed, was both frenzied and clear-headed as he himself released his seed into this pretty and alien woman. He watched Annie's long neck and the gloss of sweat along the throat, the fine arc of jaw, raised as if to bay.

"Oh Sal," he grunted, sad for Sal that though she was more beautiful than Annie, her lines had no specialty for him.

"What did you say?" asked Annie, frowning instantly. She hadn't ever respected people who, after a few days hotel loving, decided to live together. She looked for symptoms of the mistake she suspected she'd made. She clutched his left teat. "What *did* you say?"

"I don't know," Brian told her, feeling no guilt for the lie. "I don't know what I might say. I speak a new language now," he embroidered. "I live on a new planet."

His threadbare image of himself as deified, a space dweller, broke a clot of acid in my belly.

Annie pitched herself off him and fell to his side. "Tell me again you *really* have no children, Brian! Tell me again . . ."

"I have no children. And Sal . . . Sal's so pretty. She'll have men . . ." He coughed. ". . . someone anyhow . . . within a year."

Annie said, "You talk like a social worker."

She had nonetheless spread her knees to let his hand at her body's pink mouth. Her buttocks writhed with a force she would have liked to use to signal her regret for Sal, to Sal. *Am Unaware Whence Passion For This Man Derives,* she would have liked to transmit.

Twice more before Brian's return we visited the Gnome.

Both times he had piano music playing on a tape deck and fussed about Sal with teapots, cake, fruit, or wine. They did not talk about the mania linking them. They would never talk about it again. It was the sort of thing which, if said twice, blew away.

On the second of these afternoons the alternator on Sal's car went and she had to leave it at a garage near Pembroke

Gardens. The Gnome drove us home at 6 P.M. and Clytie, so willing to interpret Sal in terms of her own randy girlhood, saw him taking us to the door.

"A funny-looking little man," said Clytie. "Haven't I seen him before?"

"Please Clytie," said Sal. "It isn't an attachment . . ."

"You don't have to apologize to me. I believe, in any case, the diminutive have their points."

It was a Thursday afternoon when Brian called from Heathrow. He sounded as Sal would have expected, whiskified from the flight, and at his first slur of greeting her body bespoke her need for him. Even I caught the now familiar impulses of her belly, of her ankles, of the backs of her neck and knees; and hated Brian in measure.

Two yards away, in a thicket of public telephones, Annie Newman called her boyfriend, telling him in breathy and neutral voice that she had a lot to talk to him about. On the plane, in skies free of missiles and fighters, Brian and Annie had spoken of making it "quick and merciful." It was, as you might guess, Brian's phrase.

I knew this was bound to be a bad afternoon. I churned and danced and Sal thought it was her desire gingering me up, and sang as she put on a yellow print dress.

She watched from the window the tarnished yet golden afternoon across Clapham way. When the taxi pulled up and she saw Brian back out of it and accept his baggage from the driver, she could also see the back of Annie Newman's head through the taxi window, but presumed he had companionably shared a cab with a fellow journalist. Whereas all across the Hammersmith Overpass Brian and Annie had twitched to be at each other's body.

Sal did notice however that Brian stood among his luggage a full twenty seconds after the taxi vanished. She was forced therefore to push the window open and call to him. "Brian! Brian boy!" Like a man with a headache he squinted up at her, waved, checked the wave, and hauled his bags indoors.

Sal was waiting for him at our open door. "Hello," he said pityingly.

"Hello?" she inquired. *"Hello? Is that all?"*

"That's all," he said, leaving his bags just by the door. "Are you tired?"

"It isn't the problem . . ."

"Oh. What's the problem? Christina?"

"Christina?"

She grabbed him by the side and innocently ground her body against his hip. "I'm too easy on you," she whispered. "We'll talk about this Christina girl once you've been adequately ravished."

I noticed now that for the first time in his life he was affronted by a sexual advance, in this case the best advance he would ever receive. "What do you think sex is?" he very nearly asked her. "Do you think I can make love to anyone?"

He mustered kindness enough to pat her hand. "Sal, I didn't bring you a present."

"What did you think I wanted? An ornamental cannon shell?"

"Sal, Sal." With pressure of his chaste hand against Sal's hip he separated her from himself. "Let's sit for a second."

She agreed, coming down crookedly in her chair, frowning. I and not Brian took account of her fluent body, of what a bounty she was beside bony Annie Newman. But Brian had written her white body off.

"I'm in love, Sal," he said. "You and I aren't going to live with each other anymore."

Sal made a small squeaking appeal with her lips. Soon—in a conversational way—she asked, "Is it that girl you brought the liqueur for?"

"What girl?"

"What girl? That . . . that bloody Christina. The secret recipe girl. *What girl!"*

"That girl was a casual lay, Sal."

"Oh. I see. One of the casuals. Do they all get gifts of liqueur?"

"I know I was disgusting then. Why couldn't you see that? You were tolerant as my mother."

Sal's knees flexed and she stood. "As your mother, you bastard? As your goddamn mother? I have breasts that go pink for you, I've a belly you drop your saliva on, and a crotch that flows to your touch. Is that how it was with you and your mother?"

"I'm sorry, Sal. I've been disgusting these last six months. I'm not disgusting now."

"Good, good. You're over being disgusting. Is that guaranteed?"

"The girl . . . *this girl* . . . I met in Israel. I haven't been hiding her from you. Her name's Annie Newman."

"A journalist?"

He nodded. "An Australian too."

"Like your mother."

"She isn't as obviously beautiful as you . . ."

"Oh well. Obvious beauty's a little crass, isn't it?"

She thought, I must stop saying these sharp and narrow things. He means to go, his bags are placed for flight. "What do you mean you're going to live with this Annie?"

"I'm sorry, Sal. But these things don't operate by laws of our making."

"Oh?" Sal said, going back to drollery. "Oh, the gods imposing their will on you again, Brian? The gods do that a lot, don't they, you poor old bastard?"

I did not move in her stilled waters. Even the walls of her amnion were flexed, cartilaginous. "I *love* you, Brian. Don't you understand? You may be spectacularly unworthy, but you're my love."

"I suspect that's the way Annie feels."

"Annie . . . ah, Annie," Sal whispered.

"About your pregnancy," Brian said.

"*My* pregnancy." She adopted a bitter stage-Irish accent. "Are y'implying it's the Virgin Birth I am?"

"No. Look. It's no use being sarcastic."

"Tell me about our pregnancy, Brian."

"I'll be brutal, Sal."

"It suits the day."

"I think you . . . we if you like . . . ought to get the thing terminated."

My legs jerked. My fists clenched. I opened my mouth and a silent but, I could tell, powerful curse fell on him, on his manhood, on the bed he shared with Annie.

"No," said Sal. I was too panicked, however, to tell how deep that no ran in her, it might be just a surface and flimsy negative.

"A journalist's pay isn't good. I can't afford to pay two rents on decent accommodation. And I don't want my kid growing up in any slum . . ."

"I'll be finished my novel soon."

"According to the Society of Authors," said Brian, as if he'd saved up this statistic a long time to bludgeon me with it on the apt day, "the average wage of novelists is less than two pounds a week."

"I'll go back to journalism."

"And spend three-quarters of your money on a nanny?"

For ten minutes it became a crazy debate on incomes and prices, on rents on Streatham basements and first-floor-back flats in Paddington; and Brian saw rents and prices as crippling, while Sal argued they were no more than you'd expect in an imperfect world. Brian at last broke off this false symposium on real estate.

"Can't you see?" he asked. "I want the marriage canceled. I want its fruits canceled. Having a brat . . . it'll start Annie off on a basis of guilt over you, over the brat. Isn't that clear, Sal? Isn't it?"

In Sal the waters quaked once and began to flow again and fortify me. More strongly than ever before, I opted for birth, for its puzzles and perils. For you shall see my face, you bastard. That I promised him. You'll face my knowing eyes and my so-called baby hand will close on and claim the fingers you ram so willingly into alien women.

While I bubbled and vowed, Sal got to her feet. She

thought of internal me but also of the external Gnome, who gave her reasons a face. I did not resent that; I was glad at that moment to share a face. I was pleased that her voice, when it rose, was so low and so impermeable. "Listen," she said. "No. And don't mention it again."

"I don't want to have an existent child," he said, "that I'm absent father to. It's messy. It's cruel . . ."

"You want your weekends free, do you, Brian?"

"It's unfair to all parties."

"I said, don't mention it." She watched his bowed head. Even the pain on his face looked shallow, something he'd get over at the first pub. "Where will you stay tonight?"

"I don't know."

"Not with Annie?"

"She has a boyfriend to . . . to evict. I don't know if that will be easy or hard."

"Take off then."

"What?"

"Take off."

"Oh. All right."

She rubbed her thigh again like someone relishing a joke. "What you want is for me to act up, to seal the situation. Of course, a good wife should. I should tear the pages from the pornography you keep in the second left-hand drawer of your desk and release them from the window like a flock of doves. I ought to tell Royal Hospital Road in a high voice that you have a weakness for Alsatian bitches."

"But I don't," Brian argued. "I don't go in for anything like that."

"Well, all the better for your purposes. Then I should drive you down the stairs bombarding you with copies of your favorite novels and bringing Clytie and George and Ran cursed Singh out to stare on your discomfort. Then, as you fled to the nineteen bus, you would be free to think, How well I am to be away from that bitch. I'm sure that's the last conjugal service you came for, and I'm not going to render it."

"I'm grateful you don't," he told her, as uncomprehending as he'd always been. "Really."

She gave one of his bags a nudge with her foot.

"All your shirts must be foul. There are a few fresh ones inside. And your underwear. I suppose you've been coming in it all over the Negev."

He pursed his lips and went inside, slow and ceremonial as a choirboy in a recessional. He returned holding two modest fistfuls of cotton garments. Sal laughed at him a second, he looked so waiflike.

"I must be the first woman, hot-to-trot, that you ever knocked back."

"There are going to be others."

"Oh well. It's nice to belong to a sisterhood then."

Opening a suitcase, he put the clean shirts on top of the stained ones. "Get rid of the fetus," he said, as harsh as he could make it. "It hasn't got a future."

"Not only has it got a future," she told him, thinking of the Gnome. "It has a present. It has a past."

"Oh Jesus," he said. "All Celtic again. Soon, Sal, you'll have a nice man crazy for you."

He thought he'd said something soft to wind up the connection and quickly grasped the handles of his bags, managing it two-handed and at once.

She heard him go. Her legs twitched, wanting her to be up and screaming down the stairwell. But at last the front self-locking door of the house sighed closed.

Fearful that Sal might yet decide to tell the street something unspeakable about him, he sprinted jerkily toward the Royal Hospital, glancing over his shoulder for a taxi. At last he reached the corner of Smith Street and rounded it; and looking up at a house where Mark Twain once lived, he felt his gut unclench and sweep him forward without any sense of the impact of heel on pavement.

Meantime Sal realized that Annie might not have got from Brian a full report of his marriage, since giving partial reports had been ever Brian's way. Sal found herself on the balcony calling, "Have you told her I'm pregnant?"

But Brian was already in the Phoenix, winking at a double Scotch.

Without United Press to pay his bills, Brian was forced to a modest bed-and-breakfast hotel called the Argyle near Victoria Station. There were young Australians in the foyer, chatting loudly about whether they should visit Hampton Court or Dickens's house in Doughty Street. There were tired, ratty-haired girls with American and Canadian patches on their nylon jackets. The room had a framed calendar picture of Lincoln Cathedral, but an Anglican pallor, not a gothic oomph, infected the air. The washbasin was streaked with umber.

He had, however, to meet Annie at eight-thirty. He cherished that timetable in his cupped hands like a pauper cherishing soup; and then he lay down. My father and enemy slept till eight.

He got to the meeting place at Victoria Station five minutes early. From a minute after the half hour he gave way to panic, his armpits itched, he put his frantic weight first on one hip, then on the other. He wondered in his childlike way if Annie could snip and cauterize the nexus with her boyfriend as well as he had snipped and cauterized his with Sal. What if the boyfriend pleaded and won and he, Brian F., was condemned to lie down in the Argyle forever, without a breast to put his head against?

While he twitched beneath the nominated archway, a small car stopped where it shouldn't have in the midst of the perilous road outside Victoria. From its passenger seat a woman half tumbled, half jogged. A van, skirting the statue of General Foch, avoided knocking her down but nearly managed anyhow, since she was off-balance and had momentum. With all the traffic honking at her, she ran to Brian's side. Her left wrist was bandaged as if she had been at it with razors. Her right eye and her cheek were bruised.

"Annie . . . ?" he asked her. The bandaged wrist frightened him more than the bruises did.

"No, no," she soothed him. "I was wearing a glass bangle. It snapped."

The driver of the small car that had delivered her was still parked there, where nobody parked, in the middle lane of Buckingham Palace Road. A thin young man with a mustache. He leaned over his wheel, looking at Brian. Even intervening trucks did not seem to break his gaze. So he invited Brian to ford the traffic and face him.

"Bastard!" Brian screamed and stepped from the pavement.

"No," Annie told him. "Pay attention to me."

The thin man drove away. The world grew simpler than ever before for Brian in that second. There was his damaged darling and himself and their mean room at the Argyle to be turned by their mutual fancies and cherishings into a satrapal pavilion. And for want of seeing my ferocious and irrevocable face, he had already cut me off. In his brain a black hole had taken me. I had become negative matter.

"Tomorrow," he told Annie, "we'll look for a flat."

But he would have felt embarrassed to go around the estate agents with a bruised woman. He didn't want those blithe know-it-alls who staff letting offices to wonder if he was a woman-beater. While widowed Sal wept by the river, taking no comfort from the minuscule actions of my limbs and wondering if the Gnome could give any; while Annie slept late with her bruised face and slivered wrist, Brian went alone to an agency in Fulham Road. He was shown an "airy, bright place" one floor up in W8, one-bedroomed, "suitable for people without children," as the agent said.

This flat happened to be two streets from the Gnome's house. Walking to the corner with the agent, who was showing him how close he and Annie would be to the 97 bus route, Brian saw the Gnome drive past with Sal in the front seat. Sal's face, Brian saw, was bruised with grief. Yet he saw also that she sat with the Gnome as if he were something habitual, a chauffeur or a lover. Through all the agent's blather he read and retained the license number. He wondered if she had had secret comfort from that small driver before yesterday or if she had for solace's sake found him since. Both concepts sickened him.

On the way back to the agent's office to sign the lease he excused himself, went into a telephone box, and called his news editor.

"Clive, can you have a car number traced for me?"

"On what basis?"

"It could be a nice scandal. A hint I picked up at a party. A politician and a girl. Suggestions of espionage . . ."

"What politician?"

"Harry Steele," lied Brian, grabbing at a name.

"Christ!" The name Brian so loosely uttered belonged to a Labour messiah, a West Indian by birth. Recently he had affirmed the glamour of politics by taking a wife away from a rock star. Brian's flesh prickled in the phone closet's thick climate. He asked himself why he needed to excite his news editor with such a sledgehammer name.

"Call me in half an hour," Clive told him.

And when the lease had been signed and notarized by an Indian solicitor, and the heavy deposit paid by check, Brian called back.

"How does this sound?" Clive asked him in a febrile voice. "The car is owned by a Warwick Jones of 23 Pembroke Gardens Close, W8. Do you learn anything from that?"

"I don't know," said Brian slowly, as if he were really measuring the car ownership of Warwick Jones against a corpus of other painfully connected data. "But I'll be seeing Jones tonight." For surely, surely, Sal would not be sleeping with him this evening, so early in her widowhood. "Or at the worst, tomorrow morning."

"Is there any danger? For you, I mean?"

"No." There'd be danger to Jones.

"Well, I want a full briefing as soon as you leave him. You've got my home number?"

"Of course," said Brian sweating, lost to his profession— a profession of pygmy-truths and grand omissions—by the kind of lie that tells against a man.

Sal had the Gnome take us home that evening, though she would willingly have slept, rolled in a blanket, whimpering freely through her opened mouth, in his glacial apartment. The thought however of Clytie nodding and winking at her door in the morning compelled Sal home.

Sal wept before her television set, and the earth's torment as detailed on "The News at 9" seemed to her a mere ripening of her own loss. She had not eaten that day and did not touch liquor; she was in fact angry with herself for harboring a woe too deep for whiskey to touch. Tomorrow she might call his office, might even visit it, and whether she begged or threatened she would be messy and loud. Knowing that, she felt a disgust for herself so deep that its sharpness crossed my tongue. What does the voyager do, I had to ask myself that grievous evening, if the captain comes unhinged?

Almost for the sake of light entertainment, I watched Brian watch the Gnome as he returned to Pembroke Gardens Close a little after nine. Annie had been left lying in bed at a good tourist hotel in Gloucester Road as the facial bruises reached their richest color. Brian had told her he had to go to a press conference at Heathrow. He could not admit to his true task, since it was a sort of betrayal of his bruised Annie to want to beat up Sal's lover. Sal's lover should have been—he understood—a dead issue. In Gloucester Road he felt a flush of guilt appropriate to a young man out on his first adultery. He was a patchwork quilt, my own true begetter, of misplaced and cross-eyed emotions.

And how lovingly and intimately I hated him in the core of each of my dazzling and multiplex cells as he stood in a light spit of rain, watching the Gnome come home and enter his house. Brian counted to sixty before moving from beneath a beech tree and ringing Mr. Jones's bell himself. Even as he pressed the button he was growing confused as to whether to be polite or to be primal, to begin by sitting and talking or by beating the hell out of the Gnome.

When the Gnome answered, the formality, the New England polish of his voice, cowed Brian.

"It's Brian Fitzgerald," he said in a rush. "Sal's wife . . . I mean, husband. I think we should talk to each other."

The Gnome hesitated a ponderous time before inviting him up. "All right," he said at last. He waited for Brian at the top of the first flight of stairs. On the staircase, and after the Gnome greeted him and pointed him to a leather chair, Brian took some warning from the Gnome's blank white walls. He thought—correctly for once—that there was a toughness and fixity in a man who left his walls altogether blank.

Brian didn't sit in the chair the Gnome pointed to. He inspected his host. Could tall Sal bed down with this scrap, this fragment of man? The Gnome seated himself, half lost yet unabashed in the void spaces of his big leather chair.

"I happen to know, Mr. . . . Mr. Jones," said Brian, pushing his teeth forward within his tight jaws the way Ran Singh did when under threat, "that you've had something to do with Sal . . . my wife."

"Yes," said the Gnome. "Yes. That's quite correct."

"I don't want to be the vengeful husband."

"No. Good. There's no sense in that," the Gnome told him flatly, as if giving him bonus points for good sense. Brian's temper began then, a prickling in his belly, still a quiet tide, however.

"Have you known Sal long?"

"A long time by repute," the Gnome said with a little smile. "We met only a short time ago, however."

"You must know that we aren't together anymore?"

"She was . . . distressed. But she didn't tell me."

Brian grew confused. The separation, his chances with Annie—it was all in danger unless Sal began to tell other people that her husband was gone.

"I'm worried about her stability," said Brian. "I still worry about her, after all. I don't want her to . . . I don't know . . ." He gestured at the Gnome's spartan walls. "I don't think this is any use to her."

The Gnome thought again. Five seconds. A long time for a man like Brian to bear.

"It's not a relationship you choose to pick up or put down," the Gnome at last began. "It's more absolute than that. You must have had relationships like that. A friendship and more. Yet sexless."

This sounded like a surmise and Brian answered with an edge. "For Christ's sake, why don't we talk straight? Have you been sleeping with Sal? No, that's a stupid question and by Christ I'm going to try not to be stupid. How *long* have you been sleeping with Sal?"

The Gnome would have liked to deny he ever had but thought if he did he might then be trapped into confessing the true connection.

"You want to know for reasons of divorce proceedings?"

"Listen. Listen, sport. I just want to know. Did you realize she's pregnant?"

"Yes. I know that. I knew that fact. I . . . knew it."

"Well, mate. There's a standing bloody question."

"I would say," said the Gnome, "the standing bloody question is whether the child is mine."

"In one, my friend."

The Gnome paused yet again, as I paused in Sal who sat mute before her jabbering television. Brian willed me to be the Gnome's son, not knowing that the Gnome had already willed me to be his brother.

"An answer," said Brian. "Come on, mate. An answer."

The Gnome stared up at Brian the begetter. There was a childlike blankness in the Gnome's eyes but also there was an assessment. He felt nothing for Brian. Sal was to the Gnome a figure from mythology. Sal was *the Good Mother*. But Brian was simply an uncertain stranger, twitching for a pretext to get rough, to lay fists on a smaller man.

"It isn't, I can assure you. It isn't my child. The relationship doesn't involve adultery. I told you. It's more absolute than that."

"Absolute. Listen, mate. Don't pull any of that metaphysics on me. *Absolute!* What sort of fucking goes on in an absolute relationship?"

The Gnome smiled and shook his head. "You can't define some alliances. There's too much danger in trying."

This reply came to Brian as a gnostic and irkingly paternal answer. Brian, on his feet, clutched the Gnome's elbow, raised him from his chair, shouted in his face.

"You pig's arse!" Brian yelled. "You coy little bastard."

"Let me alone," said the Gnome in a voice of rising intonation, a little sentence but its tail raised like a scorpion's.

Brian took the stocky shoulders and tried to shake them. I knew Brian was about to be punished. Jubilant, yet in two minds, I waited for the Gnome's blow.

First, Brian found himself on his backside. No direct punch had been thrown, no particular pain felt. The Gnome had by some deft means released Brian's hold and sat him down on the hard and unadorned floor.

Brian rose, as he had to all battles since the age of thirteen, intending a simple gambit. Get him in the groin was the strategy. Then work on his warped face. But it was by a hard, raised knee that the Gnome propelled Brian back against the wall, where a node of bone at the top of his spine struck with a *whap* he felt in his anus.

Brian now got an education in what it is to suffer my kind of anger, the anger of the enwombed. For the Gnome's Asiatic skills kept Brian from making any of the impacts he desired to. Any limb he extended toward the Gnome was used to dump him against some harsh surface. He was a man in a perverse electric field.

I began to pity the bastard, far too early. That, as Sal and Annie knew, was one of Brian's gifts—to stir premature mercy. But not in the Gnome. And there was that in Brian that had outlasted the lashes of the Empire: his great-grandfather would not scream at the flogging triangle for George III. With the dregs of this congenital perseverance, Brian would not cease trying to get at the Gnome's face or at least to land a persevering boot in his scrotum.

Therefore the Gnome put him four times more on the floor, twice more against the wall. For the Gnome could not prevent himself. He fought, as they say, like something pro-grammed, dispassionately; and a neutral onlooker, if there had been one, might have thought the plate in his brain had something to do with it.

It was an encounter with the rim of one of the Gnome's empty bookcases that finished Brian. His brain grew large, seemed to rupture, and a gaseous pain leaked forth with a long torrid sigh.

"Oh sweet Christ," the Gnome said. He knelt by Brian and held him while Brian shuddered and the eyes strained to focus.

"Oh God, you little bastard," Brian said, still wanting to kill him. What must he be like in bed? Brian wondered. A terrible force. This is an absolute relationship, the little man would say, before violating Sal's sweet mass with a hot little cock. That was how Brian still misread the Sal-Gnome alliance.

Of course he began weeping.

"Please," said the Gnome, putting just two fingers on Brian's elbow. "I don't sleep with your Sal."

"Oh no, oh no," said Brian. In the clouds of nausea rose a small alp of unbeaten irony. "You're the two founding members of the W8 Scrabble club."

People are often possessed by a rash urge to trust Brian. Now the urge operated in the Gnome. You might have thought his experience of foster-parents, assassins, and intelligence bodies might have warned him off such easy impulses. Instead he cleared his throat once, looked at his murderous little hands, and told Brian his orphan story.

And Brian's pleasure in the tale was illimitable. His head cleared in one pulse of astringent joy. He did not make his happiness apparent to the Gnome, for fear of a further beating. But now he had Sal beaten, me marked off for some obstetrical abattoir. And the bastard could just manage to swallow his smile.

He refused to be driven home.

Once on the street, even with the taxi fare the Gnome had forced on him still in his hand, he made for the police station at the western end of Kensington High Street, getting there before the facial swelling contracted or the contusions lost any of their opulence.

In the station a sergeant and a constable were chatting, standing idle in a city plagued by plate-brained violence. The sergeant noticed Brian, who even managed a little stumble. "Oh, here indeed comes one," said the sergeant, and the constable found a chair and helped Brian into it by an elbow.

"Who did this, sir?"

"A friend of my wife," Brian muttered. Authentic tears stung his lids.

The constable puttered around him making noises of appreciation for the damage. "A woodener, eh. What in Christ's name did he hit you with?"

When names and places were all written down, the sergeant asked, "Do you want to prefer charges of assault?"

"God, I do."

"May I ask, is this man your wife's boyfriend?"

"Not exactly. He thinks she's his mother."

"Oh? He's a young man then?"

"He must be forty."

"Oh. And your wife, sir?"

"Twenty-eight."

"Jesus!" said the constable.

"That's what I call a case," said the sergeant.

Brian made a tormented mouth. "I know it's hard to believe," he uttered coyly.

"No, sir. The cases that come in here. Sometimes you wonder if anyone in the world has straight old-fashioned sex anymore."

When they got him tea he sank his nose in it the way a refugee might nose soup. Rising steam deliciously fingered his bruises as, a little later, did Annie. He pitched her a story about a chance meeting with a friend of Sal's, apparently in a pub, apparently while he himself was drinking whiskey to brace himself for the Heathrow job.

"I think she's mad," he told Annie, making a lumpy sound of the *th* of *think* and a juddering one of the *m* of *mad* like a man struggling to get out the words or to keep them in. "Knocking about with a killer. Well, it's been said now. She's m-mad." And indeed the word was now in the ether. Soon the yeasts of London's air would work on it, giving it a layer of substance.

"Why are you crying?" he asked Annie, though it was clear she was crying for Sal.

"Sal?" he asked. "Sal is the unkillable Celtic goddess, tough at the core, oh yes. And she's got friends. Clytie . . . George . . . good friends." Annie took no comfort. It irked him that she was not soothed. "You can't expect me to live with a madwoman."

She did not answer that. He watched her mourn for Sal and hated it. He hated it when women lamented for each other. Then Annie spoke of something that must have been, to her mind, allied to Sal. "We have to get my stereo, Brian. It's still with . . . at the old place. I hope he hasn't done anything to it."

More bruises? Brian wondered. He had lost hope in the knee-to-the-groin.

And still he had not mentioned me to Annie. He who inhabits a madwoman has no standing.

Happily, in Royal Hospital Road, grief had at last worked its sedative effect on Sal. She had frazzled herself wondering if she should emigrate to the United States. She had exhausted herself in making certain vows, such as that should he come back she would copulate like a vixen, rant like a redhead, and beset all his horizons. She slept stubbornly now, determined to spin out her sleep. She believed that the worst was that somewhere within five miles of her Brian was telling Annie that he has never known such joy in the flesh, was writing off the two years of joy in the flesh with her.

I, who knew that the worst was worse than that, signaled as best I could in the direction of Pembroke Gardens Close, of the—at this hour—fitful plated brain of the Gnome. Though I called and called, I enjoyed no reciprocated sensations from the Gnome's direction.

Since all the world slept, foe and ally in the one slack-mouthed grievous sleep, I settled to a consideration of my momentous heart, its three-centimeter extent. Before I was self-aware, I had grown it in its simple form. Unknown to me it had laid down its atrium and its ventricle, all unknown to me walls rose yet again and its primitive chambers were now four. Yet I must have, even then, even in my sleep no different from the sleep of a cauliflower, seen the possibilities of the heart, and, sensing the riskiness of drawing, in the great genetic lottery, Brian as begetter, clung to its simple defects as to a weapon.

As an instance, I let the pulmonary artery grow yes, but at a slower rate than I. Though I should have encouraged the wall to close between the ventricles I chose to keep it open. It had done no harm to date, that breached wall, and might one day provide some sort of escape. Without knowing its name, I had the aorta creep too far right above the holed wall. I now voted to retain these minute defects.

My reason was that if one hoped to rivet a man like Brian, one needed props.

The condition I fostered in my heart—we would all afterwards discover—went by the name of Tetralogy of Fallot. Wrongly, I hoped that when it emerged it might well dominate Brian and spin his nice-enough Annie off into the ether to a distance where he could look on her as he now looked on the lovely constellation of, say, the Great Bear.

"Your husband came last night," the Gnome told her to rouse her out of her silent occupation of a chair. Earlier, and as usual, he had brought a little lacquered table, placed it by her knee. On it a dish of raisins, some olives, an open bottle of Rhine wine. He had poured her a glass, neatly as a wine waiter. But she had not leaned forward to pick up the glass. Now she leaned forward at the mention of Brian.

"It got physical," said the Gnome.

Sal put a hand over one of her eyes and gave off a little whine. "Did he hurt you?"

"No. He got a bruise though. Against the edge of the bookcase there." He went and touched the site. "He's dangerous."

"Brian?"

The Gnome rapped the case. The battle with Brian had given this item of furniture some meaning. "Please, don't consider him a clown. Consider him dangerous."

I winked to my dark self. For—so it seemed—some of my transmissions had got through to the Gnome. It was to be my last wan triumph that side of the jailhouse.

Sal insisted on going home each afternoon, in the half hope Brian would turn up in the evening crying, "She's not what I thought." As the Gnome took us to his car that afternoon two uniformed policemen came in at the gate. They saw Sal on the steps, descending slightly crabwise, since her pregnancy was beginning to tell. The constables waited for Sal and the Gnome to reach them, and watched Sal and not, therefore, the way the Gnome's feet were arching.

One policeman held in his hand a document folded lengthwise in eighths. It summoned the Gnome to Kensington Magistrate's Court and although Sal did not understand that, the Gnome knew what it was on sight, being in spirit the canny unborn. He could foresee too how it would be for him if Brian stood in the witness box talking about the fetal obsessions of the accused. He knew also about the summary committal powers of police doctors. Unhappily, Sal did not.

Sal would know, and so would I at last, that on the afternoon those policemen came to Pembroke Gardens Close there was a further panic working in the Gnome. As he had confessed to us, he had made his money in strange manners and dubious company. Not only in Vietnam but elsewhere, unnecessary and unwarranted millions had come to him without his striving for them. Like any man who feels queasy about his riches, the Gnome kept a secret address— that featureless apartment in W8. Now his secret address had been given away by Brian. It was on government records and computers were free to chatter of it to one another. He was open therefore to be visited, questioned, molested by the corporate investigators and the fiscal priers of some half a dozen nations.

"Mr. Warwick Jones?" said a policeman, anyhow, that afternoon on the garden path.

"Yes?"

"Could we speak with you a second?"

"You're welcome," said the Gnome. His body was however secretly coiled.

"And you, miss. You're Mrs. Sally Fitzgerald? Good. Would you mind staying a second? Perhaps if we could go inside?"

Uniforms can begin the unhinging of those who must face them, and the police uniforms on the garden pathway seemed to Sal such a trespassing on her pain that she smiled at them with a pained, crazy broadness. They did not fail to notice it.

The Gnome feinted back toward the step, as if leading

them indoors. He hooked a foot behind the knee of the nearer constable, spilling him against the one with the summons. Then he left—sprinting—by the gate, got in his car, which his lust for survival had taught him always to leave unlocked, turned the ignition which said lust had also counseled him to keep tuned for instant combustion, and was speeding leftward out of Pembroke Gardens Close. From there, if I was not mistaken, three lines of flight presented themselves, one of these westward toward the bend of the Thames, the other north to Kensington High Street, the third south toward Earl's Court. All of them were cluttered paths. But Sal and I could tell, as the constables rose and radioed their base, that they had not got the Gnome's license number.

Neither of us believed the Gnome had abandoned us. We felt, instead, triumphant. Turning to the police with a faint smile still on her lips, Sal saw them as Brian's easily sidestepped employees. If I could have transmitted to her I would have said, "Get outside your loss, these men operate beyond your heartache."

"Miss," they said, and now they were less reverent toward pregnancies than when they first came in the gate, "will you please accompany us?"

"What right do you have to ask me that?"

"We would be grateful for your help," one of them said, pushing her forward. She walked, still believing that they were agents under Brian's control.

They hustled her from behind.

"Your husband swore out a complaint against Mr. Jones."

"My husband. I don't have a husband."

"I'm sure that's not literally true, miss. I wonder why Mr. Jones ran like that?"

They had by now put her in the back of their Ford patrol car. I could hear her heart surging, I could feel the buffets in her blood.

"He didn't want the trouble, that's why. He didn't want the trouble and the lies."

As they drove her away, the one in the passenger seat

kept one arm over in the back, the hand nearly touching her knee. "I wonder what we'd find if we got a warrant for his place. What do you think we'd find?"

"You'd find white walls and a minimum of furniture."

"I wonder, would we find heroin? Any acid?"

"Don't be absurd."

"By what we hear, he gets hallucinations."

"Hallucinations? No."

"Yes. About you."

The hand wavered before her knees. There was a male threat to it, even though it hung so slack.

She began to fight them in the doorway of the station, she grew frantic at the idea of going in there. For the smell of the place, the cut of their uniforms, still seemed to her to be crafty items arranged by Brian.

"You can call your solicitor if you want," they assured her, pushing her through the lobby.

"I don't have a solicitor," she told them in her unworldly way. It was left to me to be knowing, and I knew she should not tell them that, that in their eyes it made a vagrant of her. But to ride Sal then was to ride in a runaway wagon. No nudging, no sweet brain waves could soothe the stamping horses.

She began talking fast, saying that her husband had left her and that Mr. Jones was a friend she had known for only a week but that she found him restful to talk to. The tan walls of the station pained and panicked her the more, and the band of blue, one inch wide, that divided the nut-brown uppers of the walls from the nut-brown lowers. What did the line mean and why was it put there, so inhumanly exact?

"I have to insist on going," she told them.

"No, please," they said.

They went on pushing her persuasively, by the elbow.

"Do you realize you're trampling on habeas corpus?" she asked.

"I don't think that's the case, miss."

They got her into a tan room with a wired window, and

the lunacy of the blue line prevailed there also. I too felt the closeness of that room, it was a fever lying in wait, it prickled her flesh; the event had exactly the nature of those frightening moments in fitting rooms when her head and shoulders were trapped into some too-tight garment she had tried on. She didn't hear them say that they would fetch in a she-cop and a cup of tea or that in a little time she would be outside under the low and welcome sky. Rather their words struck like thrown stones. Before I could soothe her and with better success than Brian had with the Gnome, she drove her knee into one of the coppers' groin.

The other one, the one whose hand had dangled by her knees, slammed her down on the chair. Even in her insulating seas I could judge what a shock it was to her frame. "Muriel!" he called. A neatly made policewoman entered. "Now, madam!" she said.

Sal seemed calmer, though her brain was astray. Everyone has London pallor, she postulated, looking at the kicked constable who sweated and coughed against the chestnut wall; a pallor deep and evil enough. But it increased still if you kicked them in the balls.

"Now, madam. Do you have any reason to struggle?"

"I am not arrested or charged."

"That is an omission now likely to be attended to," said pretty Muriel, dark, and petite for a cop.

"Wait outside, please, gentlemen," she told her colleagues. They seemed to go willingly, the upright policeman waiting for the assaulted one to pass first through the door.

"I want to call my publisher," Sal said once she and Muriel were alone. "Sir Don Cale. I want him to arrange for press coverage when I leave."

"Write do you, miss?"

"I'll say I bloody write."

"Sit down. You'll get a telephone in a moment."

They argued for five minutes, Muriel crazily bland, bland as a parent who won't hear. Sal's hysteria was thereby sharpened and refined. At her core, I knew she was making every mistake available to her. From the way Muriel's pretty brows clotted I could tell that a spiraling axiom was operating in her brain. Suspected of being mad, this woman struggled and kicked and raved; and therefore she was mad.

"Where do you think he'd go, miss? I mean, it'd save us sending out a bulletin if you could tell us . . ."

"I don't know where he'd go."

"I mean, we only wanted to give him an assault writ. Do you think he has anything to hide?"

"Yes," yelled Sal. "He carries hope in a little box."

Muriel quivered, plucking at her own sternum. "Now listen to me, you mick bitch. I don't have to reason with you. We already *have* you . . ."

"*Have* me? *Have* me? Woman with child assaults constable. Your man should have too much shame to write that down, and you should have too much bloody shame . . ."

The electric blue line still fretted her though. She was sure it maintained itself by taking the oxygen out of her air, whereas Muriel looked as if she could operate on pure nitrogen, and Sal—not so endowed—lowered her head and began to weep for the abundant gritty air of the streets.

It was the tears that angered Muriel most. "You scum. Look at you! Pregnant. Who by, eh? By whom? Getting your boyfriend to beat up your husband. You scum!"

Muriel left us then, stumping out, her legs tight and righteous. Alone, Sal felt better, sure for twenty seconds at a lump that the Gnome would get us out, that he had fled to find a lawyer, a good one, who could outface police and magistrates. "Brian," Sal called, dropping her head, fingering her belly. She wanted the rescuer to be Brian.

At last a gray-haired man entered in a tired, chemical-smelling gray suit. In his lapel a snake-and-scepter pin indicated his profession. Sal noticed how he wiped his pale hands on a white handkerchief, as if he'd just come from an autopsy. Is there blood in those hands, she wondered, behind the upper lip with its ashen mustache? She decided not to watch his hands, but his kind brown eyes.

Unlike the Gnome—as I have remarked—she knew nothing of the summary committal powers of police surgeons. She welcomed him, she calmed, she pursed her lips and raised her chin.

"I'm Dr. Thompson. Have you been seeing a doctor, Mrs. Fitzgerald?"

"A gynecologist."

"No. I meant a psychiatrist really."

"Why would I see a psychiatrist?"

"I simply wondered . . ."

"Because I defended myself? My husband will tell you I'm sane, that I don't need a psychiatrist."

"Well, of course, psychiatry isn't only for the insane. But your husband does seem to be worried about your *stability*."

"What?" Sal stood up. "What?"

How was it Brian had achieved credibility in the world of police surgery? Did bruises give a man authority, did they up his stature? Sal couldn't believe it and felt that if her answers were satiric enough she could get the doctor to join in with her in laughing at the idea of Brian as a pontiff, a binder and a looser.

"Your husband says you don't actually have an adulterous relationship with Mr. Jones. He says that Mr. Jones, who is I believe at least forty, considers you are his mother."

"It seems a harmless ambition, in Christ's name, to have a young mother."

"Don't you think it an unstable one? A dangerously *unreal* one? That it does—in fact—abuse mathematics?"

"I don't know anything about mathematics. As for unstable ambitions, it's no more unstable than wanting to run for alderman."

"He is forty and you are . . ."

"Twenty-eight years old."

"And you think it's not irrational for him to believe you're his mother?"

"Oh. Irrational. That's another matter. If irrationality were a crime, my old man would be here in front of you."

"I wondered though . . . Are you disturbed by the illogical nature of Mr. Jones's attachment to you?"

Tactically astray, Sal sighed, rolled her eyes, and adopted the air and false voice of a swami. "There is a plane that is within time," she said, "and a plane that is beyond time."

"Do you believe," Dr. Thompson asked in a way which, I could tell, meant *for the record*, "that on the plane beyond time you are his mother?"

There was no chemical or electric message by which I could tell Sal that Dr. Thompson was not going to stop his plain questions, would never laugh with her. "It mustn't be the strangest thing you've heard," she said, in those forced occult tones.

"You assaulted a policeman, Mrs. Fitzgerald. Do you consider yourself guilty of assault?"

"No!"

"Neither do I. We'll have to make proper arrangements for you. *Muriel!*"

"What are you talking about?" Sal demanded, understanding too late that raillery itself might be considered a symptom.

The policewoman returned to the room. Sal noticed Muriel's lower legs, hard and tight inside their stockings and reminding you of those wooden clubs boys used to swing for trophies in rural Ireland.

"Sit down, Mrs. Fitzgerald," Muriel told her, taking her by the elbow and, with the other hand, forcing the chair against the backs of her knees. With an unclenched hand, Sal pushed Muriel's right shoulder.

"Mrs. Fitzgerald," Muriel barked, "all this idiotic resistance could harm your child."

The mention of someone as private to her as me enraged Sal. She fought Muriel off, for her arms were longer than the policewoman's. She defended her sovereign blood and her inalienable structure from molestation by a government employee, and her hands became fists and she punched one of Muriel's breasts and saw, entering the woman's harsh pretty face, the pallor she had induced earlier in the kneed policeman. She felt not at all my small fists at the amniotic wall, advising her of the size of the fabric she fought when she fought Muriel. But she had become a primitive: she saw only what she saw and she punched what was to hand. I shall fight forever, she promised herself, and people all around me will go on changing color.

But two constables quickly got her seated and turned to comfort Muriel. Dr. Thompson, from the open door, looked down on Sal with a ghastly steadiness before turning and going away. On his way out of the station, he signed a form E2 summary committal paper which had just now been typed up in her name.

12

So we traveled—her hands cuffed, mine still free and insulated by the waters of her womb—in the back of the police car. Northeast through London toward one of Her Majesty's mental institutions. Our conductors were a squad of three, two police males who sat in front, one woman who shared the back with my braceleted mother. They were cool and blindly compassionate and Sal could tell from the way they talked that their full-time work was to collect the committed from police and other restraint and escort them to an assigned hospital.

During the journey Sal would sometimes shake her wrists. "This is impossible," she would say. "This is like Kafka."

One time the policewoman said, "They all talk about Kafka, love."

It was a useful comment and helped Sal see something of the new rules. It was no use fighting here or arguing her own sanity, chapter and verse. To these three she was a package, and they probably hadn't lost a package yet, or been talked around by it or let it free.

As the car passed Ilford on the High Road, she began to despair of the Gnome. She wondered, with as much sorrow for him as for ourselves, if he was now following some other pregnant woman and pitching her his orphan's tale. And she was angry with him as well; she bunched her fingers in the effort to bounce the echoes of her rage off that plate in his cerebrum: A lawyer. Get a lawyer.

I knew there would be no lawyer. I knew.

We were Dumas's Corsican twins, the Gnome and I. It was as if we shared a placenta and swapped our visions and sensations. But like any careful children—who generally begin a closeness with the barter of small things, jacks and marbles and bits of ruptured balloon—we began with an exchange of glimpses. Small footages came into me from the whirring cerebrum of Warwick Jones, my Corsican brother, my external knight. Small offerings but with the promise of larger ones. So I had glimpses of the Gnome thinking away in a pub in Hammersmith. He knew and I knew that you couldn't let a lawyer come near your obsession. In this case deliverance could not be hired, put on a retainer. Deliverance had to be arranged in person, and the Gnome's brain circled this personal question of Sal's retrieval, head to one side as if to give some aerodynamic lift to the metallic surfaces in his head.

The policewoman smiled at Sal as we went in through the gate of Stapleford Hatch hospital; it was a congratulatory smile. Now we are delivered from you, it said, and you are delivered from the lonely onus of your madness.

Sal didn't answer in any way. She looked at the old house which made the center of the hospital and at its two wings, one brick, one steel and glass. She felt a reminiscent nausea of the kind she had known at the age of nine on first sighting the Convent of Our Lady of Mercy at Enniscorthy. All the way in the police car she assured herself that there must be doctors inside the hospital who would spot her coherence, who would laugh with her about literal Dr.

Thompson, about punched Muriel and the kneed constable, and then sign her release.

But it seemed to her now that in this mean Victorian mansion and its two ill-adapted wings there must be personnel likewise at odds with themselves.

The policewoman went ahead, carrying Sal's handbag in the front door and Sal, flanked by the two men, followed her inside, past the stained-glass panels of Artemis and Athena mourning, which the man who had built the place a century before as a home had put there without any prescience of the final usages to which the structure would be put.

In the hall they unlocked her cuffs and released her hands. On the wide floor of black slate and white marble a little box of plywood and glass had been built and labeled *Admissions Office*. The door of this office must have been the boundary of the policewoman's duty, because she left without saying good-bye, beckoning the men to follow.

Sal sat down in the office like a peaceable patient. She would not have been dumbfounded to see her father come in at the door putting his hand on her shoulder and working his thumb along her collarbone in a manner half protective of her, half demanding. Wearing a homburg to show he wasn't a farmer. "Yes, Reverend Mother, Sal's an obedient lass with just this little occasional problem of bed-wetting."

The Admissions women, a clerk and a silent muscular attendant, got name, address, and age from Sal's license, which had been taken from Sal's bag. Sal wasn't called on to say much. So she sat keeping the tremulous secret of her sanity. A bell was rung and a thin psychiatric nurse arrived. The gutted handbag was given back to Sal. Sal advised herself to be quiet. Yet a handbag is so personal, so personally battered and creased, and a seer could read your past and future out of the detritus of its four compartments. It was a shock even for me to see it, like an amputated organ, looted at the hands of a skinny stranger.

"Come on, dear," said the nurse, and they went out across the checkered floor. "I know it's all very traumatizing."

"It hurts as well."

"I know it hurts."

"When do I see a doctor, tell me that?"

"Tomorrow afternoon probably."

"Do you mean there aren't any doctors involved in admissions?" Sal halted on the landing, a hotel guest who's just found that the establishment has been downgraded in *Guide Michelin*.

"Ideally there would be, dear. But there's so much illness. So much."

"You just have to jump me up the line, that's all. I just happen to be one of the sane ones."

"But dear, no one thinks of committal any more in terms of sane and insane. If you have a husband . . ."

There was a dappling of yellow fury in Sal's vision; it was like a waft of mimosa across the stairway. "How do you think I got here? How do you think I did?"

They were already through an ornamental grillwork door concealed on the oncoming side by faded russet drapes. A male attendant who had himself been somehow concealed swung it to behind them. Locking, it made no honest jail-house clangor but a small maidenly crunch.

Sal and the thin nurse stared at each other. "It's only closed at night," said the nurse in extenuation.

That futile jailhouse panic rose once more in Sal. It washed to me and beyond me, yet I was so placed as to ignore it just as a picnicker on a riverbank ignores a dead cow floating past that introduces a few seconds of squalor into his sunny appetite. I was very cool and very sure of the Gnome, for the Gnome's lobes were jumping in the pub at Hammersmith. Therefore, as Sal was about to run back and shake the grillwork, I kicked myself off from the roof of the womb and butted my forehead repeatedly against the base of her stomach, spinning on the umbilicus away from the honest placenta so that she was aware of the contour of my head breaking the smoothness of her belly. Feeling me pound her, she thought, I must breathe

146

gently, I must fight all this alarm. A struggle might hurt the boyo!

And wait for the psychiatrist, Sal! Keep your chart clean and convince *him*. All the rest of them are but turnkeys.

Telling herself these sane things, she followed the nurse deep into the house and into the corridors of the extensions. "You'll be in Beta dormitory of Cerise wing. You share a dining room with Beige and Periwinkle. Of course, the meal is over now, but I asked them to leave something on a hot plate for you."

The dining hall vastly surrounded Sal but the tables were small like those in a motel rather than those of a prison. Natty plastic cloths punched out in a doily pattern covered the tables. This jet-age napery was clotted with desiccated sauce and gravy. The disturbed—it seemed to Sal—ate carelessly.

"Oh, it's dried out," said the nurse at the hot plate. "But it's better than nothing."

Sal chewed on marbled New Zealand beef heated to a biscuit texture, and while she chewed surveyed the windows. Each was covered on the outside with ornamental iron, more as if to protect fragile insiders from the outside world than the reverse. Sal hated the coyness of this prison and would have said so if I had not sometimes distracted her with a buffet.

She ate only two mouthfuls of the gritty beef. As the lean nurse led her down further corridors, past television rooms where silent patients watched footage of the recent Arab-Israeli war (What could it matter to them? Sal would have liked to ask) she noticed that the windows facing the front garden were unbarred but that there were television cameras housed in weatherproof boxes beneath the eaves. The sight stopped her, she couldn't absorb it: that the circuitries that prevented the filching of cake mix and Mars bars in supermarkets had been applied under the eaves of Stapleford Hatch to keep free citizens prisoners.

"This is Cerise," said the nurse, "and this is Beta. This

is your bed." The nurse pointed to it as if a duty of quietus and contentment had descended on Sal.

In Beta, ten beds stood at diverse angles to each other and on one of them three intent women, Sal's age and younger, sat in conference.

"I'll call the doctor," said the nurse, "and ask him what medication he wants to give you."

"How can he know? He hasn't met me."

But the nurse turned her back. Wearied, Sal looked at the bed and sat on it. One of the women across the ward, sweet-faced and plump, saw her and rose and joined her.

"What age is yours?" she asked.

"I don't understand."

"Your child."

"I don't have a child yet. I'm pregnant, of course. But it's my first."

"You feel aggression already?" asked the plump girl shrilly.

"Aggression? Look, I feel aggressive, yes. Against policemen and nurses and others. Is that what we mean? I've always felt aggression against someone? Once there was a nun I hated, and another time a features editor on *The Express*."

"But . . . Jesus, it's so hard to vocalize! . . . aggression against the fetus."

"Don't be ridiculous. How can you feel aggression against a fetus?"

"But," the girl said, aggrieved, "we all feel aggression in this ward. Against our own children. They said they were only putting people in here who had aggression problems toward their children. It's an experiment, to let us talk it out. Pooling our guilt. Why did they put you in here, when you haven't even got a child?"

The girl began weeping softly because some guarantee had been broken. Resist her grief, Sal counseled herself. If you get tangled in it you may end up staying here as some sort of missionary.

She said, however, "Come. Don't cry."

"Cynthia—that's the one smoking—broke her baby's hip. In a normal ward she couldn't live with that, she couldn't tell it to anyone. Dallas—the one with the touch of acne— she was from a strict religious family and she thought her baby was the devil. She beat it with the King James Bible. I . . . well, my husband kept coming home from work, finding me standing over little Coralie's cot with a pillow in my hands. Oh, Jesus Christ, what things to tell an expectant mother!" The girl could not speak for a time, the shame hissed and rattled at the back of her throat, a serpent in its own right, a masculine demon behind the soft gullet. "There are nine of us in here," she said at last, and it was almost a boast, "and we're all murderers of our own children, in thought at least."

Sal touched her own stomach, a secretive touch to which I, after a second of core-coldness, answered with movements of the arms. Were the masters of the madhouse, we wondered, suggesting a course for Sal?

"Of course," the girl went on, "I now know why I held a pillow over Coralie. I am still a child and this new child threatens me. There's the reason. The only question is, Can I grow up before Coralie does? Can I ever grow up?"

Her face crumpled once more, there were bruises of anguish under the eyes. Sal, spontaneous, thrust out a hand to the girl's wrist. "Of course you will. You know what your fear is, when everything's said and done. You're already ahead of some people." She hoped this reference of hers would travel southwest across the metropolis and sting Brian's arse as it heaved above Annie Newman in W8.

"It would be better," said the girl, "if they gassed all of us."

"Oh no," Sal told her. "We go ahead in pain. Not knowing we do, we still go ahead." How did I become a morale-booster? she asked herself. It wasn't an exercise she had time for, consoling murderous parents. Someone had to be appointed for it, yet I must keep to my objective: escape.

She showered and was given a nightdress. Suddenly Beta had its full crew of women, all of them young and pretty mothers of one or two, their hands lingering on each other as they said good night and in all their motions, whether sharp or dull, whether the grasping of a toothbrush or the sitting down on a bed, unforgiveness for themselves.

Overhead lights went out and the room was lit only by bed lamps. The thin nurse came around giving a small wax cup of drugs to each sufferer.

"This will make the night go quickly," she promised Sal, handing Sal her little pabulum—a white pill and a capsule. Some greeted their medication with open mouths, with a sensual impatience, stroking their throats; and the tiger growled once within and was doused. But Sal kept hers in her hand, where they were welcome to any pharmaceutical influence they could exert.

The lamps went out now, all but a night-light above the door of Beta. After an hour—and hours can go quickly for the aggrieved who have breakouts and vindications to think of—she got up and limped across the room like a woman with a bona fide full bladder.

She scouted the corridors, dodging the mutterings and the dots of light where duty nurses spoke in low voices. Finding a barred door open a little—some nurse on a short errand to another part of the house must have left it like that—she moved through it, though she knew it took her deeper into the house and into its core madness. For in this part of the institution the ground-floor windows were unapologetically blocked with old-fashioned vertical iron rods. This was a harder prison than Cerise, so that she could not benefit by exploring it further. In the act of turning, she saw a man of about forty years leaning by one of these windows, dressed in a gray cardigan and trousers.

He frowned at her. "Want to see the evening star?" he asked.

"All right," she said, for politeness' sake.

"In the western sky, shrouded in clouds of its own making. Not like the blatant Venuses of today. Eh? Eh?"

"Very lovely," she said, and went to move on.

"It is the evening star and the morning star, it led Captain Cook to the island of Venus to observe its transit across the face of the sun . . ."

"The island of Venus?"

"Why Tahiti, of course." He chuckled. "Ask Marlon Brando," he suggested.

"When and if ever I meet the man," she said.

"The Catholics applied the image of Venus mysterious behind her clouds to the Virgin Mary, did you know? Star of the morning they call Christ's mother, and though I'm not one to go crazy over the mothers of great men, I am delighted to find that by this imagery the sacred and profane are unified."

"Yes, yes," said Sal, a little frightened by all these crazy symbols. "That is a nice arrangement."

"May I tup you?" the man asked.

"What?"

The man put a hand toward her elbow and only by a skillful wriggle of that joint did she avoid him.

"May I tup, converge, fit close, adhere, grip, grapple, burrow and tunnel, clinch and tumble, ravish and pair?" he asked, like a thesaurus of synonyms. "Please say yes."

"Here? In this corridor?"

"All the world's a corridor and we poor gazers strolling down it, squinting for the right office to which to report ourselves. The Cancer Office, the Coronary Bureau, the Famine Committee, the Board of Highway Decimation, and the Advisory Council on Cardiac Explosions. 'Knock, knock, am I supposed to be here?' 'No dear, what you want is farther down the hallway. Keep moving, love.'"

Sal liked his patter and he was a handsome, Italian-looking man. Beyond the walls and at her leisure Sal would have been taken by him.

"Couldn't we get into the garden?" she asked. To kiss and run was in her mind.

"There's no way into the garden. And who wants bloody rhododendrons when you grow fruit so sweet." He raised his hand and with thumb and index finger touched the nipple of her right breast.

She turned away. The thin nurse and a male attendant had come up in rubber-soled shoes.

"This is out-of-bounds for anyone from Cerise wing," the nurse said.

"Come on, Mr. Elwin," the male attendant told him. "You know it's bedtime."

As they returned to Cerise, the nurse said, "Mr. Elwin has all sorts of deviant problems. He's a dangerous man to talk to, even if that wing isn't . . ." The nurse made with one hand a gesture of setting aside, of demarcation.

Sal said, "If you use school terms like out-of-bounds I'll beat your narrow brains against the wall."

"I'll get you some more medication," the nurse assured her.

At the time Sal fell asleep in an asylum, Brian was helping Annie unpack her books. He stood by a cardboard box with a copy of R. D. Laing's *The Politics of Experience* in his hand and that sight alone should have produced laughter among the stars. Yet in the whole galaxy only I laughed and that laughter was, in pitch, beyond the hearing of animals and involved as well a minute and unrecorded shaking of the head.

"I have to tell you, Annie," he said, "Sal's been committed."

"Committed? You mean . . ."

"To a mental hospital."

Annie stood still, in her hands an old copy of *King Solomon's Mines*, which for some reason she considered worth picking out from the moraine of her last alliance. She began to tear a loose thread of the binding—her simple pride in the ownership of books had been thrown in doubt.

Brian hurried to say, "It wasn't anything to do with us. The police went to talk to this boyfriend of hers. They both resisted. Sal attacked a constable at the police station and then punched a policewoman in the breast. Fortunately, we live in an age where there are certain rules and they got in a police surgeon instead of charging her. He had his look and committed her at once."

But Annie went on rumpling her Rider Haggard. She knew from her career as a journalist that there was not always cause to rejoice in police procedures as uncritically as Brian was now rejoicing.

"For Christ's sake, Annie, she ought to be able to deal with a separation without beating up the constabulary."

He grabbed her and pressed against her an erection that was intended to be all solid conviction. But she did not seem interested tonight in acquiring faith through penetration.

"You're going to see her?"

"I'm going up tomorrow. Just to talk to her psychiatrist."

"I'm sure she must feel she's already half won. Getting you there," Annie said. But how could he explain that a purpose of his trip was to inquire into the canceling of me. Looking at his scared and peevish love, he thought: Given time, even the greatest passion comes out as just another woman full of strident demands. He believed as he stood there so puissant both over Annie in W8 and us in Stapleford Hatch that he had abandoned Sal, a woman who, as God is a witness, is not clamant in her demands. Among which are, of course, the quaint demand that she be loved, that she be permitted to give birth.

"Just the one visit," he told Annie.

"Be kind to her," Annie murmured, for she suspected he mightn't be.

There seem to be two theories among psychiatrists on the matter of whether a committed patient's husband or wife ought to be there in the room during the first psychiatric session. Some say no, that marriage is a condition instituted by God and the state for the mutual lunacy of both parties and that craziness exhibited toward a spouse does not count as true social craziness. Others say that the true condition of the patient can be most easily judged by his or her demeanor toward the spouse and that the contours of the disease can be most clearly traced by brandishing the partners at each other.

It was Sal's bad luck that Dr. Carbon belonged to the latter school. He was a young man, not much older than Brian, who had been trained in crowded public hospitals. He had never known the days of leisurely curing. He knew that madness was epidemic and that Stapleford Hatch was overpopulated. He put a high value therefore on the speed of the turnover of patients. For speed's sake he had Brian there, in his pink office, before Sal even arrived. Brian thought Carbon seemed tired but professional, the sort of man you might like to have a beer and a chat with. Behind him the lines of nicely tooled psychiatric texts seemed to offer Brian the promise that the meeting would be a neat affair, that Carbon and his texts had powers over hysteria.

When Sal knocked, Carbon held out a preventing hand toward Brian and opened the door himself. Brian rose as Sal came in.

"Respect, Brian?" she asked. She was routed to see Brian there. The doctors of the other school were right—all her marital madness came to the surface of her skin.

"I asked your husband to be here, Mrs. Fitzgerald. My idea, not his. Do you mind?"

"Have I the right to mind? If I have the legal right to mind, I mind with a bloody vengeance."

"All right. Sit down a moment and tell me why."

Sal sat with all the unsure grandeur of her long bones.

"I'm sorry, Sal," Brian muttered, "that it's escalated this way."

"Escalated? Don't talk like a secretary of state, boyo! Talk about the real things."

"What real things?"

"Why . . . lust, terror . . . betrayal."

"It's the child, Sal. I know you can't handle a child."

Sal poked a thumb toward Brian and spoke to Carbon. "Do you hear that? I . . . I can handle a bady and suckle it and sing it songs all day. He . . . he can't handle it."

Dr. Carbon sighed. "It is of course more than a matter of suckling and singing songs." I could already tell, though Sal still hoped in him, that he was a member of the throw-'em-in-the-deep-end school. "They shit also. They wail in the night."

"I know that. Why shouldn't they shit and wail? Don't we?"

"When you're down, off-balance, distrait, it's a terrible thing to be faced with a child."

"Is that why you put me in that dormitory of child-killers?"

"What?"

"Is that why I'm in Beta for baby-beaters? Is that what passes in this place as a subtle hint?"

Carbon frowned, stared at her, then at his sagely linked thumbs, and again at her. He looked to Sal like someone making mental note.

"Don't be coy about it," Sal told him. "Take your pen out and write whatever you like about me. Paranoia, clinical hysteria, schizoid . . . I'm inured and immured both."

Carbon could tell that her palms itched to attack Brian because of the temperate way Brian sat, the ends of his lower lip folded in under the flabby limits of his upper in lines of discreet and worldly grief. Sal considered falling on him and wolfing those composed lips away, exposing his twenty-four remaining teeth to Britain's low and deadly sun.

Dr. Carbon did not want blood on the mat if it could be helped. He now asked Brian to wait outside and Brian went, a little hurt since he'd presumed Dr. Carbon and he were bonded by some kinship of sane men.

Alone with Carbon, Sal noticed the dust motes behind the psychiatrist's head and was reminded of plankton in the sea and of grazing whales. The sea seemed relevant to her because it had been there for the crossing yesterday, in the age of her freedom.

"Do you understand you've lost certain civil rights?" he asked.

"I can tell by the bars on the windows."

"Quite. Do you want an abortion?"

"No."

"I don't know how long you'll be here, but your pregnancy is approaching the normal limit for termination. So you have to know that it's quite possible you won't be permitted custody of the child."

She struck her stomach with both fists. I felt the blows, but in no way resented them—they stung me to resist the scalpel and, if it came to it, the orphanage.

"I *bear* the child. Who would it go to if not me . . . ?"

"Your husband . . . though in view of his new liaison
. . ."

"New liaison! . . . his fucking of a stranger!"

"Quite. So it would be a toss-up between him and the
state. Listen, you're young, you know you're beautiful.
You'll be pregnant again. But this one—" He pointed
frankly at her belly. "—this one's under a cloud. I see that
as my first duty to you, letting you know where you stand."

"No," said Sal in a subdued way. I too was subdued. It
was no use detesting him. Sitting tight in Sal's fluids and
detesting Dr. Ford had once been a harmless little sport
of mine, but this wasn't a time for sport. I sat still, feeling
for comfort the remote waves of the Gnome's machinations
reaching me from the other end of the city, from the airport motel where he sat letting his plans define themselves.

"Is it because this gentleman . . . Mr. Jones . . . thinks
you're his mother? Is that why you won't terminate . . . ?"

Sal slapped her thigh. "What does it matter why? Does
a mother need reasons, for Christ's sake? Do you inquire
of the earth, eh? Do you inquire of the goddamn sea?"

"The earth and sea aren't in a curious legal situation.
Come on, prove your health by facing up to your legal
situation."

In all her useless anger she got up like a cormorant rising,
her chin lofted in an angle of flight.

"This is a flesh deal, is it? The baby . . . it can be traded
for a clean bill?"

"I didn't say that, Mrs. Fitzgerald. I was merely recom-
mending that . . . well, the decks should be cleared."

"Jesus!" she yelled, and the word was not with her a
wanton utterance but halfway a prayer, Sal halfway expecting Dr. Carbon to be interrupted by the Christ of her
childhood, who could not, however, Himself escape the
doctors and the proconsuls.

The door opened and it was Brian.

"He!" she said. "He lives in terror and ruts like a child
sucking its thumb. Why doesn't he have legal limits?"

Her hands were turned to claws at seeing him standing

aggrieved, not by a quiver of the knuckle confessing how jaunty it made him to see her so arched and crazy. I have only to look like a just man, he knew, and she'll fly at me. I can go home to Annie with scratches to show I was married to a madwoman.

Sal came for his face. Oh, this is a bonus, he confessed, as her little finger hooked the right corner of his mouth. He could have held her by the right wrist but that would have diminished the decorative effect she had on his face. So, hands folded over his averted head and elbows tight in against his bottom ribs, his stance was that of the martyr or the defeated boxer.

They filled Sal up with paraldehyde, a drug for the demented, a drug for boozers who see the punishing wings of bats or the worst arachnid monsters crowding out the moonlight. In a word, as perfidious a drug as any you could catch in a syringe.

They did not tell us the dose, and as the tide of sticky somnolence, the treacle comber, rolled over our brains, it came to me and to Sal as well that they might be trying to kill me off with the dosage and call it a pharmaceutical accident. "Sal," I called in Sal's waters; their brine washed against my palate yet the drug was there, in solution, slackening my jaw. They might keep her drowsed till she woke without me. Then I would have some sort of wakening only in the black cove, on the arse-end of nothingness, surgical refuse in a garbage bag, Sal-less, sea-less, song-less, my marks fading on her temple walls, my story shriveled, and that grand hermetic cave of mine now mere working space for the next occupant, the newcoming artist.

For the same reason Sal fought the drug, kept her brain glowing as her muscles came unstrung. She traveled back to Beta strapped flat on a surgical trolley, her frankly mounded stomach raised to the sharp fragments of fluorescent light that fell from the ceiling. She murmured and protested inside the straps, and because paraldehyde could not unplug her mind, it set to on her epiglottis, freezing it. Sal began to gurgle and toss her head. The sweet-faced black lady who pushed Sal's trolley took no notice. Perhaps she was used to chokers.

When they put Sal, comatose and strangling, on her bed, only I answered her panic, only my gullet was sympathetic, only I choked with her. As Sal's sweet gray brain-bird fell from its perch, so did mine. We went under gagging—Sal, cosmos, and me. And Sal's last cry was to Jesus. Oh Sacred Heart, I made my nine First Fridays. She felt entitled not to choke, which is marginally better than going under feeling, as I did, that all entitlements were canceled.

During Sal's long night and mine—in fact as soon as he got back to London and before he saw Annie—Brian took his scars to Clytie's place. The claw marks around his mouth, he was sure, would work as well as any argument on Clytie and George. It was an evening of the kind he liked, a moist hazy evening when the lights shone like golden smudges. There had never been such evenings in bone-dry Cunnamulla in his boyhood. His fancy was to behold himself as if from the outside while he walked wearing—careless as a hussar—the style of a man who has breathed the air of madness and could with sorrow tell you about it if you asked.

He knew he was a winner. He had fought me for living space and for breath. So that I might not stand between the womb and him, so that he would not have to stand between death and me. One was forced to admit, there had been worse reasons for fighting wars.

Clytie and George were drinking their evening gins and tonic when Brian arrived. Offered one himself, he pondered for a while before accepting, like a man who usually refuses liquor but will sometimes drink for politeness' sake.

"Sal or another woman?" Clytie asked, pointing to the facial marks.

"Sal."

"Well, well."

In his caged-off stateroom, Ran Singh bounced about. Brian, it seemed, was welcome with Ran Singh.

"Then what's been happening with you two?" asked Clytie once Brian had his drink.

Brian told her. It was a doomed conjunction, he said, me and Sal. I . . . I am partly to blame. I . . . I love women.

"Well," said George indulgently, "who doesn't?"

"You know what the Irish are like," Brian said, drawing them into an Anglo-Saxon alliance. "They believe in exclusivity. Not that that stopped her seeing a local maniac called Jones."

George and Clytie kept silent.

"I'm afraid she's been committed," he went on.

"Oh?" said Clytie, frowning in her wisdom. She had a working idea of who was mad and who wasn't. "You mean committed to a mental hospital?"

"Yes."

"I always knew you were crafty," Clytie told him.

"It was done in my absence. A police surgeon did it."

"It's nonsense. Can she be visited?"

"Not yet," said Brian.

"This," said George gently, "is one of the areas of medical law I know little about . . ."

"After she gets out," Brian offered, "I'll go on paying the rent upstairs."

"Of course you will," said Clytie. "Not that it wouldn't be easy to let. But you ought to pay and not expect any medals."

Brian laughed, partly at himself for expecting iodine and sympathy from Clytie. "And of course the pregnancy." He came casually to the nub. "It's just got to be terminated. I mean, now we're apart, it should be done anyhow. But there's no chance she can mind a child in her present state. They have her in a ward of women who do homicidal things to their babies. I mean the warning inherent in that is plain enough . . ."

Neither George nor Clytie helped Brian by speaking. In

the monkey's stateroom, Ran Singh—who could not afford to be particular—squeezed his squeaker bear and passed it through the wire for Brian to squeeze and pass back. Poor Ran Singh's bid for friendship I saw even in my profoundest sleep, yet Brian took no notice of him.

"It has to be done soon. That's the dilemma. Because the thing . . . the fetus . . . is eighteen weeks old. Beyond eighteen, they say, it gets risky. But George would know better than I do."

"That certainly used to be true," George agreed. "Even eighteen was a little beyond the limit when I was a young man. But of course they have improvements now in procedures and anesthesia . . ." He spoke in a haze, however. There was a shift going on in the deeper geology of his mind. He could tell and was trying to trace it: I must love her, I must love that Irish girl Sal. All he could tell was that the shift had occurred in a primal area older than himself and surgery, older than Wales and high Anglicanism, as old and mythic as the impulses of the partisan women on the islands of Dalmatia who were, after all, his last abortees. All his later work had been with bones, especially with hip sockets, mere mechanistic procedures. But this was not a mechanistic procedure happening in him. As well as anything else, it was older than mechanics.

Clytie rose. It seemed she had decided to mix herself another gin, but as she did it, she turned to Brian, shaking a lemon rind at him, a poor weapon but the only one to hand.

"I think you're glad," she said.

"Come!" said George.

"I think he's glad. I don't think he wants to pay child support. Simple as that."

"Why don't you just say I'm a bastard," Brian suggested.

"Well, I've always thought you were."

"Now!" George protested. George didn't want to drive Brian out. Brian was a stimulus to George's sense of something seismic happening in the deeps.

Displeased at the absorption of his foster parents and

guest, Ran Singh began shaking the wire in a rage. He felt that Brian should console him for his wifelessness at least by playing the squeaker game with him. But though his fit was aimed at Brian, it was Clytie who acted on it.

"Darling," she told George, "it's time for 'Laramie.' Could you turn on the set for Ran Singh?"

Brian lowered his head and directed a smile at his own heart. I'm getting away with it. My adversary is all but signed over and my landlady orders the set be tuned in to "Laramie." In a world like this—he realized—you can do anything.

While Sal and I, together, slept the tainted sleep of winos, the Gnome began to work for us. Images of that work entered my shut-down brain and sat there for later viewing—the way a teletype machine, left in a closed and blacked-out office, goes on chattering forth its coils of news which will not be read until the morning shift comes on.

There was a lawyer the Gnome had often played tennis with. At 3 P.M. that afternoon he employed him for a limited task. To call Stapleford Hatch and discover the wing and ward where Sal could be professionally contacted. It took the lawyer a quarter of an hour and a deal of high-horse talking to discover where Sal had been slotted, to find out something of her state and of her psychiatric prospects.

Paying twenty-five guineas for this service, the Gnome went out onto the street certain that extreme methods of rescue would have to be used. And in Sal and me, even as we lay poleaxed in our dark daze, the same certainty was forming. The Gnome's obsession had made of the three of us a minority sect and there was no chance for us under laws that had without warning become alien.

That same night when Brian visited Clytie and George, the Gnome went around to Royal Hospital Road. Brian had left, wanting to take his scars back to Annie while their gory brightness still showed. George and Clytie were still up, sipping a post-dinner brandy, when the Gnome loosened the multiple but undeterring locks on the front door of Clytie's tall house. It was ten-thirty, an hour when a man fumbling at the door of a well-lit house looks like a tenant and not a thief. Inside, on the stairs, he trod more like a lessee considering his landlord than a man trying to soften his footfalls for reasons of stealth.

The lock on Sal's door was no challenge. Once in the flat he searched in likely places for her passport. It was not discovered in the bookcases or in the drawers of her desk. It was not discovered in the dressing or bedside tables. The Gnome felt no distress at that, in fact, loving Sal the more for being such a random girl who might have her passport anywhere at all. Smiling, he found it in a drawer of towels under the washbasin.

By eleven he was on the streets again, stepping coyly off the narrow pavement in Smith Street to make room for a spillage of fraternal boozers from the Phoenix. There was time for him to exercise his natural politeness, for his appointment with a wealthy young forger in Ladbroke Walk was not till midnight.

He hiked it. In the forger's living room he sat inspecting a hefty book of Chinese erotic prints while the forger proceeded in another room. In this wise: lifting the photograph from Sal's Irish passport, the forger transferred it to a freshly prepared British passport on which the name was Mrs. Sally Raftery. The Gnome had ordered the same first name, for he wanted to be free to call her Sal wherever they might travel.

While the Gnome surveyed a print in which a Chinese master and mistress couple in an open loggia to attract a maidservant to them, the forger granted Mrs. Sally Raftery an Australian visa.

It had not been easy for the Gnome to choose that distant continent. In the past he had made one of his unhappy and accidental fortunes there, and there he had former partners of the kind he never wished to see again. But it was a large place and escapees could live a quiet life.

Where else? America was unsatisfactory, the continent

which had denied him birth and punished his boyish honesty. Asia was likewise wrong and Europe too close to such enemies as Brian. It left the Gnome with extreme choices only—Argentina, say. And Argentina's culture might not suit Sal, who at the time of birth would need to converse with doctors and nurses. Therefore Australia!

After he had worked on the Australian visa for Mrs. Raftery, the forger prepared a further British passport, based on the Gnome's genuine American one. The name was Mr. Henry Tournay. It had been chosen out of sentimentality for a beery French-Canadian hockey coach the Gnome had at Danbury High. Even while watching the Chinese at their ecstasies, the Gnome memorialized that plump and dyspeptic whacker of pucks.

The forger now prepared immunization cards, for he had been told that the journey was to take place without delay.

Well before the wonders of the print book had been fully explored, all documents were ready at a cost of fifteen hundred pounds, which the Gnome considered a fair price in a falling currency. The residue of the night he spent in a small hotel in Paddington and, after breakfast and a successful argument with *The Daily Telegraph* crossword, telephoned an agent in Geneva who arranged for the transfer of a hundred thousand U.S. dollars to the Bank of New South Wales, Sydney, for collection by Henry Tournay. Memorializing the hockey coach further, he bought two tickets to Sydney in that name at the British Airways counter at Victoria. They were return tickets, for like Brian's convict ancestor, the Gnome intended to come back from the Antipodes once the northern world had again rendered itself habitable.

In the afternoon, he hired a car and drove to the Department of Health Drafting Office in Gray's Inn Road and, as an American hospital architect, spent two hours in a study of the deposited plans of a number of British mental institutions, especially Stapleford Hatch. When a bored girl handed him the plans even for alarm and security systems, he reflected how easy it was in liberal democracies to research proposed subversive acts. He found that only the front gardens of the hospital, where the patients took their exercise, were subject to television surveillance. He read a memorandum from a Dr. G. F. Ambrose which stated that ornamental grillwork on the windows of Cerise wing had produced from most patients a happier answer to the question, "Do you feel trapped here?" The Gnome understood that if he got over the back wall and cut the happy grillwork on a back window of Cerise wing, opposite the dispensary for Gamma and Delta wards, he had just to walk around a corner to reach Beta.

The rest of the day was mechanically spent. He bought luggage, underwear male and female, explaining to salesgirls with suspicion in the corners of their eyes that he and his wife were going to spend six months in a subtropic climate and that no autumnal wear was needed. Finally, just before shop closing, he bought pinch bar and rope, grapple, and bolt-cutters from three separate hardware shops in the East End.

He had not eaten all day and would not eat, for he went forward on a pure fuel which left no wastes in his bloodstream and no hollow in his gut. He did not doubt he could manage the performance and walk unchallenged as a Minister of Health, as Jung or Adler, in the hallways of Cerise wing.

At the same time Sal and I reassessed our bodies after the long paraldehyde sleep, and Sal lay docile for fear they'd give her more of the stuff. While the tormented women of Beta ate in the dining hall, a tray was brought to her and she wolfed the ropy meat and the custard with hands that seemed unstrung. There was a hazy excitement in her, unlike the more precise one in me. She could tell though that there wasn't time to linger at the meal, that the earth would soon shift under her feet, though in what direction she could not have told.

In Sal I frowned. My brain, though still in place, felt parched, a bare floor, patches of old and yellowed clothing blowing across the boards before a dry wind. I needed a fit and healthy sleep and, though there was much to think of and to fear, slipped into one.

Sal finished the custard, grateful for it, for it meant there could be no anesthetic in the morning, no surgical attack on me. Putting the dish aside, she sat up in her bed and crossed her hands before her belly. She spoke and the sentence entered my sleep. "How was that stuff, darling boyo? How was that stuff?" she asked, damning herself for raging and fighting and inviting a needle. She kept awake till nine, but drugged sleep is exhausting and now the genuine item overtook her.

A little later, I awoke myself. I knew that the Gnome was in the building.

14

At about the time the Gnome cut his way through the therapeutic grillwork and penetrated Cerise wing, immediately taking on the stoop and shuffle of the potently sedated, George entered Ran Singh's stateroom through the door from the guest bedroom. In his hand he carried a capped syringe holding five hundred milligrams of paraldehyde, three times death for Ran Singh. Though he had always chafed at sharing the house space and the love with a Brazilian monkey, he had not considered murdering it until now. It seemed to George, however, that if I was to vanish, the monkey too had lost its standing and should vanish as well.

Also on that Yugoslav tier of his spirit, which he had found through doctoring partisans in '43 to '44, he was still influenced by the antique rites of Mithra which had once flourished in Dalmatia and of which blood sacrifice and regeneration through blood were large aspects. On George's Yugoslav stratum therefore, Ran Singh was the animal sacrifice and substitute for me.

George picked up the poor simian's squeaker toy and squeezed it and handed it to Ran Singh. As the monkey bent to pick the squeaker up, George uncapped the syringe, pushed the needle into the monkey's hindquarters, and squeezed in the overdose. Ran Singh savaged George on the left hand, but in a few seconds his neat monkey jaw slackened and he swooned sideways. George went into the guest bathroom, washed the deep tooth wounds with iodine, and injected himself against tetanus.

He was sitting contemplatively in the living room by the time Clytie got back from a visit to her daughter's. She noticed instantly the glaring badge of scarlet and bandage he wore on his left hand.

"Clytie," he said, "I have to tell you straight. I gave Ran Singh a needle. I'm sorry, Clytie."

Frowning at him a second, she moved at a ceremonial pace and found the small body, lying inside the unlocked door of his cage on a stained edition of *The Observer*. Ran Singh's hair was brilliantly russet under the fluorescent lighting of the stateroom. She wailed and wept, lifting the small body in her hands. "This is your child, you bastard. Do you understand that? You've killed your child."

In appealing and denouncing, she twisted the body without knowing she was doing it.

"I could tell you that the vet advised me to do it," George said in a monotone.

"Well . . . well? Did he?"

"No. The truth is Sal can't come home childless and be happy with us for keeping a monkey. A monkey at such expense and trouble."

"Trouble?" Clytie shrieked.

"One got sick," said George, his eyes and voice neutral. Pretending to be callous because his profession had taught him how well callousness stanches debate, how it satisfies the grieving who can go away saying, "My God, they're insensitive, those doctors." "One got sick of the shit. And of explaining him to visitors. And of saying, 'Don't be disturbed if he jerks off in front of you.' "

But even demented, Clytie knew George better.

"It's those Yugoslavs," she screamed. "Those Yugoslavs . . . those bloody Yugoslavs made you do this."

"What a ridiculous statement."

"Get out!" she told him, sobbing.

But an hour later George had managed to soothe her with an injection of her own, though she pretended to suspect that he'd charged the syringe with a lethal dose for her as he had for Ran Singh. When she fell asleep muttering, she was still blaming Tito's partisans.

The Gnome was now in Cerise wing, but a long corridor and two corners removed from Beta ward. Around the first corner, he found a nurse staring at him and by instinct made a little trumpety tune with his lips. But the nurse frowned after him and, level with a TV room, he stumbled in and took a chair at the back of the group. Of the dozen patients in the room, only two were watching the screen, where the comedians Morecombe and Wise performed in black and white. The Gnome sat boop-ooping away, looking at a stringy-haired girl who herself watched the performance with a drunken and unlaughing fixity.

A trolley whirred down the corridor as the comics on the screen were singing their keynote song. Soon a nurse might come in and ask the sleeping televiewers if anyone wanted a channel change. So he rose, assuming a stagger. It was exactly the right stagger. He knew it was exactly right and wondered how he knew, since he had never before been inside an asylum's walls.

He found Beta empty except for Sal and for one of the young mothers. This girl sat with her back half onto Sal. Her breasts nearly touching her raised knees. Her face was blue from recently abated weeping which might begin again at any second. She was not up to noticing him. He found Sal's bed.

"Sal," he said, leaning over Sal, shading her from the asylum light. She opened her eyes but they were unfocused,

169

so that she saw two Gnomes and considered both to be side effects of the fierce medication.

"Come on," he said. "It *is* me."

Already he was reaching her the hospital dressing gown she had been given, a sad checked affair. Though she was not born until 1949, the dressing gown had wrought a triumph of atmospherics and up until now had caused her to think of coy bathing on sad shingle beaches circa 1936. She did not until now see it as the raiment of her escape.

"Shoes, shoes," said the Gnome, casting about.

By Sal's bed stood the brogues in which she had been captured. The Gnome forced them on her feet and muttered his instructions.

Sal's young and consummate brain was burning up the opiates now, the drugs they had forced on her, and my own brain-bud too was ringing clearly and sweet. The grieving girl did not turn to us as we all left Beta. Ahead staggered the Gnome, Sal after. They did very well at pretending to be two individual *dérangés* who by accident were cruising the same corridor at the one time. And the Gnome's gait was so authentic that no one stopped him, though a nurse emerged from a night station to ask, "Where are we going, Mrs. Fitzgerald?"

The plural *we* that they used on helots and idiots and paraplegics, thought Sal, and decided to put the nurse right. For Sal had no fear anymore, she knew she could get away with the Gnome even if she took time to instruct the nurse in grammar.

"Television room," said Sal. "And *I* am going, we are not."

"Television. Not wise," said the nurse.

"For Christ's sake!" Sal complained.

"All right. But it goes off in forty minutes."

The Gnome was waiting for her at the window he had doctored. He opened it and Sal took the sharp air on her face. Dislodging the ironwork he led her over the low sill quickly—it was no problem for long-legged Irish girls. The Gnome then took time to replace the grille from outside, being studious at it; and so restored to Cerise wing its whole skin.

Climbing the wall brought on dizziness and short breath. But she managed it in no more than ten giddy seconds. On the way southwest, back across London in the Mercedes, Sal obeyed the Gnome and changed in the back of the car, putting on the loose blue trouser suit and the marginally too-large mules he had provided with the idea of making her traveling comfortable.

"You see the makeup bag?" he said. "I thought you might be pale. The drugs . . ."

"Am I pale?"

"You're very pale. Very."

Turning on a small interior light, she found in a mirror by the backseat that her face seemed juiceless. Anger and savage drugs had drawn off her moisture and under each eye was a patch of dead skin. In the makeup bag she found some moisture lotion, gathered a daub on her index finger and carefully stroked her sere flesh. Then she applied a beige makeup to give her an instant tan and next blusher to the cheekbones. They were the most expensive cosmetics she had ever used and she enjoyed the luxury of them. As she saw her face achieve a look of health under these preparations, as she looked down at her lower limbs in the expensive clothing, she began to laugh at the joy and thoroughness of the escape and the Gnome laughed with her.

"Expense is no object," he told her, as if he himself had minted that aphorism.

Sal sat deeply in the plush backseat. "Where are we going?" she asked.

"Australia."

"Oh." She considered this lightly. She thought the distance involved was about the right distance from Stapleford Hatch. She wondered whether Brian could be depended on to come seeking her at such a remove, and wondered as well if she wanted him to. "This is a real coup," she said. "This is *really* a breakout."

They left their car in Cromwell Road. Standing together

waiting for a taxi, they looked like an expensive couple; their leather luggage signaled *airport* to passing taxi drivers and they did not have to wait long.

Two miles above Surrey her brain felt fresh-born to her. "Do you know?" she asked the Gnome. "I've never flown first-class before." She looked around her. A dozen or so first-class gentry were stirring, releasing their abdomens from seat belts, anticipating Martinis and vintages. "I'm going to drink a little," she told the Gnome.

"A little. Yes." Though he kept a mad idea of what she was, he still had a sane care for her health.

"The drugs go very badly with alcohol," he said.

She chuckled at him for fussing. But after two sips of the Veuve Clicquot the Gnome ordered for her, she fell asleep. Above the French Alps on a Bahrain heading I caressed the walls of Sal and savored my permanence there. And though my passage out of England depended on four Pratt and Whitneys developing horsepowers such as might once have provided all the cavalry of Europe and Asia with impetus, though my headway depended on a cunning shell of metal and on dazzling hydraulic and electronic systems, I believed that Sal was my true conveyer, Sal my benign ship.

This was my longest and most momentous journey, and I took thought of my brotherhood with my ancestor Maurice Fitzgerald, who had also once been transported to the Antipodes, not knowing what manner of forests he might move among on his arrival, not knowing what animals he might see. We had both, Maurice and I, been assigned a narrow billet by higher authority. A king and a parliament had assigned him an eighteen-inch width of bench to lie in, and I too had been granted by fathers and doctors a small and statutory width and patch of night. A rumor among the convicts said that till just the year before last *Minerva* had been a slave ship, and Sal herself had till just now been written off to the black trades of psychiatry. Maurice knew that though he and his brothers lay in a slave's eighteen inches, although like slaves they were linked together by spans of chain, they would not be sold for a good price at the voyage's end; they lacked even a market value; and I—I knew from the attacks of the past week what my value and standing was.

Yet considering what it was, *Minerva* too was like Sal, a benign ship. The Irish gentlemen on deck who were exiles and not common convicts, who had surrendered to an amnesty for rebel leaders or who had given their gentlemen's oath that they would not slip over the side, felt some guilt about their kinsmen in the hold, who had to sleep on their sides under each his one blanket and, if overcome where they lay, to puke or excrete in their chains. So the rebel general Joseph Holt arranged for his one and a half hundred fellow countrymen to be allowed on deck each day without chains. Dr. O'Connor arranged for the opening of the ventilation ports and the washing down of the convict benches with vinegar solution; the Reverends Harald and Fulton, knowing that the one hundred and thirty boys in the hold were decent young men and minor rebels, and the twenty-five women were harlots or trained pickpockets, persuaded the captain to build that thin wooden partition between the male and female prisoners, the wall to which Maurice objected.

And, as Sal said in her unfinished book, the Officer of the Guard, Lieutenant Cox, was kindly. Going broke had increased his natural humanity, though he was an efficient man and his Redcoats, as subject to flogging as any convict, would have an eye out for untoward groupings and movements of convicts. It was a convict ship, yes, but a nonpareil of convict ships. And the rations were full weight, because, although captains of such vessels might often short weight the occupants of the hold on food and sell the quantity saved by these means on the beach in New South Wales, Captain Salkeld had a firm Presbyterian conscience.

So Maurice, afloat now, had no one to detest in his ship world, as I had no one to detest in mine. All hated tyrannies, all poisonous institutions had been left ashore, and Maurice spent his evenings imagining the country he was traveling to, discussing with himself whether it would be new world or convict limbo, and wondering if there, because of its distance from the European norm, oppression might not be transmuted to something else and law turned upside down, the way Christians believe things are for the meek who inherit the earth.

All he resented was that well-meaning timber partition and he intended to penetrate it. In the coming world, he knew, every man would be responsible for his own morality. The timber partition insulted and incited him.

He said to Danny Galvin, "Those girls are the one race with us."

"Are they now?" said Danny. Danny was not used to city women, and they were all frightening city women behind that timber, their laughter never had clear meanings, always arose from fast and flashy Cork City relevances Danny could not grasp.

They should not be walled up like the dead or like the table of the law, those women. Maurice rasped the stem of his spoon against his anklets, giving it not a cutting but a gouging edge. Never, on his way upstairs for mess duty or for exercise, did he omit to take the spoon and gouge an atom or two of wood out of a target spot on the partition from beyond which came the mysterious laughter of the women.

Pressure poppings in the ears woke Sal. Dawn stood over Asia Minor. The plane, out of Europe, edged down over the mountains of Elburz, toward Tehran.

"You missed dinner," said the Gnome, smiling, approving. "But the hostess tells me that there will be breakfast after Tehran."

A surge of blood into my graciously folded hands and into my legs tucked up fakir-wise told me that Sal was still excited by her rescue and now further stimulated by the altitude and the alps beneath her. She stared at the ski slopes far below and at the volcano of Demavend. Above the outer suburbs of the Shah's city, we were no more than a pulse in the last half hour's sleep of the Persians. According to what oriental suppositions do the suburbanites of Tehran lie and love, rise, breakfast, and go to their work? Sal wanted to know. She wanted to know everything.

"Can we get out? Can we walk around?"

"No," said the Gnome. "There are armed guards. They are preparing for the great oil war."

"Oh."

"But we'll go upstairs to the lounge. You can walk around. You should. There's the danger of blood clots in the legs . . ."

Sal thought, If this were some conventional attachment, I would find him oppressive.

It was dawn in Tehran but still the small hours in London, and in their flat Brian lay against Annie's back. Neither of them slept. Annie wore a nightdress in which she looked angular, but which evoked tenderness toward her from Brian. For Annie the nightdress was an intended layer of separation. She doubted Brian had been won away from Sal; she doubted he ever would be. She thought he talked about her madness as if it were alluring. She saw it as a glamour she couldn't match.

At the same time Brian stared at the creamy triangle of flesh that showed between the nape of the gown and the beginning of her hair. By means of oblique light from the living room—for Brian never slept without some sort of light—he had been admiring its dim creaminess for hours. Sometimes pressing his nose against it in a small gesture of adoration. He was so scared of losing Annie, of being driven back to Sal and to the fact or memory of me. "My little Jewish feature writer," he said. "Still wakeful, are you?"

"Yes."

"Do you want me to make tea?"

He made it barefooted, wearing only a shirt, and by hard

thinking while he waited for the water to boil, found himself—with some surprise—the owner of yet another fresh, bright decision.

He carried the tray to her bedside. "I've got a confession to make, Annie."

She smiled the quick sort of smile a victim might give before the fall of the blow.

"Nothing terrible. I've had a vasectomy, that's all. Does it matter?"

Like the lie about Sal this also was a lie. Sal was not pregnant, he had told Annie, because he believed Sal would soon not be. He was sterile because it had come to him while he waited in the kitchen that he should soon get himself doctored. He would make the appointment in the morning, perhaps have it done at lunch time.

"You should have told me earlier," Annie complained.

"You won't believe it, but I'd all but forgotten. Does it matter?"

"It doesn't matter now. How do I know what it will matter next year?"

He stroked her elbow as if he believed the core of her sensuality were located there. "No," she said, "I'm desperate for sleep."

For Sal had, as was just, taken Annie's healthy sleep away and slept it at a height of five miles. Annie was left blank, loving but not trusting the man with the crooked grin who took her teacup from her and pummeled her pillow before she lay on it.

Propped on one thin arm, crooked about the shoulders, bruised beneath the eyes, she resembled the patient Sal recently was.

As Sal exercised in the plane's cocktail lounge, the men of first-class watched her and wished that cruises were more leisurely, that there were time to meet such women as this on B deck under a series of moons.

Meanwhile, in my ample cells I retold the journey of

Maurice Fitzgerald. Bearing him, *Minerva* sailed in a convict fleet, but storms broke up the pattern. Salkeld found himself alone when the sea settled and the sky cleared, on a bearing for Cape Verde. One Tuesday afternoon a Portuguese man-o'-war from Rio sighted them and tacked on a course to intercept, Britain then being at war with the Portuguese. The Irish gentlemen, who had the run of *Minerva*'s quarterdeck, helped Salkeld and Cox count the enemy's guns. Fifty-four, they decided. Wives and children were sent to their cabins, and Salkeld and Cox discussed if the convicts should be chained to prevent their breaking out and abetting the Latins, or unchained for easy escape when the ship foundered. Captain Salkeld asked the Irish gentlemen to help him man his eight deck guns, and though they agreed they already foresaw a future for themselves as Brazilian grandees. For the bark was trim and should catch *Minerva* up against the shore of the Gambia within the two or more hours of light that were left.

Cox, though petulant at the Latin warship for complicating his immigration, chose to unchain the felons. He spoke to them and warned them to be still under pain of being shot in the head. He withdrew, the hatch was closed, and it seemed somehow that within the hold the prisoners were entirely their own men for the first time in all the months they had inhabited *Minerva*.

Through a gouged hole in the partition, Maurice Fitzgerald—in the manner of his great-grandson—had spoken up a tubercular red-haired girl called Mollie Finnane. Mollie was, no doubt, a small thief and perhaps a Cork prostitute. Other acquaintanceships had been made through that small hole and finally the women, who had some hold over the ship's carpenter, had been able to borrow a pinchbar and loosen a section of paneling. Now four men, Fitzgerald, a trembling Galvin, and two others, were admitted through the paneling. All the ventilation holes were closed down and each of the four couples beneath their blankets, which had kept them half warm through storm and ague and dysentery, were as private as couples under the stars in a harvest field; more private than that, private as ants. Above them the sound of men running, the grind of gun carriages. But they themselves were creatures well out of that surface world.

Mollie smelled no worse than he. In the hold's dusk she was properly moist and subterranean as he. "What's your crime?" she asked as part of the small talk.

"There's no criminals," he told her, mouthing her belly, "except the ones who are on the face of coins."

Maurice gave her all the seed of his imprisonment while the gun crews primed the cannon above them. Lieutenant Cox's snipers, already posted in the crosstrees of the mast, could see the fluky coast of Africa as a hazed line. Anything could happen here—the winds rose and died without reason, favored one ship, slowed another to an amble. At half past four a blast of air circling out of the jungle shoved the blunt-nosed *Minerva* southward. The Portuguese captain conceded Salkeld had got into a special wind, and all his own tacking did nothing to close the distance. In the hold Mollie and Maurice Fitzgerald heard the Portuguese broadside as a distant thud; its impact with the water shook them by the shoulders. Women screamed and men whistled. Invitations were uttered to God to bless the guns of the foreigners and to blow this Protestant, this Hanoverian slave ship to splinters. An old woman of thirty-five, in a coarse government-issue dress up to her chin, began singing a tribal death wail.

"Oh, is it time then to go?" she sang in the old language.

"Into the dark cave
And take with me
The eyes that have beheld
Spring's sweet attack.
The flesh that knew the sunlight and the wind . . ."

The Portuguese had not closed up to Salkeld when the dusk steamed out of the mouth of the Gambia and ended the matter, the ambivalence of Irishmen on deck and in the hold. Fitzgerald and Galvin and the others climbed out of the women's quarters, the paneling was replaced. The Reverend Fulton and Father Harald offered two-edged thanks to God over dinner and General Holt said the gallant things a rebel general should say. "I advise you, Captain Salkeld, not to trust me with a cannon at any future time."

We were three hours out of Tehran when the police knocked on Brian's door a little after 6 A.M. London time. Soothed by tea and by Brian's diverse lies, both Annie and he were profoundly asleep, and he went to the door dragging trousers on. There were plainclothesmen there. They had got his address from Sal's doctor, they said, and they regretted to tell him that Sal had jumped hospital. Where might she be? Her old apartment, Brian suggested. The blood of his face burned up pungently, stinging his eyes. He was aware, through the walls between the living room and the bedroom, of Annie's listening presence. Parents in Ireland, yes. The Galley Arms, Liscannor, County Clare. We'll get the Irish constabulary to check the place, they said.

Brian knew she wouldn't go there, that she was too proud to satisfy them that way. For Irish parents always expected that one day their pretty daughters who had gone to face the world would limp home soiled and sorry.

"There's a friend," he said. "Mr. Jones . . ."

They sighed at the Gnome's name. You could tell they hadn't traced him. They thanked Brian and left, and an instant after the door closed, Annie appeared in the living room, clutching her own thin shoulders.

They would argue for an hour, then all day she would stay remote from him. Yet he was not unhappy about the asylum break. Once recaptured, he was sure, Sal would receive an added sentence. Dr. Carbon, who was the sort of man who designed a neat society, would see to it that she was not permitted to bear children.

Before Brian had finished his slack day's work, a second dawn overtook the three of us above the brown core of Australia. A land was revealed, striated brown and gray, and all its watercourses dry. Yet it was radiant in that first light, it had the impact on Sal of a God or a grand concept as she leaned over her breakfast, staring at it with her left eye.

"It looks . . ." she muttered, not finishing the sentence.

"It looks like Buddha," said the Gnome, for he had seen this country before, had hunted minerals in its deserts one winter. "It looks as if it would eat you whole. And without giving a damn."

She laughed at that; I laughed within her. We were out of range of Portuguese men-o'-war.

And as the sun grew higher, the Gnome informed us we were over cattle land, then sheep and wheat land, then forests and mountains, and then the temperate coasts. A city showed itself aport the jet's nose; it looked falsely ideal, falsely promising in the morning sun, as if it were boasting, "Look what has been made of the chains and blood of Maurice Fitzgerald."

"We have to get you to a gynecologist," the Gnome insisted as the plane dropped and the towers shone beyond her window.

"Tomorrow," she said. "Tomorrow."

There was a young man to meet them, a lawyer or accountant who, it seemed to Sal, managed the Gnome's investments in the country. He had brought his own car and drove them toward the city. It was spring and, despite the smell of tanneries on the roads from the airport, Sal traveled with the window down. The young man spoke sagely of politics—the right and the left were polarized, he said, as if this were the only country where it were true. The trade unions still dominated the Labour Party, he told the Gnome, only more so than when you were here last. "A downturn in mineral exploration," he said, like a man who had seen a dozen booms, outlived a dozen slumps.

"Investigators from Corporate Affairs came into the office one day," he said. "They wanted to know where you were. I said in England."

"I should send my thanks to Dabney," said the Gnome.

The boy lawyer nodded. "Dabney's always asking me whether you're going to come and when."

"Tell him nothing."

"Who's Dabney?" Sal asked in a dream, raising her half-closed eyes to the sun.

"Dabney is a geologist Mr. Jones once employed," the boy explained.

"Dabney is a crook," said the Gnome.

"It was just," the young man muttered, "I noticed you got me to reserve us a suite under a fictitious name."

"That has nothing to do with minerals. It's all a matter of . . ." He gestured toward Sal. ". . . the connection between this lady and myself."

The young man smiled, half he smiled for Sal, who picked it up and unabashedly smiled back. She could tell she looked so wonderful, with all the beauty of her escape swelling in her, that he too would have liked to spend days with her in a suite at the end of a corridor.

"I have a twenty-eight-foot sloop. Perhaps, Warwick, you and the lady would . . . ?"

"The lady . . . Sal . . . is pregnant."

"Oh."

"But of course I can come sailing," said Sal, correcting the Gnome.

We occupied a suite above the harbor, two bedrooms—which may have mystified the young executive—and a living room. With Sal's eyes I looked down on the dazzle of the harbor, trying to delineate the place Fitzgerald had known. When *Minerva* sailed in, the city was a hamlet at the earth's end. Of every three men who lived in it, two were in chains. The harbor was grand and melancholy and the nearly silent village was lost in the folds and hillocks of one of its minor bays. A surgeon was rowed out from the shore and looked at each convict's eyes, teeth, throat, and genitals, and a sense of a hinterland pressing so close and menacing on the subdued township, on this poorest beachhead of empire, made you wonder if the surgeon would let only the infested land on the continent.

Through Sal's eyes I tried to develop the sense-of-place that Fitzgerald had acquired, looking from the well deck of *Minerva* as the surgeon demanded he say, "Ah—ah—ah!" The sense that there were none of the familiar gods here, none of the gods of the peatbog to demand the bodies of virgins and the arms of war—items such as Fitzgerald's master had dug out of the bogs in Meath. The gods here were the gods of some other race and were indifferent to any sacrifices you might possibly make. This frightened Fitzgerald even though he pretended to be a man of reason and to be above tribal, peasant feelings.

Yet though Ireland had been full of ancient gods, ghosts, heroes, plaints, wails, and songs that stung the pith of your soul, still people suffered there, villages daily expected decimation, children—cut up by dragoons—hung by the feet from the tops of market crosses. So he considered, winking across the deck of the beneficent *Minerva* at the now-pregnant Mollie, that this country turned such an empty face on him because it meant him no malice. I, his less innocent great-great-great-great-grandson, employing Sal's eyes to look from our high window, saw other rooftops, saw foreshores and spinnakers on the water. I had Maurice's experience to go on, and so knew that there was no princedom on earth where anguish could not make its run.

Most of those first days we spent by the pool, under tall glass walls that fielded the gustier winds and transmitted the sunlight to Sal's shoulders. To an onlooker, the Gnome and Sal may have looked like people waiting for a conference to begin, a journey to start. In the meantime, they both read with absorption—paperbacks from the downstairs newspaper shop. Sal—once more in the manner of a traveler—read all the trash she somehow had missed reading while living with Brian. The Gnome read only murder stories, buying three after breakfast each morning and closing the last one with a little plaintive grunt after dinner. They read so much in each other's company that none of the staff doubted they were married.

While selecting his paperbacks in the morning, the Gnome would inspect the three morning papers, looking for a back-pages paragraph which might say either "CORPORATE AFFAIRS SEEK AMERICAN MINERALS SPECULATOR" or else "BRITISH ASYLUM ESCAPEE SAID TO BE HERE." Though he knew there was no call for such a paragraph, he was always pleased to find it missing.

During the days in which Sal consumed the best-sellers of the past two years, police were watching the Home Counties and the Irish seaports and keeping contact with the constabulary in Clare. After a week they began to drag ponds on a common near the hospital. Since they had no reason to suspect her dead, they did not tell Brian about this search. He was therefore left free to attend the vasectomy clinic on Thursday afternoon. Under local anesthetic he watched a doctor hook out through incisions on either side of his groin the two spaghettilike strands of the vasa deferentia, sever them, and return them to his body. For the rest of the day he limped a little. There was a dull pain at the base of his stomach, but it felt to him like a worthy pain. Now he had only me to face; his flanks—so to speak—were safe.

That night Annie, who did not know what he had suffered just that afternoon, noticed that during their lovemaking he uttered groans that nearly had about them the timbre of suffering.

At the end of Sal's first week as an escapee, when the Gnome had begun looking for a furnished house, Brian returned to the clinic in Palace Gate for a sperm count. At United Press it had been a hurried morning and Brian had had to get out three stories and spend stretches of time talking to Belfast on the radio telephone. There had therefore been no time for him to take the sterilized plastic jar to the lavatory and produce a sperm sample. He got to the clinic five minutes early, however, and, rushing past the receptionist at her desk, found a toilet at the end of the corridor. Its handle proved immovable. There was a notice on the door: "Please apply for key at reception desk." Yet he knew it was beyond him to do that, for he suffered from too much nicety to ask a girl for the key and hand back to her a little later not only the key but also a small bottle of his seed.

He went back out onto the street. A pub? Too rowdy, too swinish. Around the corner in Kensington High Street, he was sure, there were department stores.

He sprinted to the main door of Biba's, propping whenever women propped before windows and stood still with their mouths a little agape, galvanized by the exactly right garment. Inside there were not many men, but a girl in the information booth told him that there were men's toilets on the third floor. Reaching them, he found a cubicle, locked himself in, dropped his trousers and felt a sudden onset of grief. It seemed a pitiful end for a breeding Fitzgerald, here on the third floor, hidden between two slabs of that false brown marble they use in institutional lavatories, reading the entirely expected scriptures on the back of the door, the telephone numbers, the promises of fellatio, the statements of sexual creed, the too-hairy drawings of female parts; and it was the thought of Sal, now a mad stranger, that came up behind his left shoulder, surprised and aroused him.

As he worked there, retaining the sterilized bottle, now open, between the little and fourth fingers of his left hand, he wondered what this image of Sal signified, for Sal was not meant to be alluring to him any more.

He let his genitals drop when he heard a hiss—*Sssst!* He looked to left and right, his slack penis hanging between his thighs. *Sssst!* again. Of course, he thought, in a women's department store the men's toilets might be a sanctum for strange males. His eyes jerking at the task, he inspected the walls. There were no spy holes. The door was intact. Hot water cisterns, he told himself, could make a noise of arresting sibilance like that. And if there were no holes, then the hot water cistern must be the hisser; and he began to feel affection for the decent, sexually uncommitted mechanisms that brought hot water into the washbasins outside.

Yet as Brian returned to the task there came a too-exactly timed *Sssst!* Now he looked upward. Above his head, leaning over the wall from the cubicle to his right, was a smooth-faced, slightly flabby Indian. He looked a wealthy man, he wore an expensive brown pinstripe, his shirt was silken, there were rings on his fingers.

Brian fled the cubicle. Still shackled at the ankles by his dropped trousers, he had nonetheless lifted them by the moment he stepped forward into the mirrored richness of the third floor. Even in the corridor he was still not zipped and looked after that while walking crabwise among potted plants that fringed off the coffee shop. He saw a lift before him whose doors were creeping closed. Too strenuously he struck them apart with his shoulder. The dozen women who peopled the lift all frowned or averted their faces. They didn't like his male haste or the rattly impact he'd made with his shoulder.

As the lift hissed on arrival at the ground floor, he noticed that his sterile sample jar still stood between the splayed little and fourth fingers of his left hand. He pushed it away into his suit pocket, but the faint musk of the twelve women all around him pervaded the lift like a judgment, as if they knew he had failed to make a sperm sample on the third floor.

For this reason, once the doors had opened, he felt bound to let all the women out ahead of him. Yet he stood on the balls of his feet, wanting to push a few of those who disembarked so leisurely, so queenly. The crowds around jewelry, cosmetics, scarves, and accessories seemed maliciously thick and, weaving among them, he must have been visible from the stairs.

"Sir!" he heard behind him. The man, the Indian prince, was on the last half dozen steps. He had no shame, that man, his call was as loud as a lumberjack's. Yet it had, too, an Asian sybarite softness to it which stampeded Brian all the more. "Sir! Could I please see you for a moment?"

"Hell!" Brian screamed, bruising his hip on the corner of the handbag counter. He moved stubbornly, brutally, like in fact a rugby halfback, and the young, pretty women of London showed their style by dancing out of his path.

He turned left as he went from the store, walked down the High Street, rejecting the tube station as a refuge, seeing an opening for a man with pace among the traffic. And as the Indian called to him yet once more, too loudly, making people frown a little, Brian sprinted like a thief, weaving his hips among the vehicles, a dazzling halfback's run which left the satrap isolated from him by two murderous currents of traffic.

And now, to put a seal on the Indian's loss, he entered a branch of the Midlands Bank. He spoke to the girl at the inquiry counter. "Is there a toilet?" he asked, gagging but in his more articulate, most British accent. She narrowed her eyes at him, his sweat worried her. "I would like," he explained, "somewhere to sit and take my asthma drugs." He noticed that she had very small yet elegantly molded breasts. "I'll give you the key to the bank officers' toilets on the first floor, sir. Could you return it to me after use?"

The place was so clean and he found a cubicle that had no writing and no holes in its walls. Good old Midlands Bank, which promoted only those men who knew how to control the creative itch in the company's toilets. Yet though the jar was still possibly sterile, the sample would not provide itself. The sober footsteps of accountants arrived and went. They all washed their hands at length after their postlunch wets. Two of them chatted about the Credit Union's outing to Windsor Safari Park. "I don't know whether I ought to go," said one. "I have a vinyl top on my car. I believe some of the monkeys are tough on vinyl . . ."

At last, by taking all his clothes off his drying body and compounding a woman of Sal and Annie Newman and the girl who had given him the key downstairs, he managed to create a small deposit of seminal fluid and capture it in his jar. Going downstairs he was overcome by giddiness. The unknown sexual warrior.

"They have a grace," Sal muttered, more to herself than to her visitor. "Those boys. They have a grace."

The boys who had pleased her straddled their surfboards two hundred feet below us. The muscles of their backs were legible even at this distance through their black wetsuits. Clustered on a firm swell of ocean, waiting—patient as monks and as silent—for the exact wave. Sal too was beginning to learn which waves suited them. It seemed to her to be always one that rose to a sharp but not too concave peak. Its underbelly was first blue, and then jade, and ribbed with froth. The riders, when it came, had only seconds to read its contour and straighten their surf craft. But if caught, it carried them standing upright along the apex of its water, down its jade underface, and into the cylinder it made when crashing on itself.

"They might look decorative," Sheila Dabney said. They had been sitting there on the sun deck for an hour and a half now, and the more Sal grew enchanted by the board riders, the more Mrs. Dabney's mouth turned sour in her thin, pretty face. "In fact, they're a blight. Most of them on welfare. Our taxes subsidize that . . . what they're doing. You're watching a subsidized art form, in fact. And I don't think it deserves to be that."

"It doesn't matter," Sal said. "It's Saturday today. Saturdays aren't paid for out of taxes."

"Saturdays are just like any other day in the fiscal year." Open-throated, Mrs. Dabney drank off her glass of white wine and then made a mouth as if she had received from it nothing more than the taint of acid. At the far end of the sun deck her twin nine-year-old girls and their young brother swung a rope.

> "Not last night but the night before,
> Twenty-three robbers came knocking at my door.
> When I got up to let them in,
> This is what they said to me,
> Spanish lady turn around,
> Spanish lady touch the ground,
> Spanish lady do the kicks,
> Spanish lady show your knicks . . . !"

The decking shivered as they hopped. I liked the neatness of their skipping action; with little bobs of the head I answered those three, those prancers in jeans, those singers of whimsical and stupid songs.

This house, leased as a refuge for Sal and the Gnome and me, was a vertical one, three-tiered, affixed to a cliffside. The struts of the sun deck where Sal stood so delighted rose out of a jungle of palms, of banana trees, of twisted bushes with black cones, of *Monstera deliciosa* with their great green phalluses such as had inhabited the Gnome's first dream of Sal.

Inside the house the Gnome and Mr. Dabney were in conclave.

"Your husband," Mrs. Dabney said, "didn't seem so pleased to see mine."

"He isn't my husband," said Sal.

"Oh, I thought he was your husband."

"No. I suppose I'm a subsidized art form as well." Sal said it to challenge the woman.

"No. No, you're very beautiful," pretty Mrs. Dabney said, looking at her with full blank eyes. Sal couldn't tell what was behind them, envy or desire. What place had beauty in the fiscal year?

"Your husband . . . ?" Sal asked. "I've heard his name . . ."

"They were in minerals together. The whole continent seems to have gone sour on poor Dabney. He got the whisper your husband . . . I'm sorry, your *friend* . . . was in the country and it made a difference. He's been happier since he knew. We're all grateful . . ." She pointed even to the bouncing nine-year-olds. ". . . for these little improvements."

When Dabney and his wife and children came to the door an hour and a half past, the Gnome had tried to hold them there, had ignored the children and been morose to Dabney and the wife. Sal made up for his lack of a welcome by taking Mrs. Dabney and the children into the kitchen and opening lemonade for the children. I felt a certain aerated sting of pleasure on my own palate as the lid popped and a little pungency of soda gas was released into the air. Sal spoke loudly, for she could hear the Gnome in the living room continuing to give sparse greeting to Dabney, and wanted to save the children from hearing their father treated this way. "It should never have happened," the unyielding Gnome had said. "A geological *mistake* of that magnitude? I don't believe it."

Dabney spoke low; you could almost believe he had brought his spouse and infants here as hostages, to mollify the Gnome. The Gnome, it seemed, was not mollified.

"Of course I sold half my holding," we heard the Gnome call at some stage. "I wanted to buy in elsewhere. Such behavior isn't inconsistent with good faith."

But we could never hear anything but the intonation of Dabney's reply. He sounded like a suppliant, a man seeking a favor or a job. Facing Sal in the kitchen, Mrs. Dabney had stared limpidly at her. An expensive woman in a vivid caftan, Mrs. Dabney's eyes were shadowed and there was evenly applied pancake in the pores of her facial skin. Yet decked with all these fruits of marriage, she was willing for her three children to overhear their father's abasement.

It was Sal who needed to hurry the children out onto the sun deck. And as she closed the screen door she heard the Gnome again. "I rode my holding down to the ground. *Down to the ground.*" Ranting like some businessman she had never met and wouldn't want to. "Do you have any wine?" Mrs. Dabney had asked at her shoulder.

About noon the surfers began to leave the water, coming ashore, toting their boards above their heads.

"Must be lunch time," said acid little Sheila Dabney. But Sal knew something subtle had happened to the currents, that the swells were no longer of use to the riders. She felt an urge to defend those boys, the way you might defend a favorite writer you've never met. Before she could, the sliding door opened and the Gnome and Dabney stepped onto the deck. The Gnome turned his green eyes, vacant of comment, on Sal and went to watch the skipping children. The rope spun so wildly it resounded on the deck planking like a whip. The girls, like their mother, had quick, lithe little bones.

Dabney himself was smiling. His eyes swung gratefully toward the Gnome; he might have liked to have emerged with his hand on the Gnome's shoulder to show his wife how brotherly the meeting had been.

"Darling," said Dabney, "Mr. Jones is going to the west with me. You know . . . the new site . . ."

His stained ginger hair was tousled—you would have thought that the debate with the Gnome had been physical. His close-set eyes glittered, but Sal pitied him, for he carried his sudden joy as if it were a symptom, an affliction.

Now the Gnome began swinging one end of the jump rope and the Dabney girls performed their double jump act. Dabney beamed at the scene, but on Mrs. Dabney's cheek stood a tear the rainproof skin would not drink down. Her husband pecked the top of her head and grinned at Sal.

After taking thought, Sal grinned back, mistrusting. For he was like Brian, and you never knew what crazy things could exalt him.

What exalted him today, as we would all know in the end, was that in Western Australia, he was sure, he could murder the Gnome.

In W8 the police still called. They seemed to come in the early morning or evening, when Annie either still lay abed or the flat was full of the savor of her cooking, when, that is, warmth and heartsease were growing in the small apartment. Brian would go downstairs to try to keep them on the doorstep. Yet somehow they always had a manner about them, plainclothesmen, that got them upstairs and into your living room. Unlike uniformed coppers, who behaved like society's servants and shuffled at the street door, detectives entered like consultant surgeons.

While they were there, Annie lay deep and rigid in her bed or stood immobile, holding in her breath, by her frying pan on which she had, at the first rasp of a police voice, turned the thermostat down.

Brian sweated in the middle. He tried to be anguished enough to prove to the Metropolitan Police that he pitied Sal, yet to prove to Annie that he wasn't haunted by her. In front of them, he felt as if he were under a suspicion of noncompassion. Once they went he would return to Annie —perhaps poking at a tuft of chopped mint with his forefinger, biting the lobe of her bloodless ear. And though playing at being happy and at ease by the sink or the bedside, he sometimes felt that I had bludgeoned him just by drawing my breath and blood from Sal. Likewise it sometimes seemed to me that he had clenched his brain and the waves that were thus emitted came forth as a solid weapon. Tugged into orbit by gravity, they circled as my impulses sometimes had, reaching a telegraphic speed and striking and stunning me—among other times—as Sal stood at the side of the road above the hanging villa waving farewell to the Dabney twins and their clumsy little brother. They fell on me like murderous criticisms, like a threat to cancel my ontological license, they nudged me back toward a vegetable status. If I had not beaten them off by some small sane margin, if I had let them enjoy their proper impact, I could well have become a drooler for life. You will see my face, I threatened and promised him again. You will face my canny eyes.

Before dawn when the sea was still purple, Sal heard him moving in the house. She found him in his dim bedroom, his bed already made, the covers pulled up. He was packing. His crisp-collared shirts lay in a rack on one side of the suitcase. There was stacked underwear that looked as if it were fresh from the factory, and cotton socks.

"I didn't want to wake you," he said.

"Are you sure this Dabney can fly properly?" The Gnome did not answer.

"In Kalgoorlie," he said. In Kalgoorlie they would pick up their light plane and go prospecting. "In Kalgoorlie the whorehouses stand behind great tall palisades of corrugated iron. I mention that just for the sake of the picturesque."

"And Dabney says it's copper out there?"

"Dabney says it's copper."

She knew the story now. She had been told it on the beach two days ago, after the Dabneys had gone home, after the Gnome had asked her why she kept so silent and she'd answered, "Because you humbled Dabney right in front of his family." The Gnome had then grown frantic to explain. "I was humbled too," he said. "I was humbled too." Four years past he had been advised to buy shares in a copper company. The geologist's report on the copper site promised good veins of high content. The geologist, however, had been Dabney. In the desert in those days there had been a small corps of experts like Dabney, writers of geological fiction. And on the basis of the fictions, companies were floated, ghost ships and rogue ships on the sea of stocks and shares, vessels of uncertain and fantastic configuration.

On the London Exchange the shares based on Dabney's report reached fifty-three pounds sterling, having been forty Australian cents each at acceptance. On the day they reached fifty-three pounds, Dabney—who never bought too heavily into any of his fictions—owned a modest 25 percent of the shares, the Gnome owned 40 percent. Dabney then sold off all his holdings, and the Gnome himself was able to trade off half his in various profitable ways.

There came a time when the world began to understand that the data were fiddled and that two out of each three mineral companies were creatures of air, unconnected to any deposit in the earth. When everyone began selling his Australian mineral shares at once, the Gnome—still following that idea of the justice of things which had put a plate in his brain—dutifully rode his holding down till it was worth nothing. Dabney was indicted by Corporate Affairs, but there was some technical malfunction in the indictment and he was never brought to open court.

Now, as a sort of atonement, Dabney had found a copper vein in a long spine of antique rock called Warburton Ranges. The idea of pumping Consec's (that was the company's name) shares all the way up again appealed to the Gnome, Sal could see. Not in the hardy, gut-slapping manner that belongs to a man sure of his occupation of the earth. It appealed to him as an assertion of the innate balance of things.

I could have told them, drawing on their own histories, that balances are not so neatly reasserted. I could have called on brokers in all the earth's stock exchanges to uphold my point of view. Yet five-thirty was a rarefied hour in that vertical house among the *Monstera deliciosa*, behind windows touched by the first diffused gold of a sun that had traveled from Peru. Besides, a taxi driver began beating his horn from the cliffside road above the house.

The Gnome didn't go at once. He had an apology to make. "I . . . it's been lonely for you. We all expect mothers to live like nuns . . . it isn't just."

Sal said, "I am an escapee. I want to lie low."

"Mind the boy," he told her. It was the first straight-out imperious thing he'd ever said to her.

As soon as the taxi drove away she found herself free to behave on impulse. Her impulse was to go down to the surf. Usually—because it was getting easier to see she carried a baby—she wore a one-piece suit, half skirted, of the kind favored by tall, carrying mothers. Because there would be no one on the beach, she wore a bikini this morning. She put herself in a toweling wrap and took the steps that ran through the palm groves to the sand. She encountered, with her face moist, fresh spider strands that parted with a snap you could all but hear. Underfoot the beach was soft. Foam ran pinkly across the tide line like protozoa washing ashore one ancient morning. The sexual cuteness of her bikini demeaned this moment, and she took off the top and the bottom.

Beneath the froth the waters had an antarctic bite to them, for it was still spring. They stung her ankles and, striking her pubis, took away her breath. I could feel when she had got no deeper than the hips the contrary currents that were running that morning. But Sal was not alarmed by them. Her eye was on the point, some twenty steps farther out, where the waves had the correct configuration and would lift a naked mother and take her back to shore. That was the mark she struggled for, though the currents pushed her legs all ways.

Falling under a wave, she hooked her heels into the sea floor, and permitted a current to drag her a little way toward open sea. She surfaced among dark ridges of water where there was no foam. I, like a wary elder, was shocked at the distance she had got from the beach in her drunken dawn mood. But what shocked her was that a contemplative boy sat out there, astride his surfboard, back on to her, lifting and dropping in the face of the ascendant sun. Sal began swimming shoreward. She might even, as the locals said, catch a wave. But the caught wave took her to the bottom, so deep here, slapped her over brutally, punched me where I rode, and let us surface frightened.

"Jesus!" Sal said. The shore seemed remote to her too now. Her sea ecstasy had ended. She swam again and the shore receded. The rules of motion had turned on poor Sal this lovely morning. Now she had to call on the meditative board rider.

"Hey," she yelled. "Hey, Mister! Please!" Like the Irish waif the sea had made of her. Since the desperate are all equally unclothed she had forgotten her nakedness.

Anyone who saw Sal from a height, with, say, a gull's eye, in the growing dawn, would have noted she traveled in an avenue of teal water, a seagoing current moving contrary to the richer blue of the shore-going water. The reposeful boy had in fact a taste for perceiving things from a height and from varied angles. Though thirty yards from her, and well out of the contrary current, he knew as soon as he heard her that she was sea-bound.

Sal saw how he turned his board and paddled through the water with long easy swipes of his arms. She thought he was mocking her by taking his time, she was sure there was a half smile on his dark face, but we would learn it was just the way he worked.

In the time he neared us, disappearing sometimes behind swells, I tormented myself with pictures of what I might still become—a fetus in a sunken mother, a mariner in a drowned submarine. Sal lost to me, all her circuits and senses waterlogged, Sal swaying thoughtless in the middle deep, borne by forceful currents, cuffed and twirled by smaller and subtler ones. At the amnion I would kick and hammer, like some biblical leper, recovered, hammering for admission on the gate of his home city which plague has left empty and dead.

The biochemists, Sal knew, therefore so did I, considered us all small lakes. We brought with us from the sea, one morning like that exquisite morning in which Sal and I were drowning, the moistures and minerals of the sea, even the potassium, even the salts. We became ourselves rich lakes of wild and plentiful cilia, of browsing bacteria, of hearty corpuscles, and of those flabbergasting denizens, the chromosomes. Yet in returning to the sea so recklessly at dawn, before there were any flags up, any lifesavers on the beach sitting by their surf reels, a lake could lose itself. Now, having ambitions toward being a lake in my own right, I had been against this swim from the second she dropped her bikini bottom on the sand.

When he reached us, the surfer vaulted into the water; Sal faced him across the board. He said plain, comforting things.

"Yer in a rip, love. Why'd yer get in a rip?"

"Don't lose the board," said Sal.

"I won't lose it, it's tied to my ankle. Length of nylon. No, no, listen. Loosen yer arms, love. Loosen 'em! That's right. Why'd yer get in a rip?"

Sal shook her slicked blond hair and wasted her energies on being peevish. "If I'd known it was bloody here, I wouldn't have got into it."

He nodded, looking over his shoulder, assessing the sea. His hair was woolly, his long face reminded her of pirates or Italians. She saw in him, even in this dangerous water, the easy charm that marked Brian. She wasn't pleased to see it, thinking it was an antipodean disease, wondering if there was much chance of rescue in it.

"That's cool," he said to himself. "Listen, honey. Paddle with the left hand. We'll get out the side way."

But he was not able to ease us out of the current. At its edges, where it met the normal water, there were eddies. We were spun back into that outgoing thoroughfare of water. Whenever they failed, he smiled at her. "Stop grinning!" she yelled at him. She imagined herself and the charming boy adrift on the surfboard in the open Pacific.

The rider could see that Sal was tired now. "That's cool," he told us. "We'll just ride it around the headland into Whale Beach." He had time to shrug in these elements that had us by the scrag. "Let *it* do the work, eh love?"

Propping her chin on the board, Sal cried, adding her lake salts, if you like, to those of the grand sea. The surfer had not convinced me either. How did he know it would take him around the headland and into the next beach? How did he have the rashness to treat it as if it were scheduled transport between A and B?

"Listen, get up on the board, all right? Go on, get up and rest. Go on, sling yer top half across the board, go on. Yeah. Now lift the other leg. Come on, I've got yer knee. Come on, across. No, I'm holding it. Good!"

At first she sat the board tautly, her hair smeared across her shoulders. Her breasts stood forth, the node of her pregnancy showed. The board moved beneath her with an intent like that of a trusty horse.

"Now," said the board rider, accepting her nakedness as one should, as one of the bounties of a board rider's dawn. "Just be comfortable, just be nice. We'll let *it* do the work."

Sal let her back loosen so that now there were fleshy dimples at the sides of her spine base.

"What's your name?" she asked.

"My name's Jason, love. All the accountants were calling their kids Jason when I was born. My old man was an accountant." He laid his face against her hip. "Jesus, yer a lovely one, aren't yer?"

"I don't know. I'll tell you when I get home."

"Yeah, yer look like Leda and the Swan, something like that. And yer've got a kiddie coming, haven't yer? What a picture of motherhood, eh?"

She laughed at him and liked the sound of the laughter. The waters had not after all yet stolen her throat from her, and we were already off the point and, as Jason had promised, the waters were turning us north.

"Are there sharks?" asked Sal.

Reproachful, he stared at her. "Put 'em out of yer mind. They only turn up if yer expect 'em. They pick up yer brain waves if yer think of 'em. Seriously."

Well, it sounded rational to us. The rules out here, even

on our small island of fiberglass, were of another order than the rules of the mainland. We quashed in ourselves the image of great preying fish.

"Do yer know," he went on, "they're all company directors live up on the cliffs, old Scotsmen and Poms and so on, who think the country's going to hell. They get up early every morning to see if they can spot a dolphin or a whale, and what they'll see is us. The S.S. *Motherhood.* Jesus, if I could get off this wetsuit without strangling myself, I would. Then we'd look right. We'd look like some sort of omen, like a myth or something. Jeeze, it'd give the old bastards a lift. They'd go down to the club at lunch time and say, 'Yer know what I saw this morning?' See, I'm the barman at the club around there. Whale Beach. The Moby Dick. Oh Christ, yer've got those lovely thighs. If yer drowned and come up on the beach, even the coppers would have wept." His arm over her knee to steady the board, he took a handful of her thigh, somewhere between knee and pubis. "They feel fit for biting, eh? . . . What's yer name . . . Sal? . . . they feel fit for biting, eh Sal?"

Beneath a high sandstone cliff, this grabbing of her thigh seemed normal to both of them. And though I winced a little at the way he handled her I was still frightened enough of that vent of water we rode to think that a rescuer had some rights.

Soon a further beach was in sight, socketed among sandstone cliffs. The tide took us parallel to it for a time, before Jason kicked and stroked with his free arm, and we could tell from the different tension of the water that now dealt with Sal's dangling legs, from the way the board sat, that we had been released from the rip. Among the breakers, Jason had Sal lie prone—I too extended myself and stroked within Sal's waters, as if our momentum could be affected by my effort. So, by riding waves under his guidance, we reached Sal's depth. Here, at the land's touch, she became conscious of her nakedness. At the end of the beach some rock fishermen worked on their tackle, tying on spinners and so on, cutting octopus up into strips. A cup of coffee stood steaming on the hood of their sedan. By such signs we knew the enchanted voyage was over.

Jason told her to sit on the sand by the board. He whimpered a little seeing the way she folded her body on the sand, her knees drawn up as close as they could be to her chin. He ran to the surf clubhouse, a brick building with a garage where rescue boats were stored. He opened somehow the window into the garage and came back to her holding a red-and-white rugby shirt, the sacred number seven on its back, and a pair of shorts which had been used for some sort of mopping or polishing. Because of her pregnancy, the shorts nearly fitted her, and as she stepped into them, Jason, with a tender swipe of his forefinger, knocked the sand out of the down of her right leg.

"There!" he said. He pointed to a white bungalow high up on the slopes above the beach. It belonged to a businessman in Sydney who rarely visited, he said. He himself rented the flat underneath. She ought to rest there, he said, and then he would take her home to her husband.

"My husband lives in England," she said.

"That's cool," he said.

He walked splayfooted up the beach, his wetsuit unzipped to his brown navel, the board tucked beneath his arm, his right arm around Sal's shoulder, since her legs weren't biddable, and she had begun to shiver. At the head of the beach stood a closed kiosk where at high summer ice cream, pies, coffee, cola would be sold to surfers. A station wagon had been parked there, all its doors eaten by rust.

"I know this fellow. I don't think I'll wake him—I mean he was stoned when I closed the bar at midnight last night. We'll just borrow the car, eh?"

He unlocked it with a piece of wire, started it by lifting the bonnet and—it seemed to Sal—by simply touching the engine. He was so much in command of the beach and sea world that she felt the need to lean against him as he drove to his flat. He had promised her soup and coffee. But as soon as they were past the clutter of glass flotation bulbs from fishing nets, conch and abalone shells, lumps of sandstone strikingly striated, remnants of cuttlefish and skeletons of toadfish with which his doorstep was cluttered, as soon as they were in his bunker in the hillside, beneath the rich man's holiday house, in the long room that was all his living space, among the faint mustiness of its subtropic molds, both Sal and our host understood together that the coffee and soup could not be instantly provided. They went to his tidy bed, which must have been—like the Gnome's bed—made before dawn, and he put her down across it. She noticed on the wall above a strip of batik cloth—we would find he had bought it while riding his board in Indonesia. The formal caresses of the Asian gods who peopled it offered her nice precedents. Jason had taken off his wetsuit, his genitals and buttocks lily-white among his brown limbs. She touched his belly, he touched hers, with the exact tension a woman who has lost her love, been called mad, escaped wild tides, requires. He was tender with his hands, sharp with his mouth. As he rode in her, uttering sounds that sounded like groans of protest because his occupancy would soon end, and as she herself came to utter those plaintive noises that have always seemed to come not from Sal but from some grand and defiant beast—queen doe or mother boar—inside her, I sat neutral and closed my mind. Not that I was not as willing as anyone to celebrate Sal's continuance.

17

Like a woman avoiding the mad impulses that can come with the dawn, Sal slept the next morning till after six. On waking she lay for some minutes, feeling her body, complimenting it, with a touch like Jason's, for being soft and animate today, when it might so readily have been sea meat. These little congratulations over, she got up, put on a robe, poured herself a glass of orange juice, and took it with her out onto the decking. Below her, among the shrubs and palms, she could hear an animal moving, but by stretching she could see that it was a man in a brown suit, waist-deep among the wide perforated leaves of the *Monstera*. Feeling her eyes, he looked up. She could see his striped tie.

He called, "There's a pool of sewage down here. It must be a cracked pipe."

He was a young man, dark-complexioned like Jason, but the skin itself paler. No surfer.

"What are you doing there?" she asked.

"I was trying to find the back door, Mrs. Jones . . . I didn't want to disturb anyone. Is Mr. Jones there?"

She did not answer him. In Kalgoorlie the sun had not yet risen, but the Gnome lay beneath a sheet on a bed in an upstairs room of the Royal Hotel. Behind the bed head, the French windows stood open to catch any movement of air from the street. Out there, under a sharp desert sky still star-crazy in this last hour before dawn, other old pubs with their wrought-iron pillars, together with awninged butcheries, bakeries, merceries, all sedated with the moneys filched from eighty years of miners, kept a silence of bank vaults.

The Gnome slept with eyes open. He dreamed of Sal exactly as she was at that moment, on the deck above the tropical plants and sea, the day's first nutriment in her hand. From the adjoining room, where Dabney slept, there was no sound. Dabney had threatened at the snooker table downstairs last night that he would probably snuffle in his sleep because of a cold. But the desert air must have cleared his passages. The Gnome seemed to hear the faint crepitations and creaking of Dabney's sleeping brain. It was because the ultimate arrangements had been made that Dabney slept so well.

"Who told you any Mr. Jones lived here?" Sal decided to ask now.

"We called on Mrs. Dabney last night. She said she visited Mr. Jones and yourself here on Saturday."

Sal said nothing.

"I'm from Corporate Affairs," the young man said. "I can show you my identification, Mrs. Jones."

"I'm *not* Mrs. Jones. She *knows* I'm not Mrs. Jones. Look, you ought to come up out of the jungle for a start."

"How?" asked the boy, like someone genuinely helpless.

"For God's sake, climb the slope again. Come to the front."

He climbed like someone feckless, tangling himself in a huntsman's spider web, laughing at himself in the thick glutinous mesh, clutching a fern to haul himself farther up the slope. Waiting for him at the front door, Sal could hear branches snapping in his path. At last he reached her. He said nothing, being interested in a resinous dab of tree sap on his suit coat. He scraped at it with his thumbnail.

"I don't suppose I can come in?" he muttered, worrying over the sap.

"No."

"Surely Mr. Jones is in?"

"No."

"We could wait outside all day, you know," the boy told her with a slow crooked grin.

"Then you'd find out I'm the only one here."

"Dabney's away too. Mrs. Dabney doesn't know where. Is he away with Mr. Jones?"

"Look, I don't know."

The boy had now taken his coat off, the better to inspect the tarry damage.

"Oh Christ!" he said, deciding it was a grave dry-cleaning problem. "Look, I didn't get up early and go crawling round in sullage on a vertical bloody slope just to be stone-walled by you. Do you know how much a new suit costs in this bloody country, Mrs. Jones? For someone trying to get on in Corporate Affairs? At least a hundred and fifty dollars. Damn all to you. Try being on my wages and see what a new suit does to the grocery bill."

"Clothes won't make a career for you," Sal told him. "I'm sorry for you if they think they will."

"Look, Mrs. Jones! I've been doing this for seven years. Months in the field, getting the evidence. Months at the desk. And when you get to his front door, whoever he is, there's always a cold, blond woman fronting for the bastard. She doesn't know where he is. She's always in a long gown and looks as if she just had a cool drink. And she doesn't know where her corporate criminal is. I might be new to you, Mrs. Jones, but you're not new to me. I've seen you in a hundred architect-designed front doors. Mute, full of contempt, dismissive. I've faced a hundred of you corporate harlots, for Christ's sake." The boy hurled his coat at an oleander bush. "See, there's you, you, doing the fronting for him, then there's the politician you'll call to put pressure on us, then there's the Queen's bloody counsel who knows the judge. Yesterday, Mrs. Jones, a woman from Ultimo—do you know Ultimo? It's not a beachfront suburb, I can tell you that—she got six months for lifting a Beatrix Potter figurine from a store in the city. Prior record, oh yes, she'd lifted kids' shoes last year. She was on a bond, you see, unlike certain gentlemen of your acquaintance. Six bloody months she got. Two kids—they'll go to institutions."

It was probably a true story. But Sal said, "Oh, for God's sake, the melodrama!"

But I could tell how well he was succeeding with her, playing her sentimental social conscience, and I bounced about trying to impart to her that he was performing, that the stained suitcoat could well be just a stage prop.

He retrieved it from the soft branches of the oleander. Turning away, "I'm sure there's no need for me to tell you," he said in a tight voice, "to let him know I called."

The boy was already halfway up the stairs to the street and she could not avoid calling to him. "There was a geological error," she called. She couldn't tell why she wanted the approval of this stranger in a stained suit.

He leaned against the railing but did not turn to her. "Oh, there always were in those days. The blokes like Jones and Dabney were out to milk the world. There was always lots of speculative money around, to pay for geological errors."

"Look now, come inside. Not that I'll answer questions, but come inside and have some coffee and clean your suit before you go."

The dark boy rubbed the back of his head, helping the decision to form, then turned and walked past Sal into the lobby.

"I'm a poor girl too," she muttered as he passed her.

When she closed the door, his back was to her. He looked down the long living area toward the glittering ocean. By the set of his ears I could tell, though it seemed Sal couldn't, that he was smiling to himself.

It was a lucid morning at the vertical house, and over

the mountains of iron and copper in the west, a fierce dawn; but in W8 Brian and Annie occupied a moist Monday afternoon. They had come home early, and were dressing for a movie premiere at a Haymarket cinema for which Annie had been given tickets. She had borrowed a formal gown from a friend to wear that evening. Trying it with and without a bra, she was neither way satisfied. She sat in old-fashioned satin knickers smiling and frowning at herself in her mirror, and thinking that for a girl who was not ample she had been lucky in love. Her luck, however, was about to be canceled. For I could sense, in the subtleties of the ether that lapped Brian's ears, the imminence of policemen. When the bell went, they both thought, Policemen are about the only people who come to our door. We ought to have a party and set up again a decent ratio of citizen to police bell pushers.

Brian dragged off his dress shirt—how could he face them in apricot flounces? He dragged the shirt he had worn to work that day from the bed and buttoned it on.

"Let's not answer," he whispered to Annie as he buttoned the cuffs.

"They'll only come back," she said, "and wake us early tomorrow."

Brian admitted them. Following them back into the living room, he said, "I don't know that these continual visits are necessary. They're very upsetting to my girl. Would it be possible to call me down to the station whenever you want to talk?"

"If you prefer that way. Most people don't."

"I prefer that way."

One cop nodded, the other brought up the business of the meeting. "The CID believe they have the man who forged passports for Mrs. Fitzgerald and Mr. Jones. He identified Mr. Jones from a photograph. Of course, he never met your wife."

"He has a record of the passport numbers he used," said the second policeman. "They were on two passports used two months ago by Mr. Tournay and Miss Raftery, passengers to Sydney. The forger remembers he forged two Australian entry permits. The Australian authorities themselves issued no entry permits in the name of Tournay and Raftery. Does your wife have any relatives in Australia?"

"Australia," Brian muttered. Land of the crazed editorials. It seemed such a dangerous latitude to him, and its name released his submerged concern for Sal. She fled that far? She was as frightened as that?

"You can't send the police *there* after her," he said. "The police are pretty ham-fisted there."

"She's not the criminal," said the second policeman. "Jones is the criminal. He's broken immigration laws in two countries, abducted an inmate of a state asylum. The Corporate Affairs in Australia want to talk to him about a mineral swindle . . ."

Though he'd been roughly treated by said Jones, Brian could still sense the Gnome was a tender and reliable man. Yet mad. Was she living with a madman? Or had she gone to Queensland and shamed him, Brian, by visiting his parents?

"She doesn't have relatives," he said.

"Would she visit your parents? Your relatives?"

"No."

"Do you have parents there?"

"Yes, but she wouldn't visit them. I would have heard if she had . . ."

"Do you have their address, Mr. Fitzgerald?"

"My parents don't know about . . ."

He gestured over his shoulder toward the bedroom where Annie sat catatonic by a mirror she had only just—two minutes ago—informed of her beatitude. He gestured northeast toward the institution at Stapleford Hatch.

"Mr. Wallace Fitzgerald," Brian said at last, "Glasmere via Cunnamulla, Queensland."

"No street or number?"

"It's not a bloody housing estate."

The one who was making notes looked up from what he

had, the address of Brian's childhood. "Could you tell us when Mrs. Fitzgerald will come to term?"

"Term?" Brian winced at them, raised a finger to his lips, and again jerked his thumb in the direction of the bedroom. The note-taker smiled in a compassionate way, shook his head, yet spoke straight on, punishing Brian—Brian could tell—because he thought him a heartless bastard.

"When will the baby be born, Mr. Fitzgerald?"

Brian closed his eyes and leaned against a bookshelf.

"You righteous bastard," he muttered, "get out!"

"When, Mr. Fitzgerald?"

"February," said Brian, "middle of February."

He had been harried into uttering my birth date. By mere lasting, by the cunning escape arranged by the Gnome, by the evasion of the riptide, I had beaten him. Now he stood like a surgery patient, pallid, bent at the hips, yet his knees locked as if any movement might tumble his viscera onto the carpet.

"Don't let them go pestering her in the labor ward," he muttered at them.

"I'm sure they won't," said the one who had been my pointed object, my honed blade. "As I said, she's the innocent one."

Brian began raving. "You smug bastard. Happily married, are you? Never get a policewoman up against the filing cabinets, never fuck a vagrant? Like to shoot the queens and the adulterers, eh? Like to join the force in Argentina? Get out, get out . . . !"

Tucking into their breast pockets the address of the senior Fitzgeralds and my own birth date, the plainclothesmen went before he had finished raging. When he turned, Annie stood in the bedroom door. Her breasts were bare, her thighs in those old-fashioned knickers she had put on believing they would give the evening some sort of ambience.

"Oh Jesus," she said, and even I could sense the edge of her pain, its taste on her tongue. "There aren't any possible explanations."

Sal made coffee for the Corporate Affairs boy, and they sat drinking it, a tide of saffron light transmuting the legs of his trousers. By various transmissions and coaxing movements of my limbs, I advised Sal to let him argue and not to answer. He thought she was a corporate harlot? Let him. Let him rage to his colleagues at lunch and his wife at dinner. (He had a wife for he wore a thin gold marriage band on his finger.) About rich men's bitches.

But he had hurt Sal's peasant pride.

"You can say you're just visiting," he said, kicking at the carpet and punching the suede arm of his chair. "But there's a quality here the rest of us don't enjoy. What you call a geological error gave you this, Mrs. Jones, put that cup in your hand, and the coffee in the cup . . ."

"My name is Sal," Sal told him. "I am not Mrs. bloody Jones."

"There are ordinary people," he said, uttering a scenario, "who sold their houses to put money into Comsec, rode up with it. One fellow on our books, at one time maybe notionally worth, say, a quarter of a million. Then came hurtling down when the shares fell. A dismal little bloke with no sense of quality. Went under to a heart attack."

In my cool cave I thought, Good, it's going on so thick he'll lose her soon. She'll begin to laugh.

"I suppose you put the morning aside," Sal asked him. "For what?"

"To occupy me, so I can't call on those lawyers I don't know, or the politicians I've never met."

"You really do want me to believe that you're a decent working girl."

"I don't give a damn what you think, I know what I am."

"Just the same, you could indicate your good faith to us by spending the day with me. We could drive out to my place for lunch. Lunch with the wife, I mean. She's a nice girl, good company. Pregnant herself. You are pregnant, aren't you?"

"It mightn't be convenient for me to spend the day with you. Have you thought of that?"

"I just thought . . . if you're interested in proving good faith . . . and you seem to be . . ."

"Sod you. If I spent the day with you I'd speak about the . . . about Mr. Jones."

"We won't even mention the man."

She got up to fetch her bag, her two passports, her sun hat.

"I live an hour's drive from here though," the Corporate Affairs man warned her, as if he were really indifferent to her traveling with him.

"I don't get carsick," she told him curtly. As they left she ran ahead up the steps and waited on the pavement for him. It was up to him to close the door of the vertical house, as if *he* were its possessor.

In the bar of the Royal last night, the Gnome played pool with pub regulars, winning eight dollars from them and taking it in shy wonderment, as if eight dollars made all the difference to him. But Dabney had not mixed with the miners and mechanics. You couldn't have told from his strange contiguous eyes whether he was being sullen or pensive.

This morning at the airfield, however, he moved like a man who had resolved his thoughts and absorbed his resentments. He wore a silk shirt and a tie. He walked around the rented aircraft laying a hand gently on the flaps and the tail elevators. It was already a standard desert morning, no cloud, the tarmac in front of the hangar already throwing heat upward, the low yellow-brown hills already bending and wavering in the ruthless light. But Dabney had time to praise the aircraft. "Cessna 172. For my money the best small plane in the world." Serenely, he dipped a gauge in both fuel tanks and was satisfied by what he read. He beat the gas cap back in place with the heel of his hand; he

211

opened the cabin doors so the heat would not accumulate inside.

He walked off, measuring his steps, as if he intended to live the whole hot day and must save some energy for evening. He filed his flight plan on the telephone in the aero club. In the gaps of his conversation with flight control, he would wink or smile across the room at the Gnome. His ease seemed to be that of a sane man but was instead the ease of someone whose struggle is over, who has nothing ahead of him but an easy killing.

Soon the Gnome and Dabney were half a mile above the mine shafts northeast of the town. The last mines, the last poor cattle homesteads scuttered away beneath them. The earth ahead of their flight path was ocher and uniform and bowl-like. There was no feature to diminish it, to make of it a lesser sister to the sky. And earth and firmament ran peers and twin absolutes, hard to focus on, all the way to that weird notional place where parallels meet. Dabney acknowledged a call from Kalgoorlie control. He sighed as he hooked the receiver in place again. He had come all this way away from his neat, bitter wife to find the right place to be frank in, the climate for talk.

"It was so easy in those days."

"Easy?" the Gnome asked.

"To float a mineral company, I mean."

"It would seem, from our experience, that it was easy."

"All some geologists did was sit in the pub. They talked to the aboriginals, and asked them to bring in any green rocks they found. Then there were false assays, rocks that came from over there . . ." Dabney pointed toward the western limits of the earth. ". . . were assayed as coming from over here. No one in London or Tokyo or Brussels knew how big this country was, how free of supervision a geologist could be . . ."

"So, it was all a lack of supervision? All this trouble we've had?"

"Even the respectable companies wanted you to juice up

the data from anomaly maps. Oh, I used to send out technicians to do chemical tests. But you can do anything you like with the results. And the same with electromagnetic tests. For Christ's sake, Jones, it was like one of those Roman rituals, when a priest used to try to read the outcome of battles in chickens' guts."

"Is this some sort of admission?" the Gnome asked him.

The Gnome sat, all that way above the desert, neat hands on knees. The twin set of controls trembled in minute ways before him, for the hot columnar air jolted the airframe.

Yet, though he seemed so serene, there was that old orphan sickness in the Gnome, the sickness at being easily cheated by those who had a sense of proprietorship over the earth. In his neat, unmoving hands he knew that if he began to beat Dabney he would not be readily stopped until the man's jaw had gone, the man's brain been widely bruised. And secretly, up against the shadow of that metal wall in *his* brain, he considered how the bad money of Gia Dinh had bred, more recklessly than bacilli, bad money in this desert.

"I remember," Dabney said, "that you weren't bullied into investing.

"No. I wasn't bullied."

Yet it had been so easy for them. A London broker invited the Gnome into the city to meet a principal of a promising mineral company. The principal had been Dabney.

"You even seemed flattered," Dabney recalled, "when we invited you in as a director."

"Why not?" said the Gnome, dismissing the snide memory. "I'm not a man who gets many invitations."

Dabney set his teeth as if the Gnome's innocence offended him. "I can also remember the pleasure on your face when we flew you into Sydney. And elected you chairman."

The Gnome closed his eyes and there was a second of pain registered at the corner of his mouth. "Were there any traces of copper there at all? In the field?" He gestured toward the infinite brown earth. "Were those anomaly maps you drew up complete works of fiction?"

Dabney couldn't stand all this candor. He loosened his tie, took both hands off the controls, and hit the radio housing with the butt of one.

"That's what gets me about some of you bloody people . . ."

"What bloody people?"

"Americans. Your kind of American. You have to have things explained . . ."

The Gnome nodded, admitting it. People had thrown grenades at him because he was slow to take explanations.

"We," said Dabney, pointing downward at the unpopulated desert, "we believe that everyone is a liar until it's otherwise proven. Our attitude rarely leaves us disappointed. Convict origins does it for us, that's what we're told."

He pushed the plane into a small banking movement, just for the convict jauntiness of it .

At that hour Sal and I drove west with the young man from Corporate Affairs. On the low hills where Maurice Fitzgerald had once observed society as it was run by kangaroos stood lines of brick and plasterboard houses, each symmetrically moored within the picketed and paling-fenced boundaries of its quarter acre. There were no clouds above these hills. There were, it seemed, no clouds between these streets and the desert ridges Dabney and the Gnome sat above.

"This is the helot quarter," said the Corporate Affairs man to Sal.

"Come on," said Sal, shaking her shoulders. "It looks all right to me. Have you seen an Asian slum?" She had not seen Asian slums herself.

"Oh, it's not as bad as an Asian slum," the boy admitted. "But have you noticed the big sky? Unfenced. You can't squat down under that and fence off a tiny pocket of dirt, the way it's done here, in this street—in my bloody street too, because I'm a helot. It upsets the balance between the earth and the sky, it causes malicious electric effects . . ."

Sal made rusty violin noises.

"I just wanted to tell you," said the boy. "There can be great unhappiness in a street like this."

She grunted. She didn't need to go on a tour of moderate urban squalor. She'd seen squalor and lived in it. She was angry at him for tricking her away from the surf and the luxuriant slopes, for it was her experience of them that was small. She would have stood on a sun deck and watched for Jason's shape among the sea swells.

On these low hills, however, over which the Corporate Affairs boy now conducted us, Maurice Fitzgerald had worked on a government farm. For the first eight weeks, he and the others worked chained, waist-to-waist, or individually chained at the ankles. This was the result of an administrative axiom that said: It takes a few months of chaining for the truth to reach a convict that it is no use bolting, *bolting* being the convict argot for *escape*. It took a few months for a man to understand that here there was nowhere to bolt to.

The fact reached Maurice Fitzgerald and he made his small speech about it, according to his custom. He told his friend Dennis and the others in their shackled line who at that time were carrying cedar logs out of the forest on their shoulders: "It means this—that overthrow is the only choice we have." It sounded to Dennis that Fitzgerald was delighted, as if he'd found the best place on earth, the climate he desired most. Some of the other felons felt easier when the chains were let off and they were no longer locked in line with him. Others again repeated his utterances in the convict compound, a timber stockade among a bowl of hills.

A priest, Father Harald, one of the exiled gentlemen who had traveled above deck on the *Minerva*, visited him one evening—for the stockade gate stood open on these hills of no escape and visitors could walk in and out and so could convicts if not chained.

"Maurice," the priest said, "I don't want you to go on

speaking about throwing over the Crown and the rest of it. It excites the boys, you know. And there's no hope for it here. No hope for all this Jacobin stuff you speak, Maurice."

"Here more than anywhere," said Maurice quietly, a real hard-liner.

"Maurice, Maurice. I was a rebel too . . ."

"Then you ought to know this. That to be a rebel is most needed when the chains bite deepest," said Maurice. He could, you see, be as orotund as Brian.

"It's a risk even talking to you," the priest told him. "They watch me, they think I'm a troublemaker."

Maurice smiled at him. "If they knew. But listen, Father, use your chances. When you speak to the boys, when you hear their confessions, tell them to make pikes."

At Easter a gentleman naturalist called Graylock came riding up to the convict station on a roan beast that illustrated the colony's poor bloodlines. Graylock carried documents from the lieutenant-governor in Parramatta assigning the convict Maurice Fitzgerald to act as an assistant naturalist. This gave Maurice—if not freedom—at least freedom of movement. With Mr. Graylock he visited many convict stations and often slept at night in the convict huts. Here he would speak and advise men to make pikes and hide them. But there was this lack in him: he could create no committee structure, no system for carrying messages. It was as if he believed that all convict souls, disconnected from each other, in two dozen stations over these hills, along the Nepean River, in the foothills, would in the same instant take fire, get the compulsion, rise up. Beyond that hope, he had no gift for arranging events.

Whatever his gifts, Graylock respected them and sometimes let him ride out alone to gather skinks and insects. Already Maurice had a passion for the kangaroo, an animal he loved not only for its fluidity but for its frank, sober, level gaze. One day, breaking through a fringe of eucalyptus into a clearing, he saw ahead of him two great red kangaroos, bucks, holding each other about the shoulders with

216

their forepaws, wrestling for position, a chance to raise a long hind leg and cut the other's body open. Around, spectating immobile, were bucks and does and, ahead of him, placed exactly like sentinels but watching the fight instead, two young males.

They are a tribe, Maurice decided. They are a tribe as are the black people. And the two male fighters are fighting for females. They are a tribe.

He studied tracks they used in migrating across the hills, and between water holes. Where these tracks crossed rock, he found the rock indented by the passage of loping ancient generations of the animals. They are a tribe and have accustomed paths. He observed that they moved in the manner of tribes, with the mature bucks and their does in the center and a fringe of young bucks in front and to the side. When a young buck felt strong enough for the task, he moved to the center and challenged an older one for ownership of does. All this Maurice reported to Mr. Graylock as he had reported his observations to his naturalist master in Ireland.

One day, once more mounted and off on his own swing over the hills, he met two young bucks engaged in what seemed to him a homosexual act. Did the God of Reason permit this? But he rode back, frowning, to report it. Maurice's image of kangaroo society did not shock Mr. Graylock but reminded him, as an educated man, of arrangements among the Spartans and of other classical references. He relayed Maurice's observations at the dinner table at Government House in Parramatta one evening after the ladies had left the table. Present was the lieutenant-governor himself, the surgeon, a wealthy sheep-farming parson who was also a magistrate, and the judge advocate of the colony. They all frowned at Mr. Graylock's story, whereas Graylock had expected them to laugh. Graylock was used to the more urbane civil servants and lawyers of London. But these colonial gentlemen had no spaciousness to them. They too saw nature as an image of God's Will as in his way Maurice had. They believed that somehow the possession of this country by the Crown had consecrated it and that there could therefore be no animal sodomy under the British flag. "What did you say this convict's name was?" the parson asked. Graylock told them and some of them remembered it.

In Maurice's day these harmless suburban hills through which the boy investigator drove Sal and me therefore offered dangerous visions, perspectives that could land a man at the flogging triangle of the local convict station.

Above the desert Dabney had been watching his time and called Kalgoorlie within twenty seconds of the moment recommended by the air-safety regulations. It was important to him to appear to be a model aviator.

To the northeast the earth was ridged with low mountains where an ancient Silurian sea had once lapped. And due ahead, warts of monolithic rock, looking to the Gnome more like the constructions of a vanished people than a geological accident. Geological accident, thought the Gnome. Geological accident.

"This source you're taking me to . . . ?"

"Source?"

"This site. Is it fraudulent too?"

Dabney of course did not know how to answer. "Look, let me put it this way. I think they'll indict us again, you and me, good and thorough. Now I have some documentation at home which indicates you corrupted me." He laughed in a friendly way at the idea of the Gnome as a big business corrupter. "I think you and I ought to get out while the question's still hazy."

"Get out? Brazil or something?"

"No. They get you back one way or another. No. I was thinking of taking us both down in the plane. Crashing it, I mean. What's your insurance like?"

The Gnome laughed softly, Dabney in a more lumpy harsh way. Twin magnates in on a joke.

"I've seen what happens to the families of men who go to jail for this sort of reason," Dabney told the Gnome. "There are schools that won't take your kids anymore.

Strangers' children persecute your own in the playground. And you . . . that girlfriend of yours . . . her kid too. He'd be at school before you were paroled."

Now Dabney put the nose down but leveled out a thousand feet above the mountains. From that height, flying westerly along the ridge, you could see a speckling of green in the deeper groins of rock; not a copper lode but vegetation. In this place vegetation seemed more of a wonder than copper, meaning that somewhere in the rib cage of those hills water lay in springs, in deep and ancient holes. A tribesman could have taken you to them, for tribes still walked these places and the hills had meaning to them as the gift of an ancestor, as the spirit home of some totem creature, snake or lizard or bird.

The Gnome, inspecting the ridge, picked up with ease this primordial flavor from it. He could not believe in it as a crash site. He noticed then, as McQueen had taught him to notice years past above the Berkshires, that the left tank had emptied beneath a level of safety. The feed switch was however still turned to it. He wondered if that were a bona fide mistake or if Dabney meant to accomplish the accident that way. An error with the switches. A credible cause. He coughed. "Shouldn't you switch to the other tank?"

"Don't be so bloody obtuse."

The Gnome leaned forward and tapped the gauge. "This is deliberate then?"

"Nineteen percent of aviation accidents occur through fuel starvation. Fuel starvation at a low height. There isn't time to switch tanks to recover. It's instantaneous. Guaranteed."

In fact the nose had dropped farther. They were so low now that the Gnome believed he saw a lizard's tail vanishing in a crevice. He leaned forward in his seat, reaching for the fuel switch, reading the notations and warnings at each switch stop. At the same time he was overtaken by an image of Sal. He saw her on the beach from sand level. A sea wind flattened her robe against her ankles, her knees, her belly at last gravid. Yet he was homesick rather than alarmed. I jolted so wildly in Sal's womb that she looked up, seeing mere pavement, picket fences, red-tiled roofs; but the Gnome did not look up at Dabney. Dabney had taken from the base of his seat a plumber's wrench. His action cramped in the cockpit, he gave the Gnome a bent-armed blow on the bone behind the left ear. Though I could tell the pain was great, the Gnome's elation reached and soothed me. For he believed he'd fallen from the plane and flew as he had flown from that grenade in Saigon. Uncertain of the exact facts of the Gnome's situation, I let his triumphant feelings into me, not knowing that they were symptoms of the bruising Dabney had just given his brain and not of any true escape.

Then the Gnome's vision returned like an old door opening, with a creak. That is, he could hear, and after wincing at the sourness on his tongue, he saw he was still in the cockpit with Dabney. Now he was frightened. He had little room in the cockpit to use on Dabney the science he had bruised Brian with a month ago in the house in Pembroke Gardens Close. He sat quiet for what Brian would call a microsecond and squinted at the rocks below him, fifty paces down, so sharp-edged in this light that their points, he believed, left blood marks on the tissues of his vision. Dabney, he noticed, flew levelly, his face composed, the wrench on his lap. His tie! I transmitted. Perhaps he could be throttled with his tie. And then the other tank could be switched in and Kalgoorlie radioed and, while the Gnome kept the plane level, parsons, Corporate Affairs men, Mrs. Dabney could all be called on to reason with the reviving geologist.

The Gnome reached for the tie, it had insignia on it, some Sydney businessmen's club. He got the knot to the rear of Dabney's neck, then lifted the tassels vertically to the cabin roof with his left hand. With his right he clutched the controls on his side to keep the nose level, since Mr. McQueen had spoken to him when he was a boy about the way distractions make pilots dip the nose, and the Gnome in his thoroughness never forgot such items of advice.

While choking, Dabney struck at the Gnome's right hand, but there was a concentration in that hand and the plane rose a little. It was then unhappily that the tank became exhausted and a great windy silence entered the cabin. The nose, uptilted a little, hung skyward, and the ridge below, the Gnome was sure, exerted salutory upward hostility sufficient to keep them there, in stasis.

But then the wing on the Gnome's side swung away beneath them, the west vanished and was replaced by a geological blur. Silurian. Six thousand million years of age, the Gnome knew. The pace of their fall kept his left hand up in its hangman situation and Dabney's neck was broken. At fifty feet, the Gnome's merciful brain replaced the jumble and glare beyond the windscreen. He believed he was falling from a young womb onto the floor of Caruso's Diner in Pittsfield, Massachusetts. The fall was long but one could see the dazzling and crystalline patterns of the outer world. Born at last, he sang to himself, as the floor struck him and he opted to breathe. But his mouth was filled with an instant and painless fire.

I did the writhing for him. Sal in fact thought it was a miscarriage. "Stop, stop!" she screamed, and when the Corporate Affairs boy obeyed, ran from the car and emptied her stomach on the grass outside a post box marked Merryman. When the spasms finished she leaned against the side of the car while the boy went inside, ringing the Merrymans' doorbell, explaining to the lady of the house that his passenger had been ill and asking for the use of the yellow hose that lay coiled like a household viper on the grass.

"Lift your leg if you can," the investigator asked her, sluicing the mess into the gutter. Through my daze, my howls of piercing silence, I heard Mrs. Merryman kindly offering tea, and the young man saying no, that we were nearly home.

All day the voices were remote as radio static, while I occupied my black den in mourning. In the investigator's little brick house, behind an exactly clipped and tended garden, I discovered that his wife was a small brown-haired girl, heavily pregnant. Normally I might have wondered about the mind inside *her* swollen belly, and Sal and Mrs. Corporate Affairs sat so closely on the sofa drinking tea, were so sisterly toward each other, that transmission must have been feasible. Instead I thundered, as silent as usual, at Sal's nonapprehension of the Gnome's tragedy. The wreckage still burned in the ancient mountains, yet Sal sat nice with the brunette, was sharp with the husband for bringing her inland for the day, and smiling when the brunette laughed with her and said, "I know his ways." I alone, in all the inner and outer world, carried the weight of bereavement. I alone wondered, as mourners should, at the meaning of a life like the Gnome's, the meaning of his torment at being birthless. His tough-minded escapes, his pursuit of Sal, his punishment of Brian, his rescue of me . . . I believed I had a right to expect that a man like that would derive from some source—for he always seemed to be endowed with sources—the strength, the craft to deal with a red-headed geologist.

It was already dark when the investigator drove us into that road above the beach. Sal, I being still a dead mourning weight in her, saw the police car parked across from the vertical house before the Corporate Affairs boy did. She tautened, though I couldn't manage to. If I could have managed anything by my own muscles it would probably have been to go to the police and surrender. Sal, however, stared at the boy as if the patrol car were another of his devices. He shook his head. "Not me. I promise you that. I'll go and talk to them." He got out and went a few yards before understanding he'd left his car in her power. He came back and leaned in toward her. "Please don't drive away, will you?"

He was there, up the road with the police, long enough to plan her capture. But she knew it wasn't running time yet. She saw him recoil once, standing straight after all that genial stooping he'd been doing at the patrol car's window. Back at last to his own car, he found Sal in the driver's seat. "Move over," he told her in a small breathy voice, the voice of a man who conspires with you, not against you.

They drove away, past the police car, on the weaving coast road.

"Those coppers say you're an illegal immigrant," he said.

"Jump at yourself," she told him. "I thought it was boardroom criminals you were after."

"How can I tell you this? Dabney was killed in an air crash today. There was a man with him. They believe it was Jones."

She was not even tempted to believe him. She inspected *his* face the way you inspect the face of a man who says something in crazy bad taste. "What sort of bastard do you think I am?" he asked. "I'm sorry to say it happened."

Now she began to fear. She said, "They have to inform next of kin before they announce these things." She believed for a second that even if it were true, the Gnome might yet be able to retain life through their technical mistake.

"They've told Mrs. Dabney. They've been waiting outside your door two hours. In any case, Jones . . . well, I suppose in their terms he doesn't have next of kin."

She still suspended belief, she was still serene, the bridge of her nose creased.

"It's certain, Sal," said the investigator tenderly. "It's been on the television news apparently."

It was too cruel. She began to pound the upholstery and to choke and her viscera, I in them, were no more to her than water that might flow away down the seaward slopes.

"It happened in the desert. But the wreck was easy to find because Dabney kept to his flight plan. I know it's impossibly hard, but you must go back and speak to the police."

"Are you mad?" she asked.

He shook his head quickly and, against all his principles, kept driving northward.

Lying with two passports in her handbag was the checkbook of an emergency account the Gnome had started for her use. He wanted to make it twenty thousand dollars but she had argued with him and at last got it down to eight thousand. Now, while the investigator was still despite himself driving away from the police and on the chance he was telling the truth about the Gnome, Sal wrote a quick cash check for four thousand dollars and waved it at the boy. He turned on the compartment lights to read it and stared at her and shook his head with a pity she could tell to be real. "It's not for you," she said. "It's for his funeral."

"He'll have funeral money . . ."

"It's for his funeral. Now let me out if you don't mind." But he would not stop the car. Driving north was as big a fall from grace as he could allow himself.

In W8 our grieving night was a fine afternoon and all day little slits of sunlight had pursued Brian from corner to corner of his apartment. He still wore yesterday's underwear beneath an overcoat he'd put on this morning and worn all day. During working hours he had kept a little hope of bullying the journalists who shared Annie's office at the *Los Angeles Times* London bureau into telling him where she'd gone. It seemed she was off doing a string of features. Where, they wouldn't say.

"When she calls in we'll tell her you want to contact her."

"Contact her? Christ, I want to fuck and comfort her."

"We'll tell her you want to contact her, Mr. Fitzgerald." Now, at dusk, there was no more to be said to Annie's office. Without the diversion of Annie's fragile presence and body his memory settled on Sal and me, his attempts on our persons spoke to him, the murmurs of crimes you thought someone else had committed yet now found they were done by you while you slept.

As the darkness began, Brian turned on no lights; their sharpness would have challenged him. Then, in the dark, he found his Scotch bottle was empty. It came to him that he could never replenish it—he could never again get to a liquor store, he doubted if he could ever again dress himself. He was terrified of the last light outside and of the noises and the faces.

All he could think of was to call George's consulting

rooms. George himself answered the telephone—his receptionist must have gone home for the day.

"Brian!" George said in a clipped way. It was meant to tell Brian he couldn't expect much time.

"George, I think I'm having a breakdown."

"Oh."

"My girl left and I don't think I can get dressed ever again. And I can't ever work again. I've been here all day in my bloody jockey briefs . . ."

"Have you been seeing your psychiatrist?"

"Me?" For some mad reason he resented the idea that his craziness had been a long-term one. He still had enough vanity to see himself as a man on whom a divine lunacy had descended last night, when Annie packed up.

"Listen," George said, judging Brian's tone aright. "I'll call through to a chemist in the area and prescribe something for you. You'll have to go and collect it."

"Don't send me out," Brian said, beginning to weep.

"Listen, is it news of Sal . . . ?"

"Sal's in Australia," wept Brian, stating it as the worst punishment she could have devised.

"My God. Listen, I have some very worried parents waiting to see me . . ."

"I'm a bloody worried parent!" roared Brian, not understanding what he'd said.

"There's a psychiatric clinic in Brompton Road. Good staff. Clytie went there in the first instance."

"Clytie?"

"She—she had some problems. She's in a place in the country now. Got very upset about Rowena. No cause for it. After all these years. Precipitated by . . . well, Ran Singh died and I thought she'd get over it quickly . . . Look, I must rush, but do you think you could call a taxi? No? Well, I'll arrange it. I suggest you get dressed if you can . . ."

A little later, Brian waited on the pavement in pullover, pants, sneakers, a uniform appropriate to the homeless. He did not know who would come for him; he hoped they would be quick. It was a police car that arrived. "Mr. Fitzgerald? We'll take you to the clinic." Brian's legs jumped but he suppressed the idea of running and got in with them. When he saw the crisp blue serge of their uniforms, a sign to him that the world was still turning, he began to weep in gratitude. Now, in Sal, in the Corporate Affairs boy's sedan, my hand was up against my mouth as if Brian could be soothed that way and I felt the small and vital pea of my heart, already overweighted with the news from the desert, give way a second, and wondered if it could ever manage and control the long seas of my blood.

The boy investigator held the check up in the moonlight, giving one eye to it and one to the road. "Sal, you put me in a position. How can you leave me with a cash check for four thousand dollars?"

Sal took it away from him. "I'll post it in then. If he is . . . he's *had* this accident. If any of it's the truth."

He put his forehead for a second against the highest point of the steering wheel. "It's the truth," he murmured.

"If it isn't," Sal told him, beyond logic, "I'll goddamn curse your house, boyo." Her tears fell on the check. The investigator halted the car and then began to turn it. Though she threw herself wildly out the passenger's side door, I did not complain of the concussion. For she was all wit now, all canniness, saving the two of us. On the ocean side of the street, the houses all sat on their stilts above a drop to the beach. Sal took to someone's steep path and felt thankful for the plentiful lantana and willow and gum trees and palm thickets. Her hair was once more stranded with the rich webs of huntsman's spiders, lantana clumps raked the flesh of her arms, sometimes she stepped into places muddy with drainage water and her shoes filled. Yet it was all, of course, nothing beside her grief or her impetus. And it was somehow a fruitful grief and told her what to do without asking her to think. Without being asked to think she kept to the edges of those tangles of vegetation between one house and another, never stepping into the full night light of the three-quarter moon or showing herself against the white wall of a house. Without being asked to think, she moved in the direction from which they had driven. Not once did she hear the Corporate Affairs man's pursuit, though he must have made one. Surely?

She traveled half an hour this way, the moon on her left, before she understood that the funeral check was still in her hand.

When the jungle brought her to the beach she moved in the shadows of the cliffs. Two lovers swam naked and silver-skinned in the municipal surf pool beneath the headland. They saw her as a shape and kept silence until she had gone and then, she was sure, forgotten. Her path took her over the sandstone under the cliffs, sizable rubble, massifs taller than she. Without thinking of it, she was further cut and bruised; I felt where I sat the intrusion of the sharp sandstone edges.

She thought of Jason. If the Corporate Affairs boy had called in the police, as it would be his nature to do and to do with sadness, they were likely knocking door to door back there, at the wrong end of the beach. She was certain, simply certain, that they would not think of the cliff base as a thoroughfare. And that she herself did was only because she had skirted it with Jason in a riptide.

After an hour or more, the lights of Jason's beach were in sight. She could see the consolidated lights of the club where he was a barman certain nights of the week. Not tonight, she hoped.

Traveling through gardens and hiding from headlights, she got to Jason's place, but it was dark. She sat weeping among the sea relics, hoping he would include her among them and give her shelter.

Returning from the beach with his board and in his wet-suit about eleven, he found her sleeping there. I too was sleeping, having soothed myself for a time with the idea of all the escapes we had managed, the Gnome and Sal and I. I pondered too for the first time how the Gnome would have been after birth, if his obsession would have been dispersed, if he would have begun to breathe in a new way, and if not, what his disappointment might have been? And of course the pleasant duty of survival had descended on me most unapologetically now. For I saw that animal sacrifice—Ran Singh's—had been made for me, that there had been the sacrifice of Annie and of Brian, and that, in his way, the dear dead Gnome had stood in my place, falling from the sky into a great fire. I was dizzy therefore with woe but somehow felt regal and soothed, enough to fall asleep. "Hey," said Jason, waking us by Sal's shoulder.

"Can I stay here?" she asked, before her eyes were open.

"That's cool," he said, but after long thought.

"Listen, I came into this country without proper documents, my friend's just been killed I think. I'm pregnant . . ."

"I know yer pregnant."

". . . and the police are looking for me." Jason had opened the door and switched on the inner lights. It looked so good from outside, the bed, the prints, the humming refrigerator.

"Drugs?" he asked, leading her in.

"No. No, I skipped out of a psychiatric hospital in England."

"You?"

"Yes," said Sal. She argued like a woman who could not afford pride. "See," she said, "you'll be able to tell in a day or so whether I'm mad and if I am you can just give me back. Oh, and I've got four thousand to last me till the birth . . . I mean, it's honest money . . ." Sal, like all refugees, looked on survival money as, by its nature, honest. ". . . and look, you've got to find out if my friend's really dead . . ."

He approached her with a solemn face, her own being misted and muddied, and kissed her hard. Then he called a morning newspaper. Mrs. Dabney was sure the passenger was Jones. The charter company in Kalgoorlie had identified the passenger as Jones. The police laboratories were examining remains . . .

How Sal howled at the image of the Gnome's ashes on

a lab table and of white-coated men sorting through them for remnants of tooth and jawbone! From a shelf by the refrigerator Jason took a bottle of Napoleon brandy and began to feed it to Sal. There were no such quick comforts for me.

In his flat under the businessman's beach house we lived with Jason for many months. Two weeks of the summer, upstairs was let to a family from the country, a large sandy-haired cattleman and his big-boned wife and their five blond children. Sal was reminded of Brian's stories of summer beaching with his family. The rest of the time, upstairs stood empty and Sal and Jason lived as privately as they wished, Sal commuting from the flat to the beach and rarely taking the minor risk of entering shops.

"That's cool," he would tell her the few times he led her among the summer crowds at the beachfront shopping center. "They've all got better things to do than look for an escaped madwoman."

Sal chose also not to go near gynecologists; she knew there was a chance she'd be traced that way. There was a risk in avoiding doctors, but it was nothing beside the risks of Cerise wing at Stapleford Hatch.

The only visitor we ever expected was the Gnome—that he would come up from the road, along the path flanked with *Monsteras*, waving a neat hand, averting his green eyes, risking a grin.

It didn't happen.

Time and chemistry were relentless that summer. Time evaporated under the high summer noons, and as for chemistry—to myself and to the muscular cells of Sal's womb ancient hormonal delegates, not open to bribes, came down from the pituitary. Calcium, going its own and ancient way, took altered form in the bones of Sal's pelvic cavity, softening them for the day they would provide me with passage. The chemistry of my growing meant that I had expanded to occupy all that wondrous uterine lake which had once seemed so broad and spacious to me; and in that acorn called my heart a certain wizened artery grew to a more adequate caliber than it had, up to now, enjoyed.

It snowed in early December in London, on the day Brian, finding at last that there are joys that can only be properly had outside the walls of sanitariums, left his hospital. Going straight to Fleet Street, to the London bureau of a Sydney newspaper chain, he asked the bureau chief for a job. "We don't normally recruit into the bureau direct from the British press," said the chief. "Not a job here," said Brian, "a job *there*." The bureau chief's secretary wrote down Brian's credits—it's amazing what a listless career will add up to when put down on paper—and Telexed Sydney. A week before Christmas, Brian had an antipodean job and, on the second day of the New Year, feeling already at least the foreshadow of the summer sun at his shoulders, he left London forever. It was a hot January in the Southern Hemisphere and a hard month for working journalists. Brian was now a feature writer on an evening tabloid called *The Sun*. Its fatuity was restful to him and let him do all the decisive things outside office hours. Of which, first, he employed and briefed a lawyer expert in immigration matters, telling him Sal would be found and would most likely be found sane and in need of immigration counsel. He made sure that if Sal presented at any hospital on the continent under either of her names or even under a false one it would be reported. Third, he searched for a psychiatrist who would be likely to certify Sal sane if that were needed.

All these exercises were a form of expiation and they required of him some humble admissions. For example, he told the lawyer that it seemed Sal should never have been committed. "It was one of those situations," he said "where a woman was extremely provoked, by the police surgeon, by the psychiatrist. By her husband."

The lawyer told him, "What you have in your favor is that it's a very emotional case."

How it fitted Brian's oblique transit through life that Sal found *him*. She saw his name on a feature article in a newspaper Jason had brought home from the bar one small hours. She did not read the article, she wanted to believe it had been written in his London agency and bought by the local paper. But the next day, she telephoned the tabloid and, being connected to him, heard his voice but did not say anything in reply.

Knowing now that Brian sat in a newspaper office as close as Sydney, writing feature articles, made her hold back with Jason. It depressed me as well, for though I had banked on Brian's turning up, Jason was such a lovely man, such a simple, eager man. As an instance, he brought home to the flat booklets of prenatal exercises he had got from the Baby Health or borrowed from the shire library. He put Sal through them page by page, looking solemn, dividing his gaze between Sal and the book. "No, no," he'd say and go to her and adjust an arm or a hip.

Three days passed before she told him that Brian was in the country and in possession of a job and a telephone number.

"Do you want to contact him?" Jason asked.

"Not till the baby's born."

Jason said that was fine. He laughed and touched her wrist. He was so thankful.

The ancient cells worked on as free agents in Sal and me. They were both too minute and too potent for our wills to touch, our planning to impair. On a thundery evening in February, through communications of their own, they directed me crown first toward Sal's cervix. Abundant hormones massed in the vicinity of Sal's long ribbony uterine muscles and within two weeks, at 4 A.M. on a Thursday morning, the sinews clenched, became dense little cubes, and impelled me forward by the buttocks, the feet, the small of the back. I touched the amnion in wonder, a wall and throne and seabed it had once seemed to me I would never lose but which was now shifting and ejecting me. I touched the placenta which had been my farm, my pabulum, my commissary system. I felt a furious excitement, appropriate to a journeyer.

Jason led us to his old, rarely used Ford, Sal walking briskly as if it were a matter of pride. And as she walked I could feel the directions of her tides, the movement of her uterine sea in which I sat, no mean fish, no mean commonwealth of parts.

It was an easy journey at that silent, star-struck hour, Jason's hand on the gear stick all the way, Sal's right hand on Jason's, left on her belly. Jason smiling and saying that things were cool and Sal grimacing back.

Four months ago, if you had told Sal she might fall in love with a boy who had only one adjective, she would have laughed. She was then certain that she could not be taken with anyone who wasn't good with words. Now she had learned that silence too has its exquisite vocabularies and that in these Jason was accomplished.

The hospital stood with the sea behind it and all its lights on. So it resembled an anchored liner and it increased Sal's excitement and mine and I found my lips mouthing for her breast. In one of the books Jason had fetched home to Sal, he'd been tickled to read that the fetus was referred to in medical texts as "the passenger." It had interested him more than Sal, who smiled with him just because most of what he said was a sort of child's gift, and children's gifts have an appeal that has nothing to do with quality. The sight of that hospital, however, seemingly awash, produced in both of us the tremulous, fussy, near-drunken elation of passengers.

We went in dazed, Sal, myself, Jason carrying his booklets on prenatal exercise as if they were passports. She used Jason's name, calling herself his wife, feinting off thereby all the continent's police forces. While the paperwork was done, my head and shoulders bisected Sal's waters, making two seas, before and behind me, and I thought of nothing, my mind was on my limbs, nicely coiled, and there was that sensual delight still in the hydraulic pressure of the waters on my buttocks, my feet.

For Sal, though, it was *hurry, hurry, Mrs. Jason*—clipped questions, sharp edges. Nurses in the prenatal ward worked on her soft flesh like mechanics, demanding and collecting her urine as of right in a metal vessel, shaving her pubis barbershop smooth, running enema tubing into her anus, reading blood pressures, applying to her belly a metal horn, hearing my sluicing heartbeat, calling "ROA" to each other.

"ROA?" muttered Jason, taking a step forward in his green gown. The letters were an echo from a book he had read more thoroughly than Sal had. He did not know whether they were a good echo or a bad.

"It's presenting well," a nurse told him in a compact way, as if she had never bled, never wept, or ululated with desire. Jason looked out from beneath an anxious dark brow and wondered should they have come here, if Sal maybe should not have settled with giving birth in his bunker. He did not doubt there was a book on midwifery in the shire library.

A young doctor came next. He frowned at the sparseness of Sal's medical history but palpated the uterus and, on finding my poised shoulder, smiled at Jason. His gloved hand went to Sal's shaven genitals and he felt the cervix and the waters pressing behind their membranes. He grunted a little as if the pressures were inherent to him. He looked away into a speculative mid-distance. "It can happen quickly," he said as a warning to Sal.

I spent the meantime in an ecstasy, singing songs to myself; I, vaulter; I, humbler of summits; I, the good and splendid mariner. My manhood and scholarship inherent in me, waiting to unravel. My mind banked, simpled down, brought to a point.

On sighting the crown of my head through the bulging membrane, they wheeled her toward the labor ward, and on that journey her inland waters burst out. I felt their rushing about my ears and thought, not of triumph, but of great beached whales. This was a frightening image and a new impairment of my breath gave edge to it. I did not like my dry beach, yet it was a little while before, dragging the placenta from its wall, I was ejected between Sal's thighs as far as my nose under lights that ran molten over my brain. And born thus to the nose, I felt my blood jolt and writhe within its channels and thought, Is this pain, this anguish of breath-lack, the condition of the beast? Does it explain all Brian's iniquities? Is it what Sal means by original sin?

But then I knew it was my heart. That I was a victim of the heart.

As I was levered forth I was no longer the voiceless newborn, I was identified with Maurice Fitzgerald at Toongabbie Hill in the spring of 1800. My problems with the ether became his, I shared his problems of the blood. A week past a court of inquiry in Sydney, in questioning Irish convicts, had found the name of Fitzgerald repeated. It had also come to the court's attention that Fitzgerald held zoological opinions repulsive to natural delicacy and good order. The members of the court, surgeons, officers, a whiskified judge advocate, ruled in a colony where convicts were two out of three men. They suffered from an appropriate cool paranoia and thought of making examples of people. They advised the governer so and the governor, suffering the same disease and being also given to the bottle and to a bitter marriage, sentenced Fitzgerald and some others to a thousand lashes to be administered seriatim, that is, with pauses for nursing the culprit back to a lacerable state of health; and the whole exemplary event to be witnessed by the assembled convicts of the sentenced man's district.

And now Fitzgerald was roped to the bole of a cedar and the priest Harald stood by touching Fitzgerald's right hand, for that had been the priest's sentence—to be associated by touch with the punished. And pressed hard against the bark, Maurice could not take breath between blows, for there were two floggers, one on his left, one on his right, and the whips had each nine strands to shock the air out of you. And for want of breath, and because he had somehow locked his brain as they roped him there, he could not utter a scream. After every fifty strokes, the surgeon inspected his head and heart and stepped back, grimacing. What did it mean, this absence of yelling?

Somewhere in the second hundred strokes, the left flogger landed some strands on Fitzgerald's neck and *then* he cried, we cried, with the only breath we had, "For Christ's sake, flog me fair!" As if there were a rule of justice even for agonies.

The lashes brought solid fire down on the muscles from the small of the back to the shoulders and that seemed, to Fitzgerald, adequate solid fire to satisfy any administrator. Yet everyone wanted Fitzgerald to scream. The lines of men and women convicts before his tree groaned and might soon scream themselves. They knew that if he screamed that would be the beginning of mercy, yet with the same mind thought it indecent of him to be so far above them, so capable of stifling his howls. The administrators waited for his scream because an exemplar had no meaning unless it yelled under the whip, and how could they sleep if beset by an absence of screams?

The priest wept and whispered to him, "Cry out, Maurice!" And I writhed and whispered. And it seemed that every witness's heart swelled as in a vacuum in the presence of Maurice's nonutterance and so did Maurice's heart, for he would have liked to yowl like other men. The firmament, cloudless above the tree, impended like a membrane that might rupture and let the high tides of the galaxies rinse over the hill, abolish officers, doctors, whip-wielders, and the entire breathless colony. Yet he would not oblige them with a shriek. They were down to his muscle, his gristle fell on boots fifteen paces downwind, and still between us, him and me, we could not scrape together a decent cry, the requisite wail, the strident confession of our existence under a lash . . . Maurice . . . Oh Maurice . . .

The child, the doctors said, suffered a condition called the Tetralogy of Fallot. This meant that the pulmonary valve was constricted, that there was a septum or hole in the atrium of the heart. It was not fatal, they told the mother, and there was a 95 percent success rate. The mother would not be comforted and told them not to come to her with bloody percentages. Jason called Brian Fitzgerald on the third day and, because of the latter's untrustworthy record, gave him few details and agreed to pick him up from the ferry terminal at Manly and drive him to the hospital.

The child resided in a small hermetic crib of his own, where the weather was always temperate and the oxygen rich. His mother's milk came in through a tube in his foot, his weight was good (they said), and the starved blood which had at birth discolored his lips and fingers and feet was running at a rate approved of by the pediatricians.

The operation was performed while Jason, working by Sal's description, searched the ferry terminal for Brian, staring at a tall lean man in a denim suit and wondering was that too thin to be Sal's husband.

They did not know how to speak to each other but they were polite.

"How's Sal?" Brian asked, sitting, his knees laughably high in Jason's small car. Jason, tall as Brian, was used to the vehicle and drove with his knees.

"She's better. She's settled down. How's work on the paper?"

"Good. Bloody awful."

"Yer all right?"

"Just a bit sick. Anticipation, you know."

Anticipation of what? Jason wondered. "Wind yer window down."

While they drove, a surgeon closed the atrium in the infant's small heart with a patch of Teflon and repaired the mouth of the pulmonary valve. Both the surgeon and the anesthetist thought the procedure a success and, as the infant was again enclosed in a sterile crib, sent a nurse to tell the mother.

When Sal was discovered by Brian she was standing in the recovery ward, looking down through the thick plastic roof of the crib at her son. He could see that she was twitching for contact with the child and from her lips came an animal gurgle directed toward it. Its eyes eked open for a full ten seconds and its gaze was as level and knowing as Clytie had once said it would be.

"Sal."

"Oh, you." The smile went but her hand moved generously, indicating the child.

"Poor little bugger," said Brian.

"No. They tell me that he's fine. The doctor says he'll be able to ride a surfboard."

It seemed a strange gauge of normality to Brian, but perhaps not when you looked at the tanning of her skin. "You've gone native," he accused her but with a cautious smile.

"What do you want him called?"

"Him? I don't know."

"It seems to me there's only a few possibilities—Warwick, Maurice, Jason, Brian. That covers the ground I think."

He hoped they didn't call it Jason. He didn't want his son named for a sun-kippered cretin.

"You've had the pain," he said. "You ought to choose."

"Pain? To hell with that today."

"You have to really look after a kid with a bad heart," Brian said.

"His heart is mended, Brian," Sal insisted. But Brian shook his head.

"Sal, it's too much to ask. But are you coming back?"

"I consider the question obscene."

"But that boy . . . ?" He threw his thumb in the direction of the corridor where Jason waited.

"That boy is a paragon. Don't you *that boy* me, Brian!"

Her eyes were on him. They moved more abruptly than they used, she had a new directness from being a fugitive. And on a fugitive level, he thought, maybe that sunbleached boy out there had behaved well.

"I spoke to a lawyer," he said. "He doesn't think you'll have too much trouble with the immigration people . . . or with the question of your medical record . . ."

Her eyes stayed on him, they were a stranger's eyes, they were newly flecked as if she might in fact once have been mad. "Don't talk about it, Brian," she warned him. "Or am I to believe there are police in the corridor?"

"What do you think I am?"

"You're a bastard, you poor loveless bastard."

"I'm a new man," he said. "The way you're a new woman."

"I hope to dear sweet Christ it's so." She put her hand on his shoulder. "Now speak to your darling boy."

She left him alone with the child. At the end of the corridor sat Jason, reading *The Women's Weekly* with a student intensity. Seeing her, he got up.

"What's happening?" he said. It was no cool question. He might never be cool again.

Sal put her hand to the back of his neck and kissed him with her lips apart. "Forgive me," she whispered. "I don't know what's happening. Except that my son is a whole and lovely boy."

They kissed again. Behind them was a stairwell and they were a sight, kissing there before the tall glass wall of the stairwell, with the sea from which he had hauled her moving behind them.

Meanwhile Brian stood clumsily above his son. The baby's eyes would close but as if by an act of will come open and adopt a neutral gaze. Brian opened his hand and, making begging noises with his mouth, placed the palm, still fish-white from the time he'd spent in the sanitarium's shuttered rooms, against the plastic of the lid. He seemed to gasp and his voice came out at first aerated from too much breath.

"You see . . ." he muttered. "It's a matter of being . . . you know . . . presented . . . with people's faces. Yeah. That's what it is."

When the child slept, Brian jammed his own lids shut before reopening them to stare down like a mock patriarch.

"What's this surfboard-riding bullshit, anyhow?" he asked.